LEVEL UP

GENE LUEN YANG   **THIEN PHAM**

SQUARE
FISH

First Second

New York

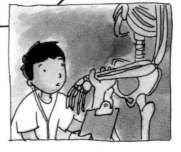

Dedicated to our brothers Jon and Thinh, both of whom work in the medical field, for being the good Asian sons.

SQUARE
FISH

An imprint of Macmillan Publishing Group, LLC
175 Fifth Avenue
New York, NY 10010
fiercereads.com

Our books may be purchased in bulk for promotional, educational, or business use. Please
contact your local bookseller or the Macmillan Corporate and Premium Sales Department at
(800) 221-7945 ext. 5442 or by e-mail at MacmillanSpecialMarkets@macmillan.com.

ISBN 978-1-250-10811-1 (Square Fish paperback)
Cataloging-in-Publication Data is on file with the Library of Congress

Originally published in the United States by First Second.
First Square Fish Edition: 2016
Book designed by Marion Vitus
Square Fish logo designed by Filomena Tuosto

3   5   7   9   10   8   6   4

http://www.jaderibboncampaign.com/

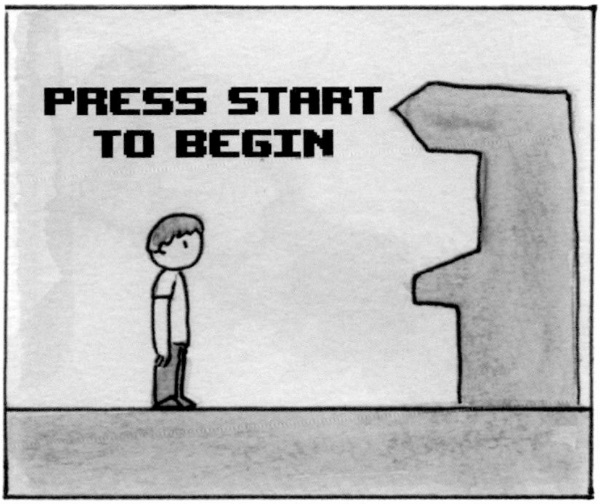
PRESS START
TO BEGIN

I saw my first arcade video game when I was six.

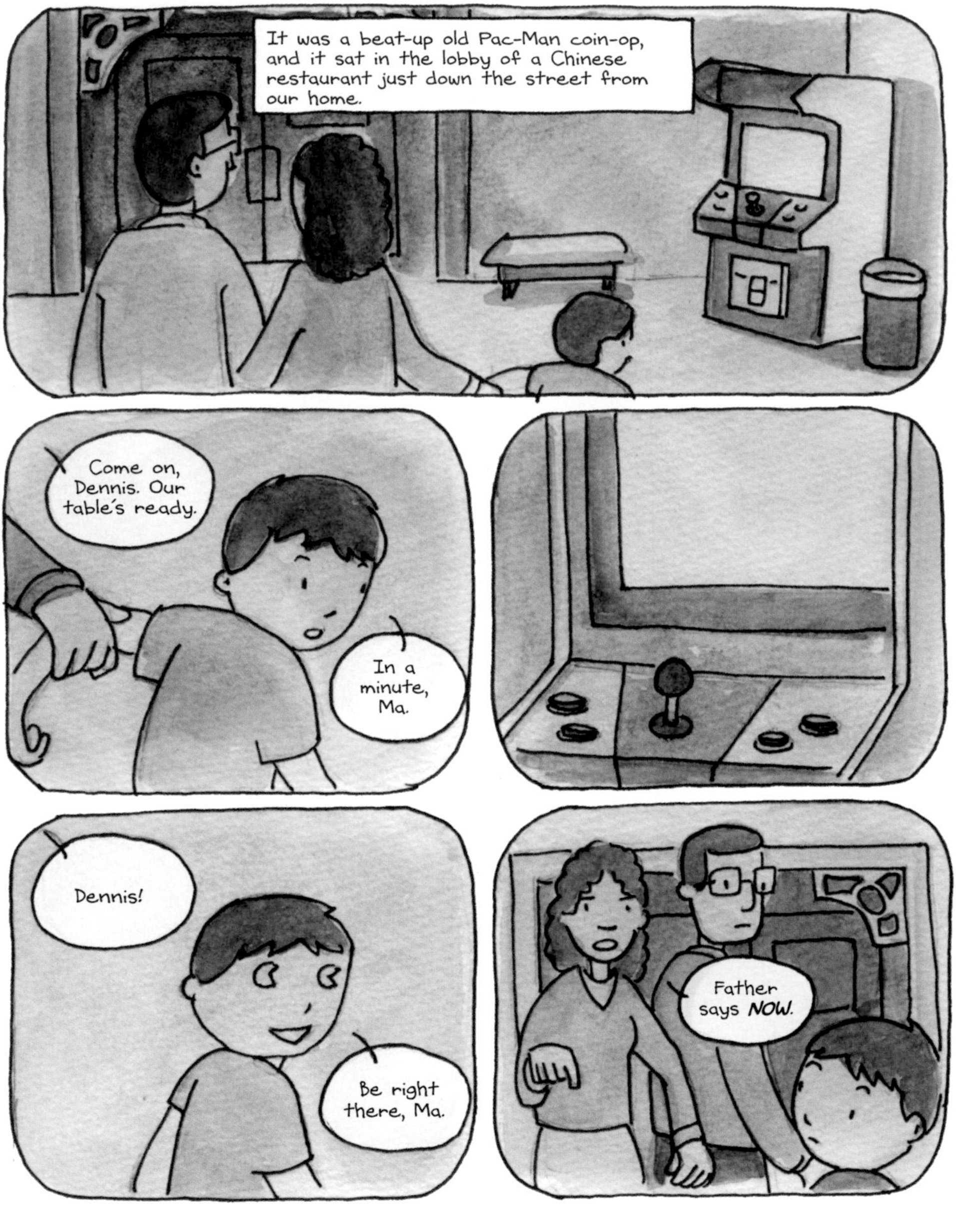

It was a beat-up old Pac-Man coin-op, and it sat in the lobby of a Chinese restaurant just down the street from our home.
Come on, Dennis. Our table's ready.
In a minute, Ma.
Dennis!
Be right there, Ma.
Father says NOW.

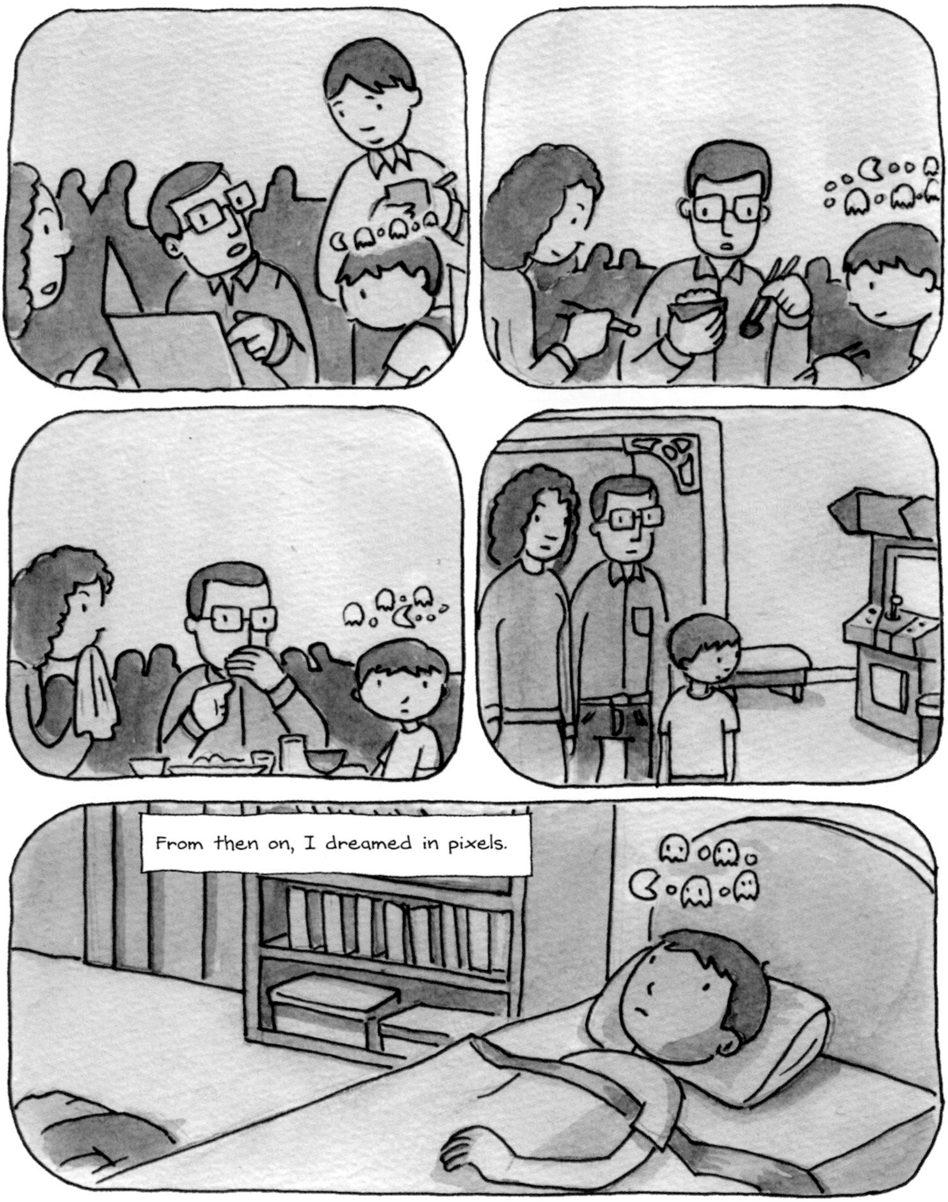
From then on, I dreamed in pixels.

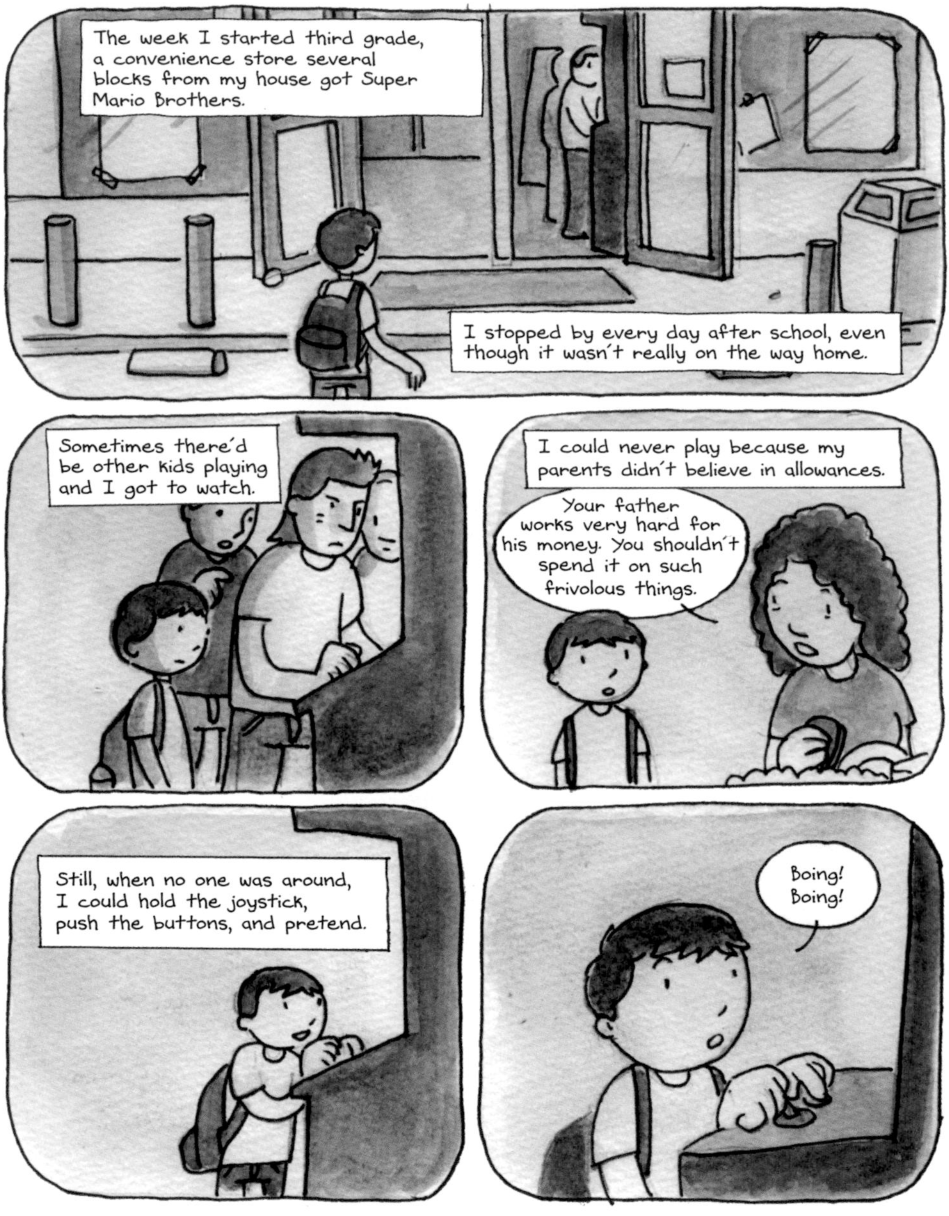
The week I started third grade, a convenience store several blocks from my house got Super Mario Brothers.
I stopped by every day after school, even though it wasn't really on the way home.
Sometimes there'd be other kids playing and I got to watch.
I could never play because my parents didn't believe in allowances.
Your father works very hard for his money. You shouldn't spend it on such frivolous things.
Still, when no one was around, I could hold the joystick, push the buttons, and pretend.
Boing! Boing!

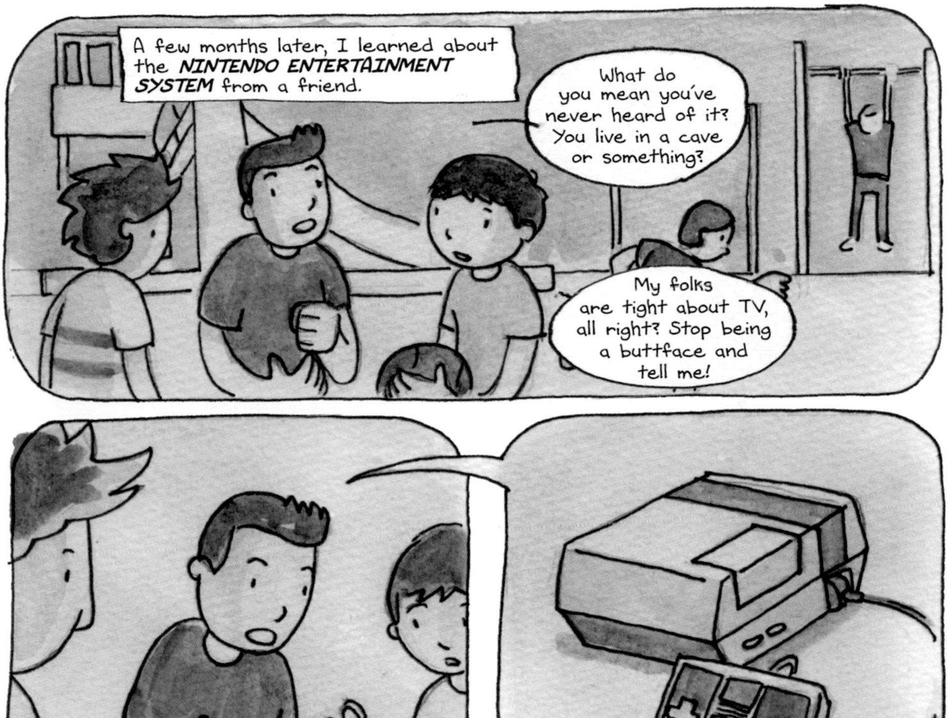
A few months later, I learned about the NINTENDO ENTERTAINMENT SYSTEM from a friend.
What do you mean you've never heard of it? You live in a cave or something?
My folks are tight about TV, all right? Stop being a buttface and tell me!
So basically, you get to play Super Mario all you want, any time you want, for FREE!
That is the single most amazing thing I've ever heard.

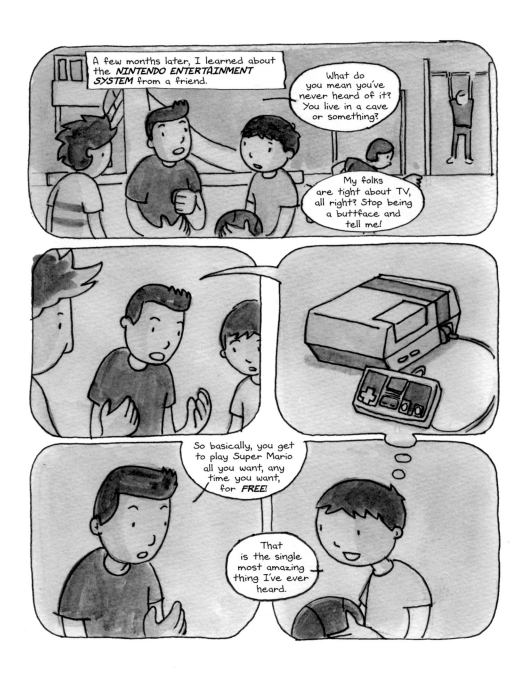

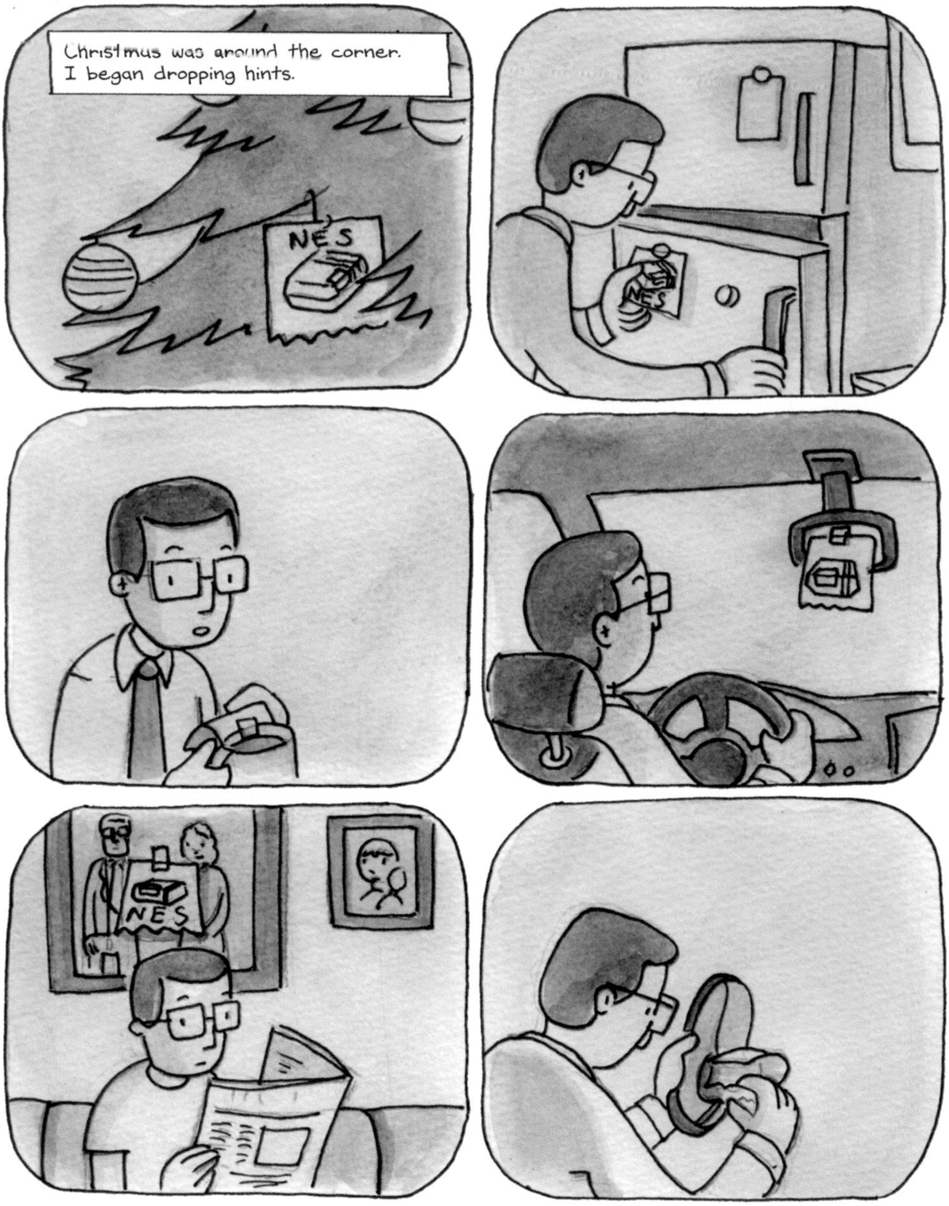
Christmas was around the corner.
I began dropping hints.
NES
NES
NES

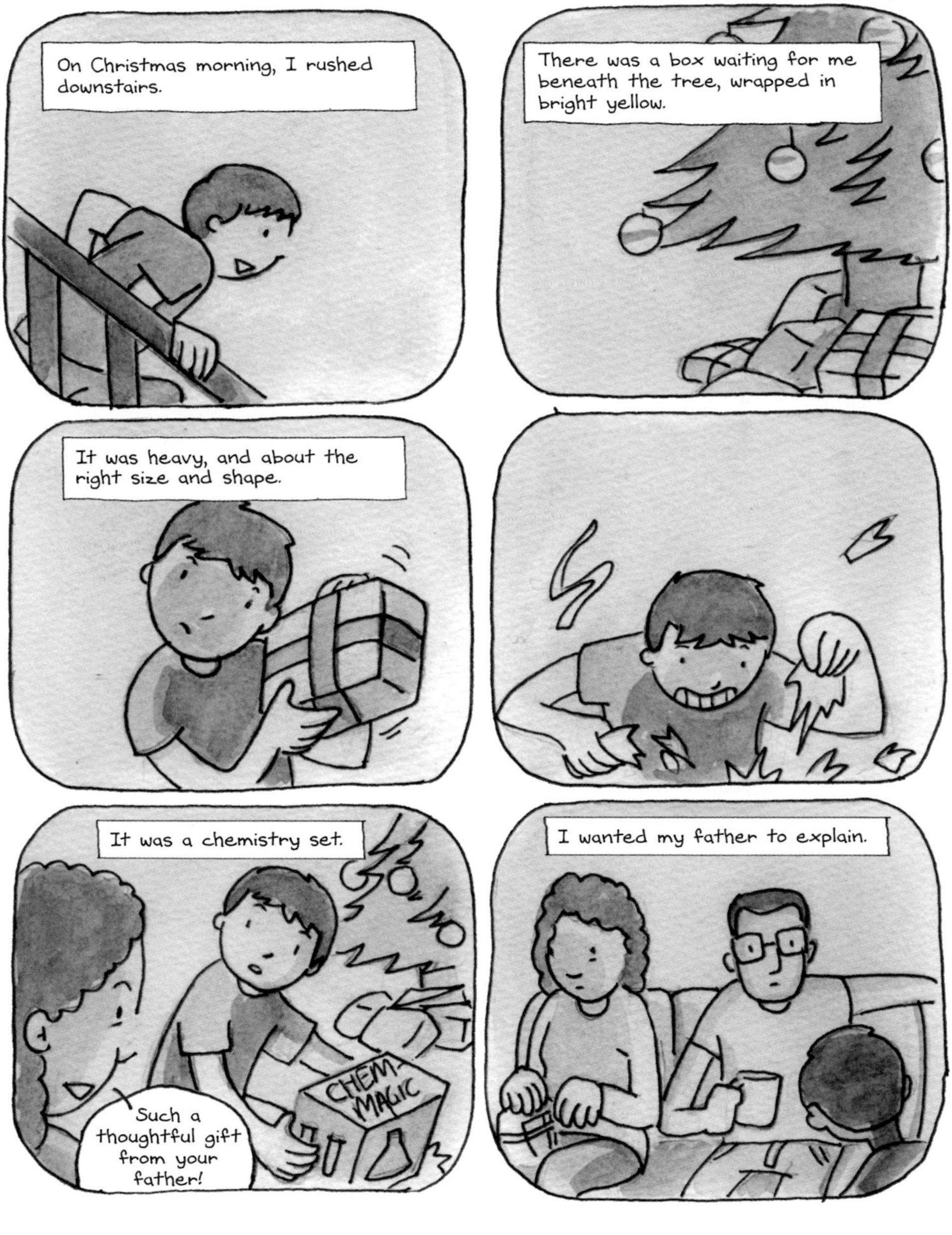

On Christmas morning, I rushed downstairs.
There was a box waiting for me beneath the tree, wrapped in bright yellow.
It was heavy, and about the right size and shape.
It was a chemistry set.
CHEM-MAGIC
Such a thoughtful gift from your father!
I wanted my father to explain.

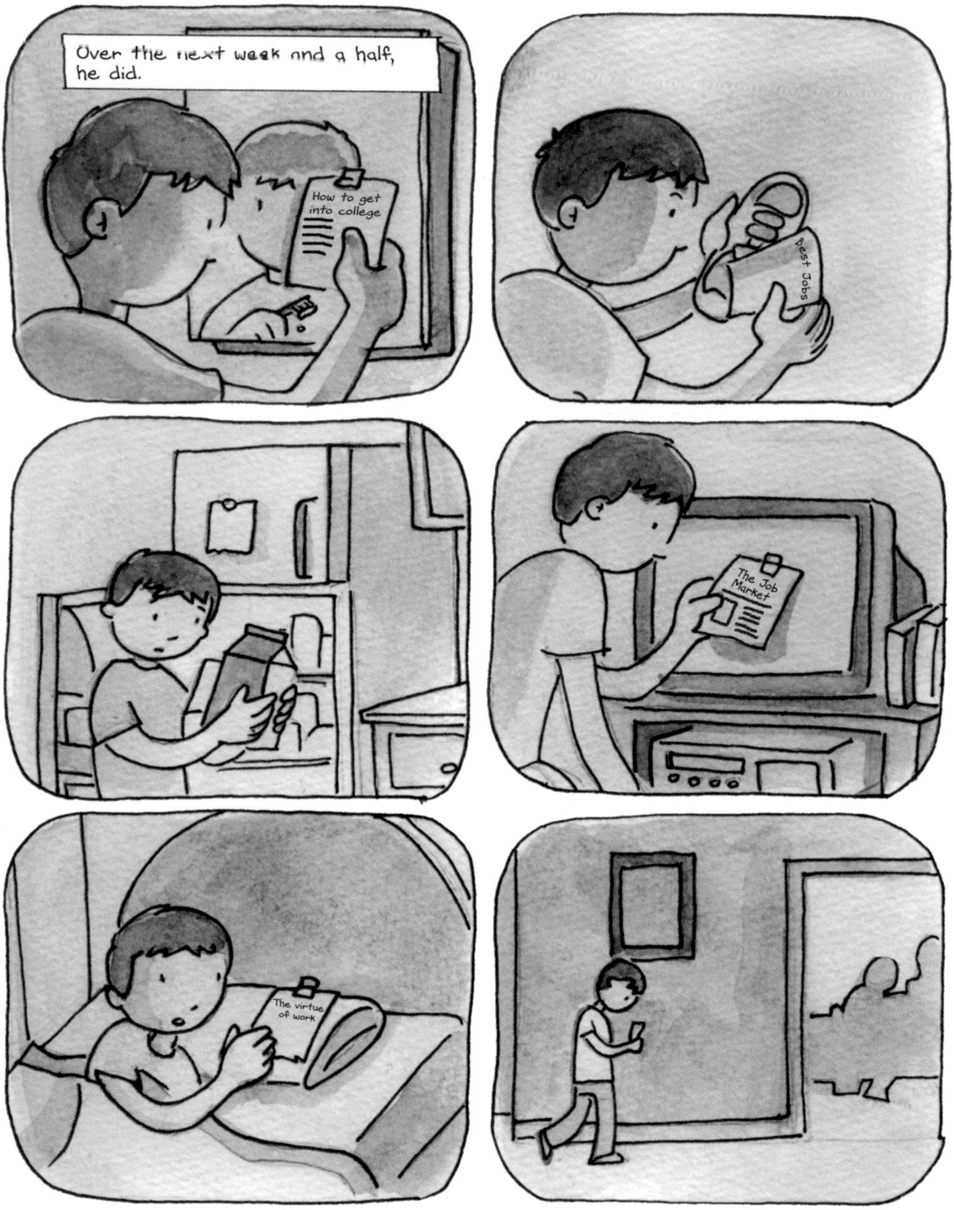
Over the next week and a half, he did.
How to get into college
Best Jobs
The Job Market
The virtue of work

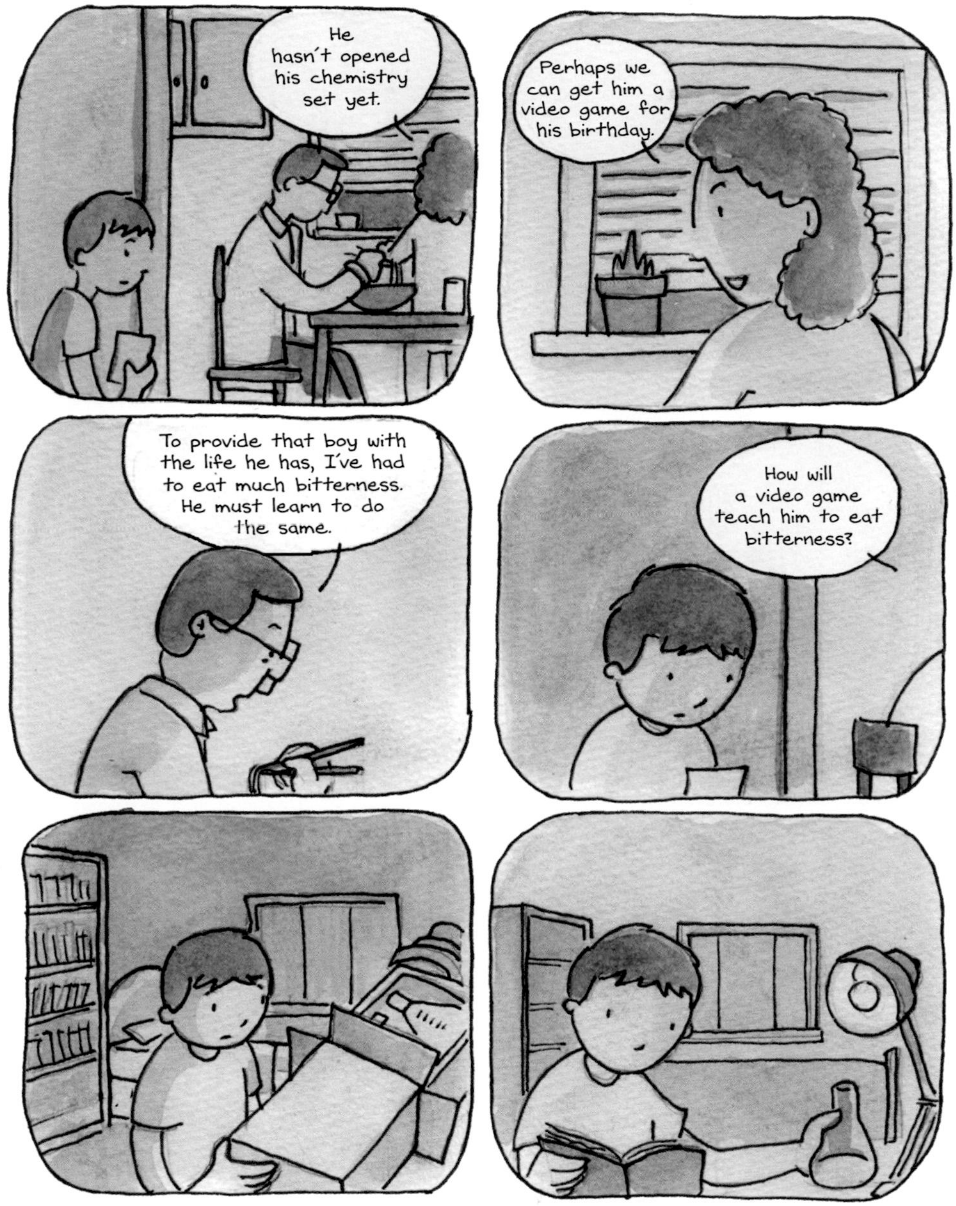
He hasn't opened his chemistry set yet.
Perhaps we can get him a video game for his birthday.
To provide that boy with the life he has, I've had to eat much bitterness. He must learn to do the same.
How will a video game teach him to eat bitterness?

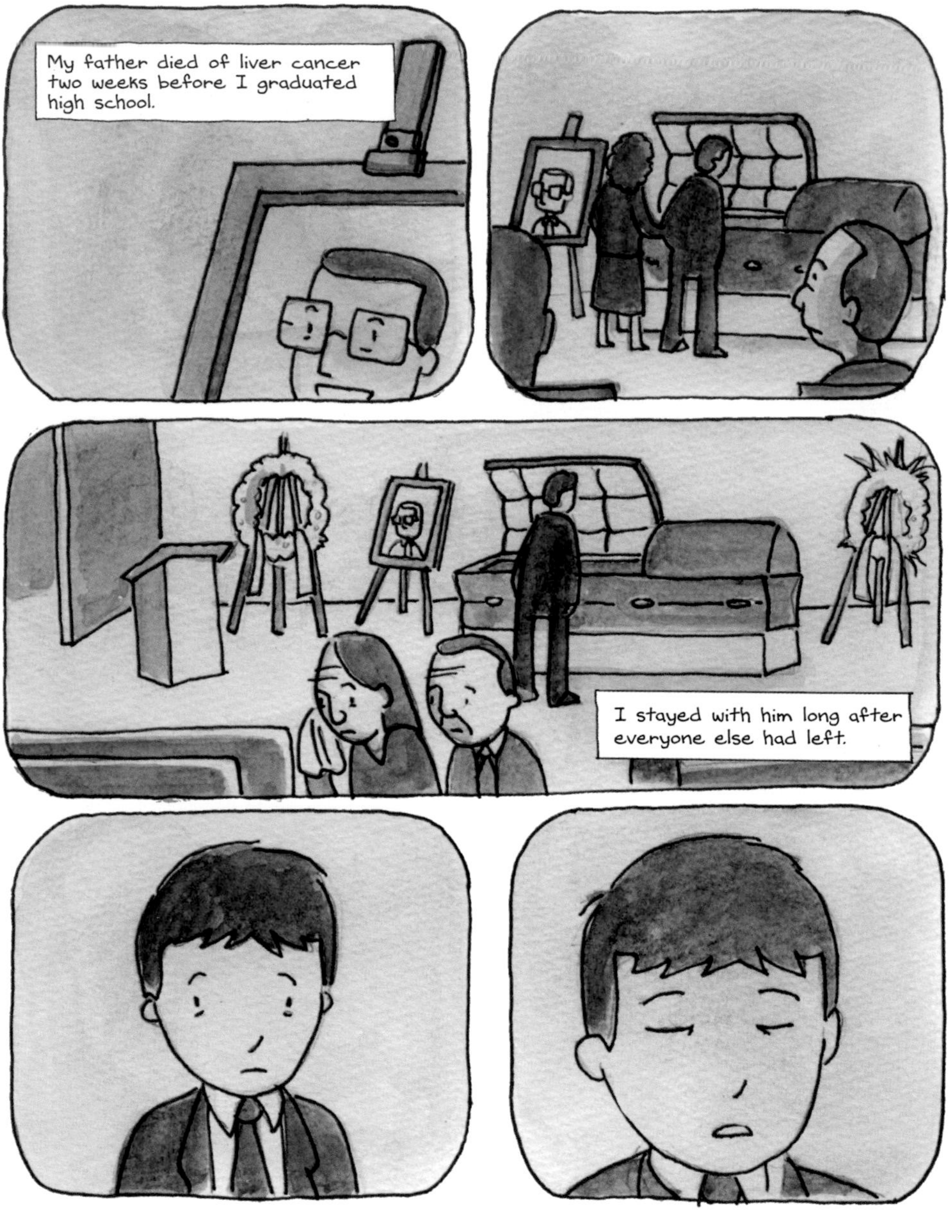
My father died of liver cancer two weeks before I graduated high school.
I stayed with him long after everyone else had left.

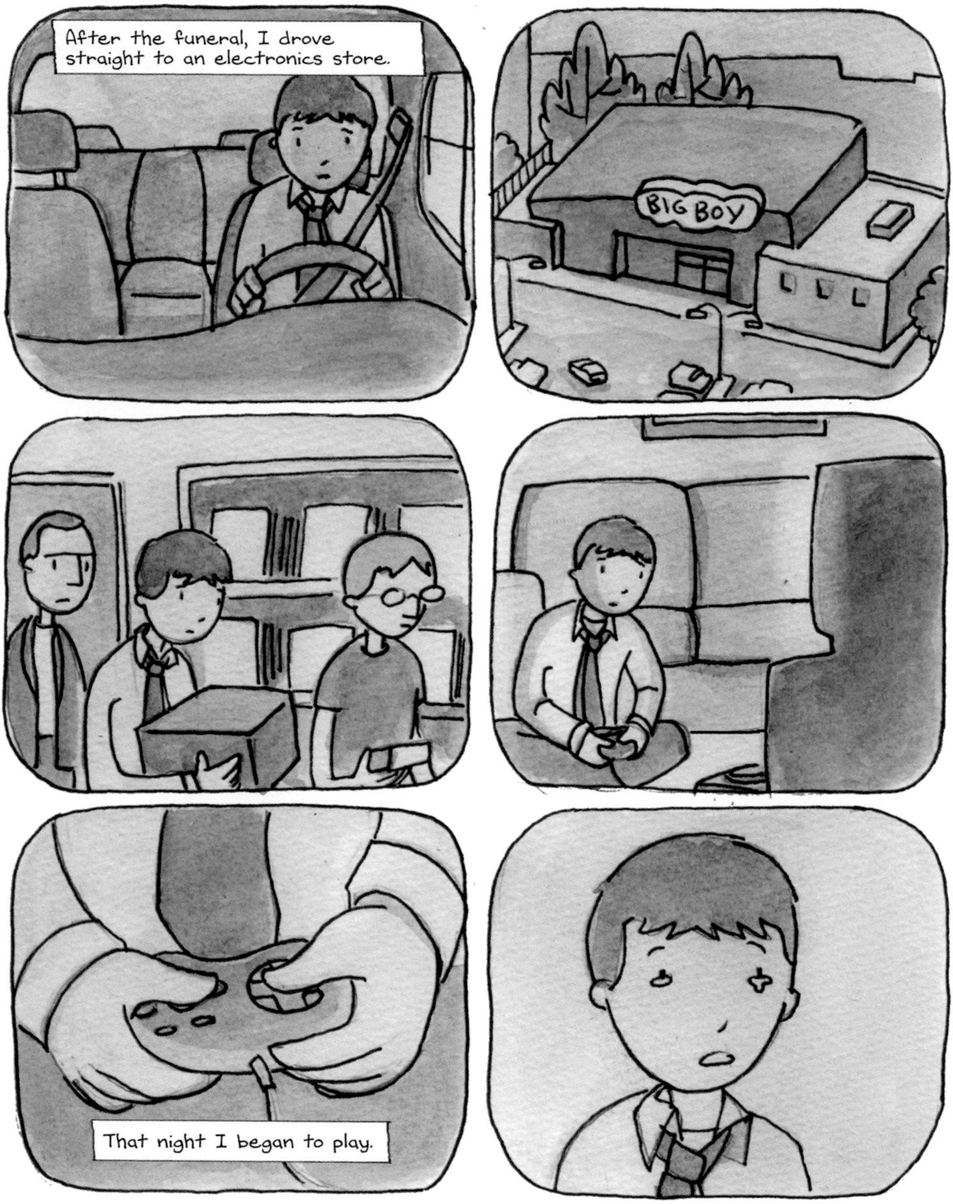
After the funeral, I drove straight to an electronics store.
BIG BOY
That night I began to play.

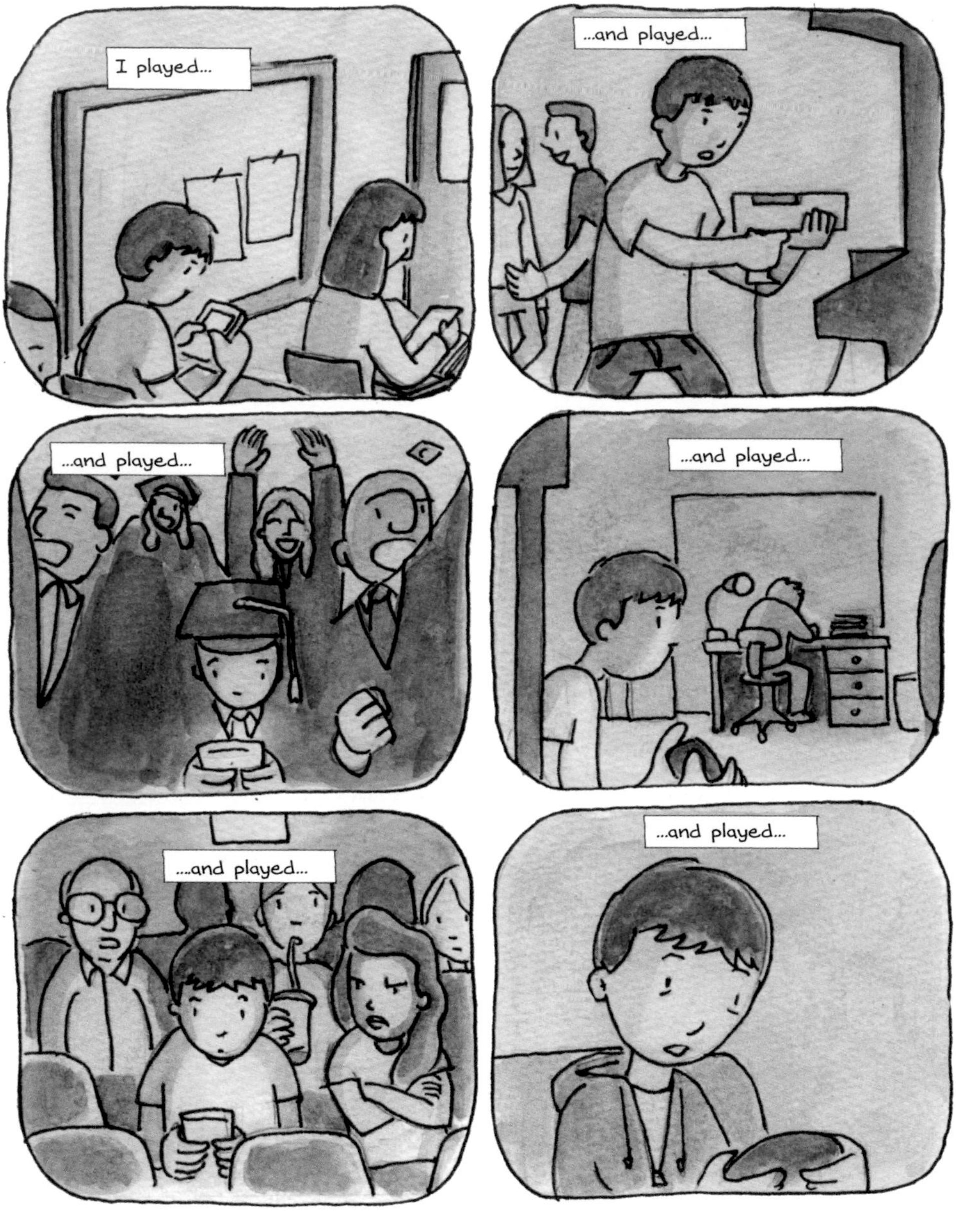
I played...
...and played...
...and played...
...and played...
....and played...
...and played...

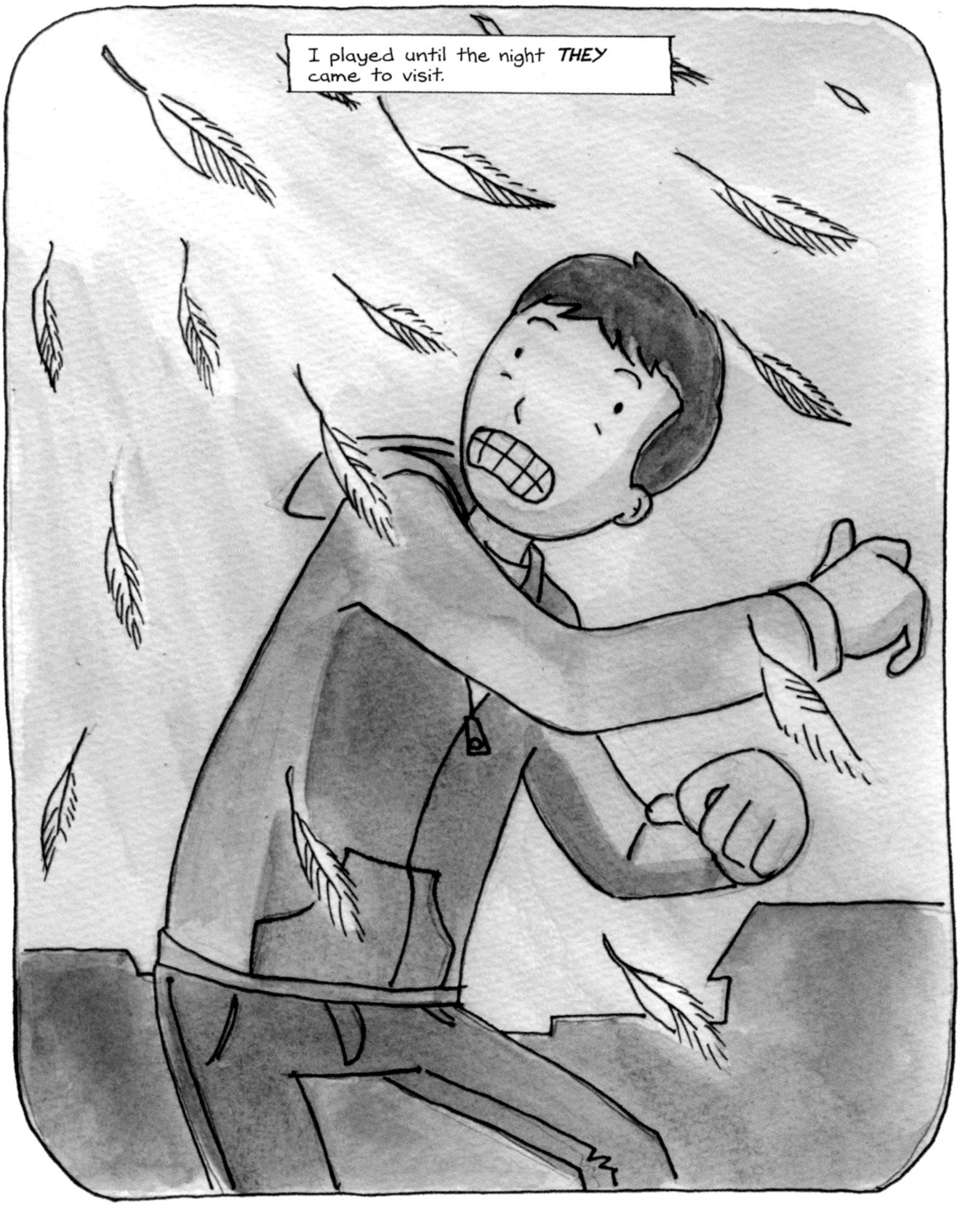
I played until the night THEY came to visit.

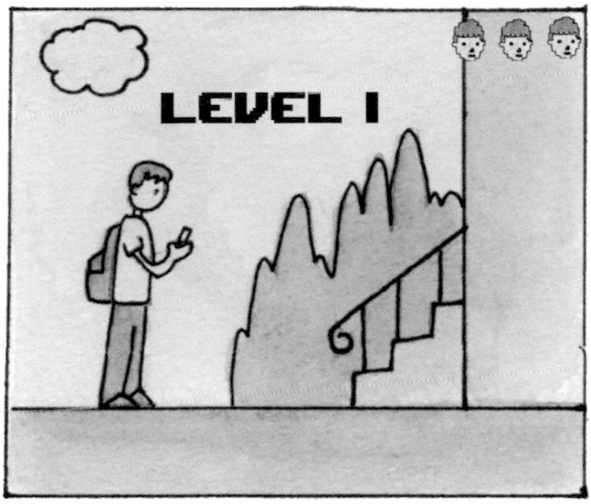
LEVEL 1

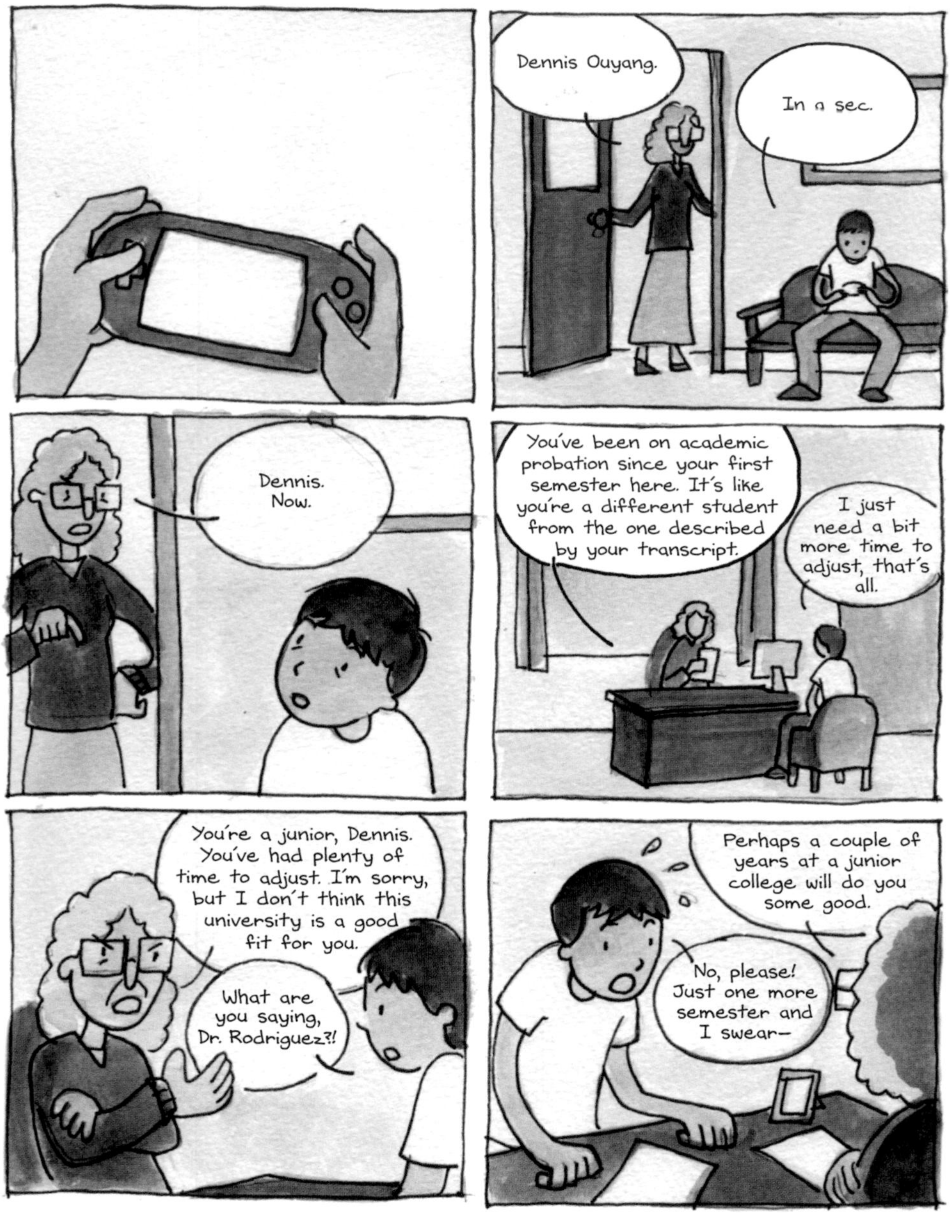
Dennis Ouyang.
In a sec.
Dennis. Now.
You've been on academic probation since your first semester here. It's like you're a different student from the one described by your transcript.
I just need a bit more time to adjust, that's all.
You're a junior, Dennis. You've had plenty of time to adjust. I'm sorry, but I don't think this university is a good fit for you.
What are you saying, Dr. Rodriguez?!
Perhaps a couple of years at a junior college will do you some good.
No, please! Just one more semester and I swear—

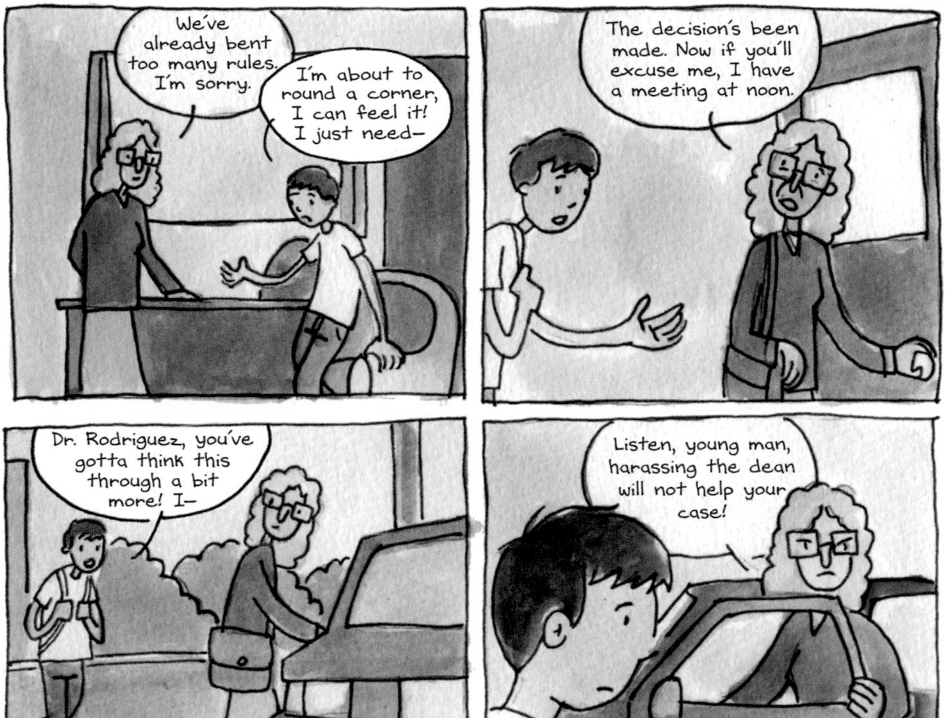
We've already bent too many rules. I'm sorry.
I'm about to round a corner, I can feel it! I just need—
The decision's been made. Now if you'll excuse me, I have a meeting at noon.
Dr. Rodriguez, you've gotta think this through a bit more! I—
Listen, young man, harassing the dean will not help your case!
You haven't had your priorities straight, and now you need to face the consequences. Good-bye, Dennis.
Nice car.

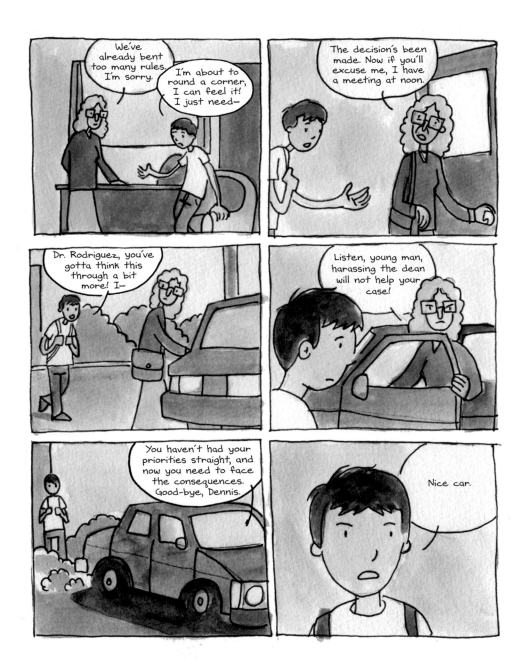

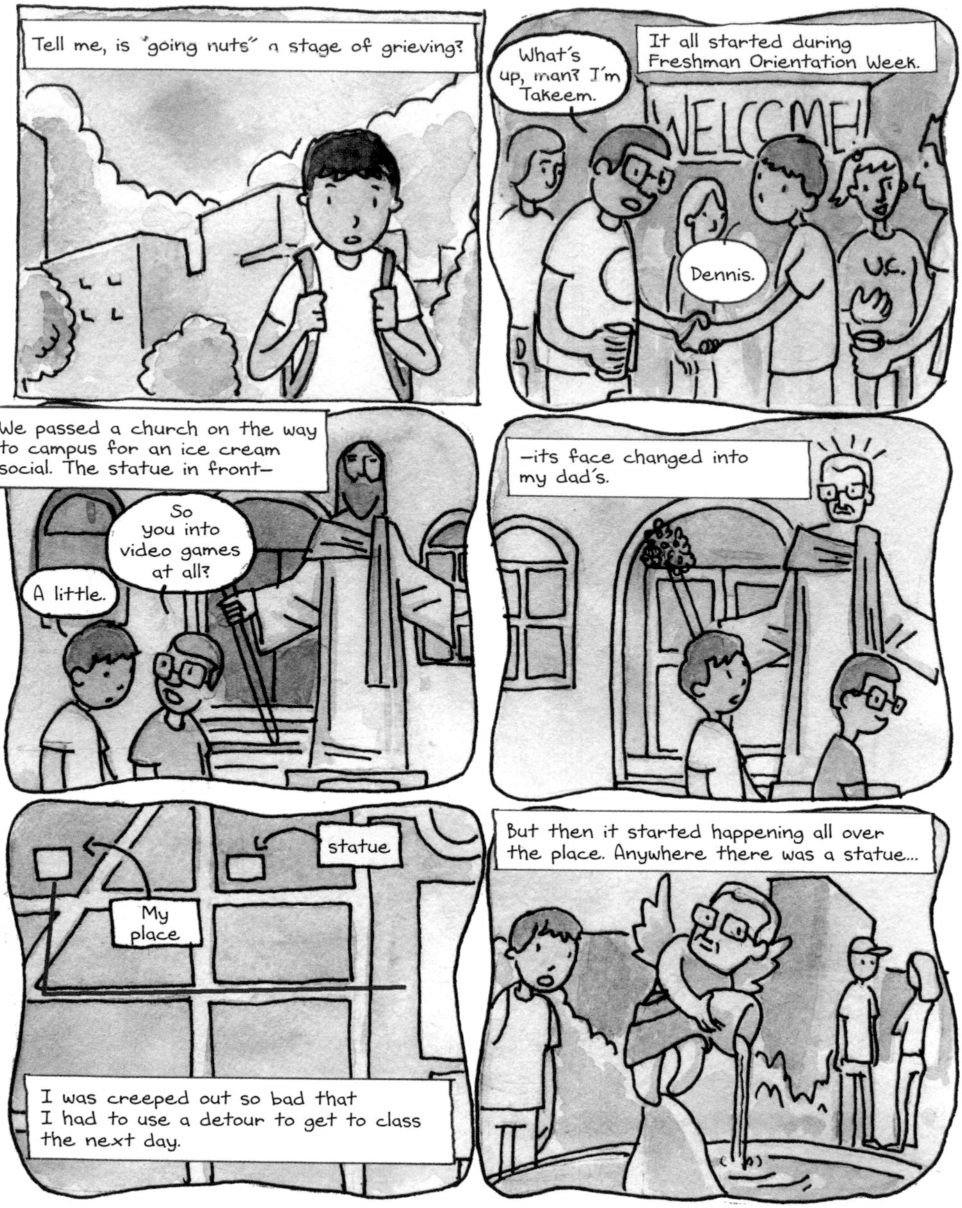

Tell me, is "going nuts" a stage of grieving?
It all started during Freshman Orientation Week.
What's up, man? I'm Takeem.
WELCOME!
Dennis.
U.C.
We passed a church on the way to campus for an ice cream social. The statue in front—
So you into video games at all?
A little.
—its face changed into my dad's.
statue
My place
I was creeped out so bad that I had to use a detour to get to class the next day.
But then it started happening all over the place. Anywhere there was a statue...

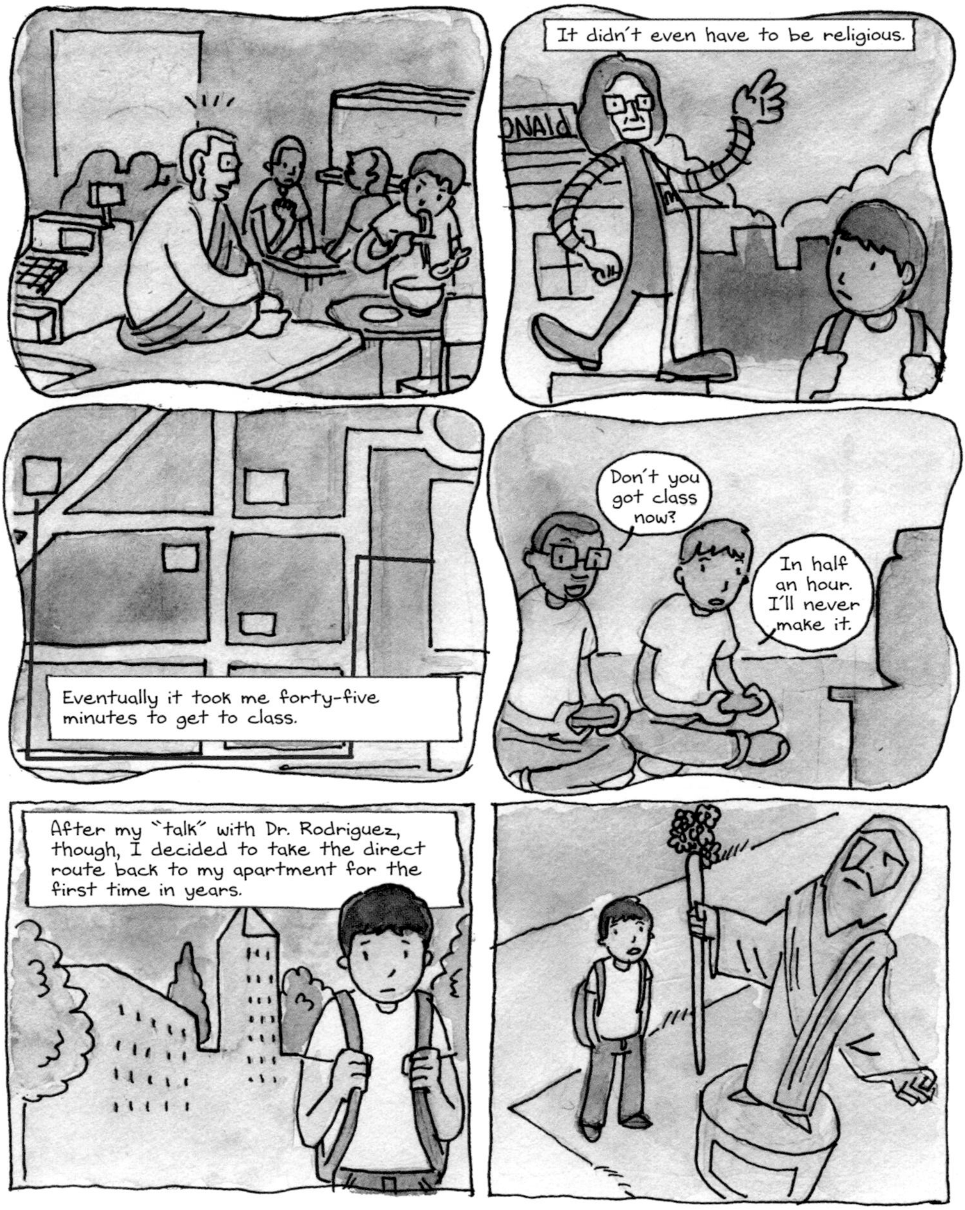

It didn't even have to be religious.
ONALd
Eventually it took me forty-five minutes to get to class.
Don't you got class now?
In half an hour. I'll never make it.
After my "talk" with Dr. Rodriguez, though, I decided to take the direct route back to my apartment for the first time in years.

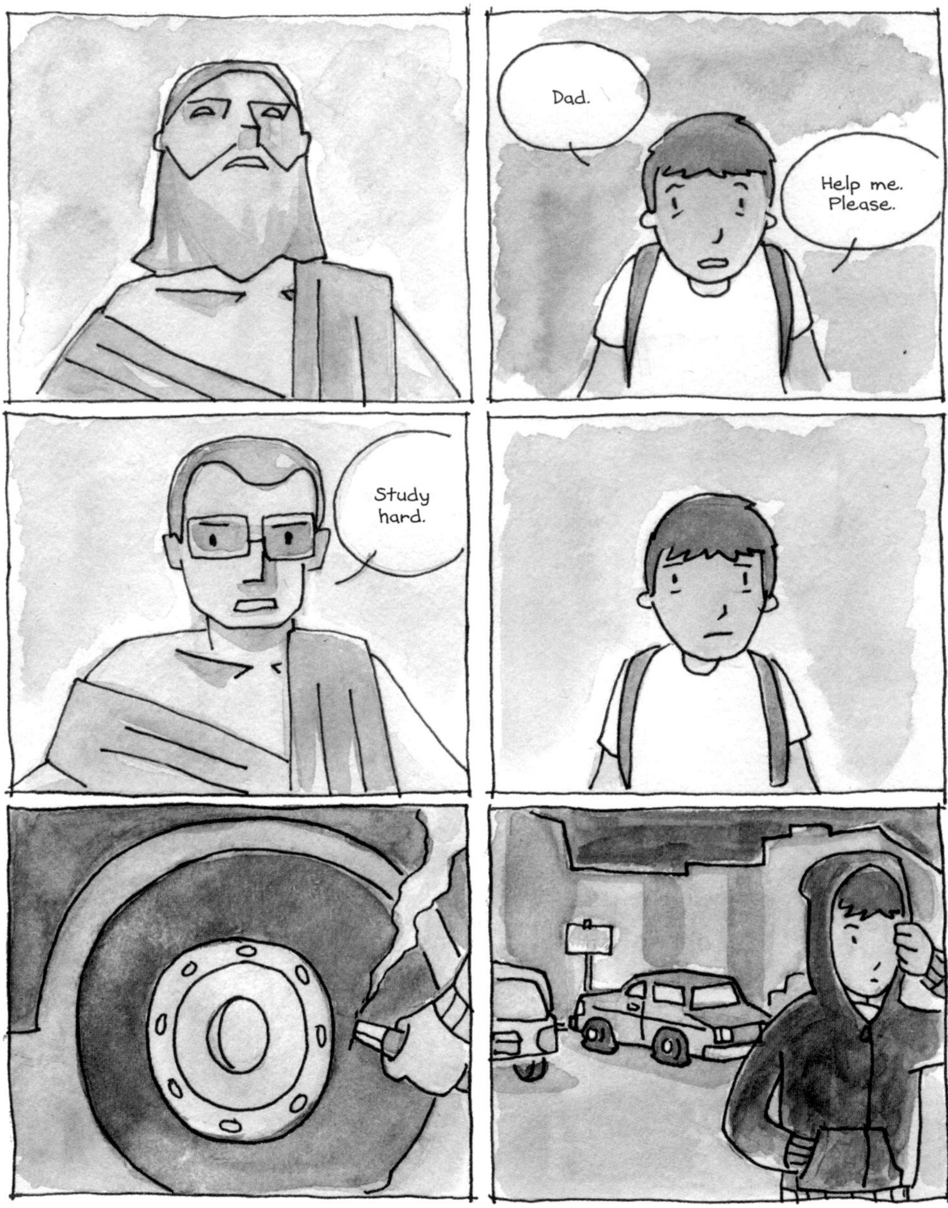
Dad.
Help me. Please.
Study hard.

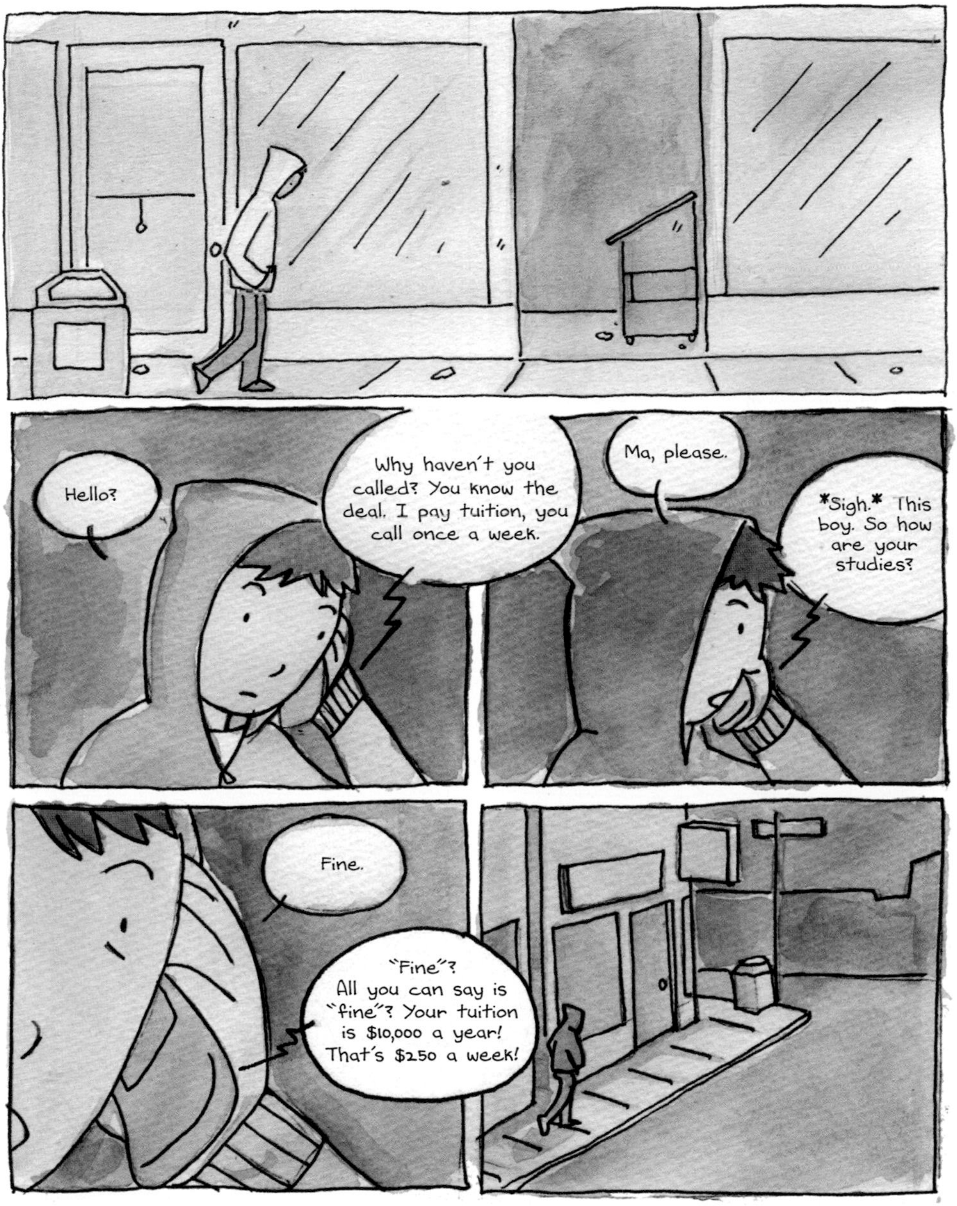
Hello?
Why haven't you called? You know the deal. I pay tuition, you call once a week.
Ma, please.
Sigh. This boy. So how are your studies?
Fine.
"Fine"? All you can say is "fine"? Your tuition is $10,000 a year! That's $250 a week!

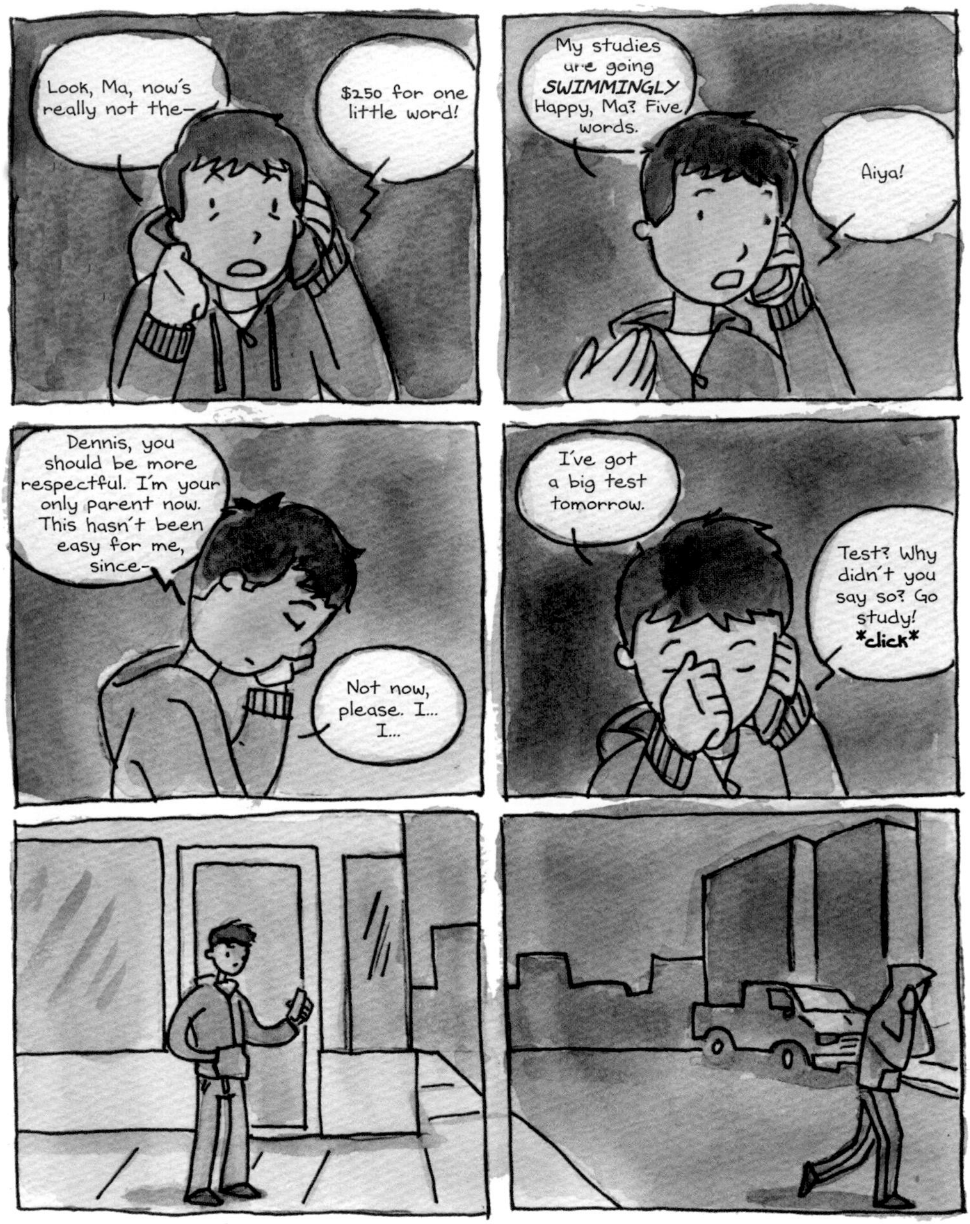
Look, Ma, now's really not the—
$250 for one little word!
My studies are going SWIMMINGLY Happy, Ma? Five words.
Aiya!
Dennis, you should be more respectful. I'm your only parent now. This hasn't been easy for me, since—
Not now, please. I... I...
I've got a big test tomorrow.
Test? Why didn't you say so? Go study! *click*

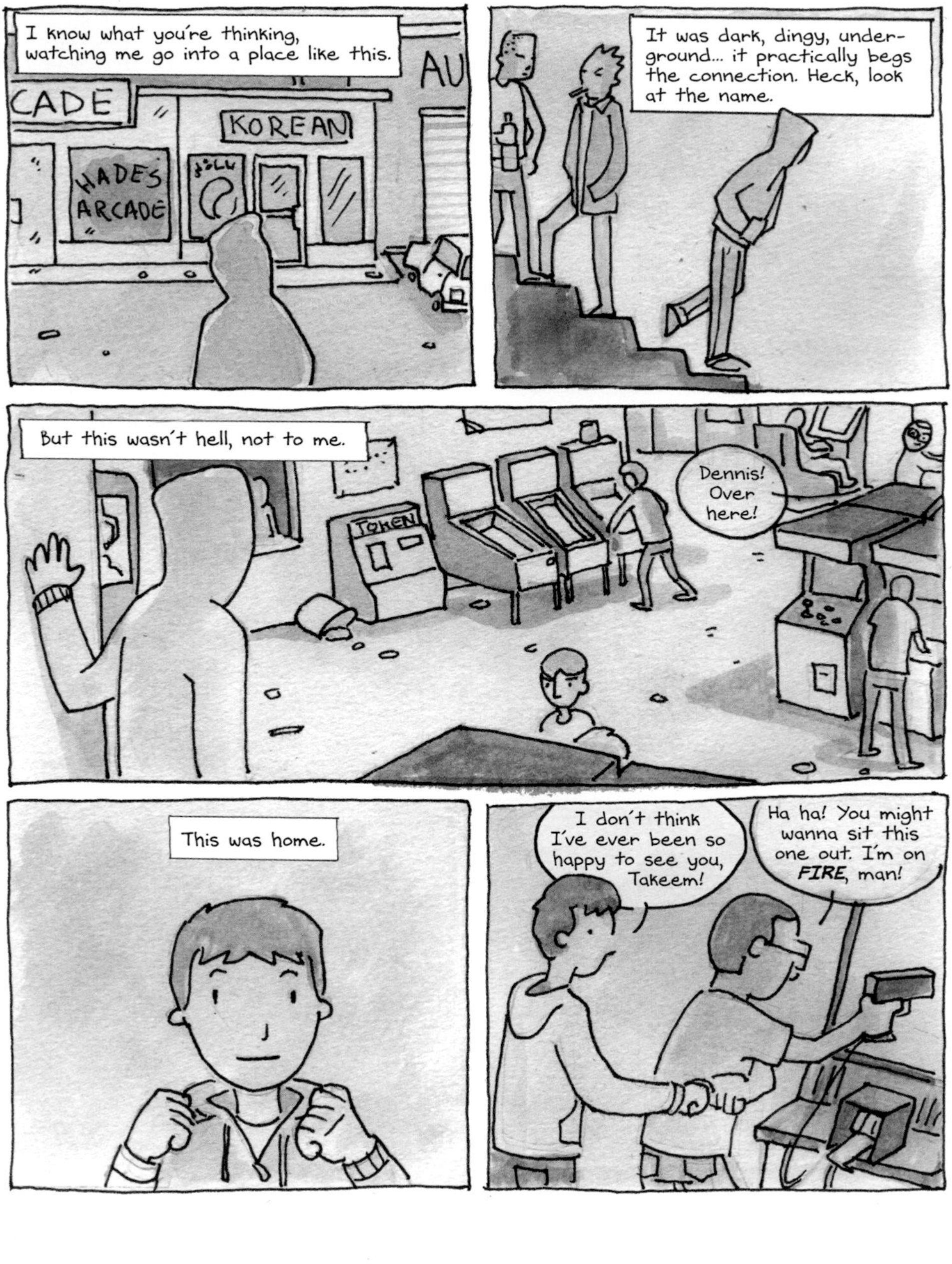
I know what you're thinking, watching me go into a place like this.
CADE
KOREAN
HADES ARCADE
AU
It was dark, dingy, underground... it practically begs the connection. Heck, look at the name.
But this wasn't hell, not to me.
TOKEN
Dennis! Over here!
This was home.
I don't think I've ever been so happy to see you, Takeem!
Ha ha! You might wanna sit this one out. I'm on **FIRE**, man!

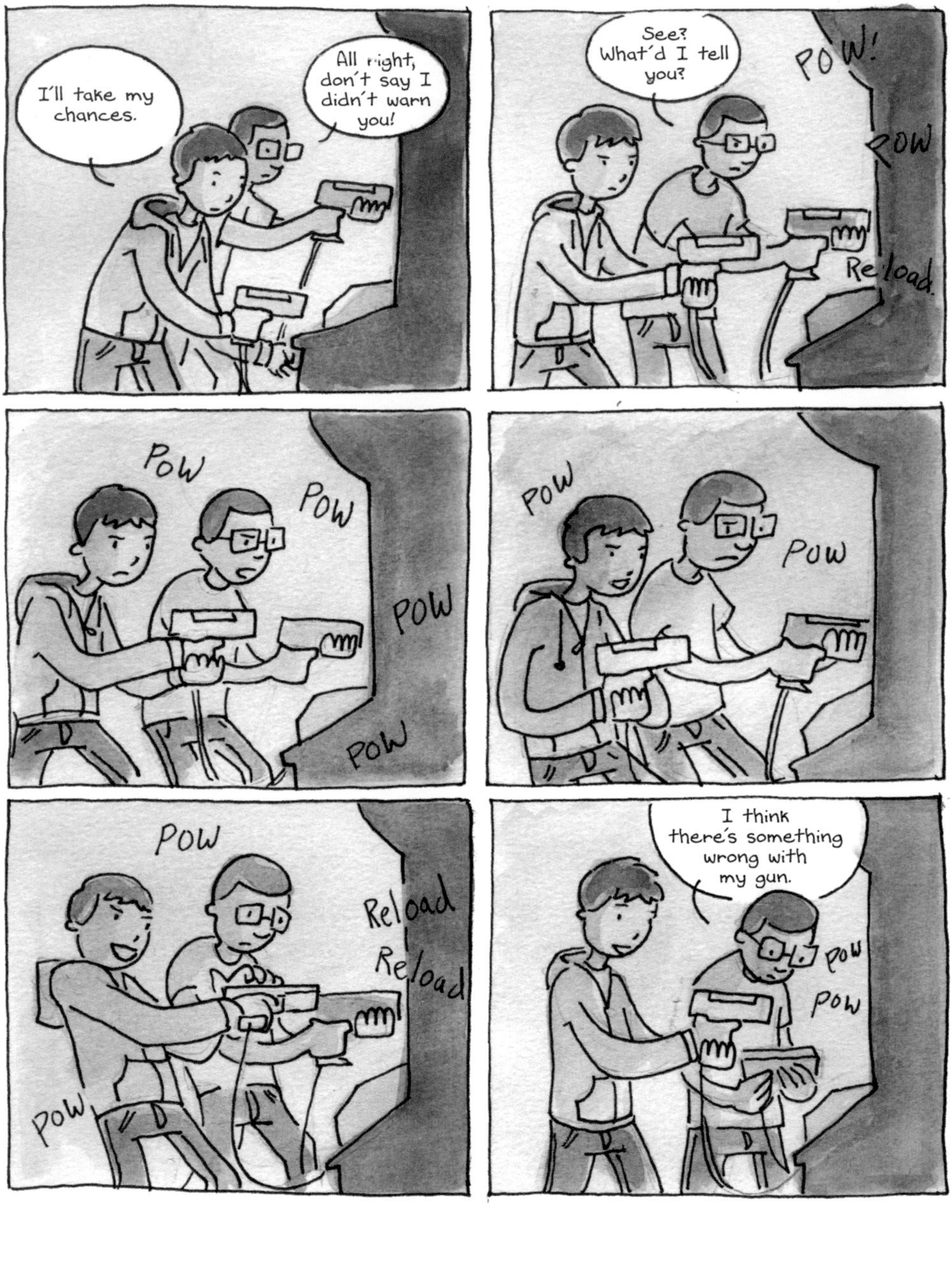
I'll take my chances.
All right, don't say I didn't warn you!
See? What'd I tell you?
POW!
POW
Reload.
POW
POW
POW
POW
POW
POW
POW
Reload
Reload
POW
I think there's something wrong with my gun.
POW
POW

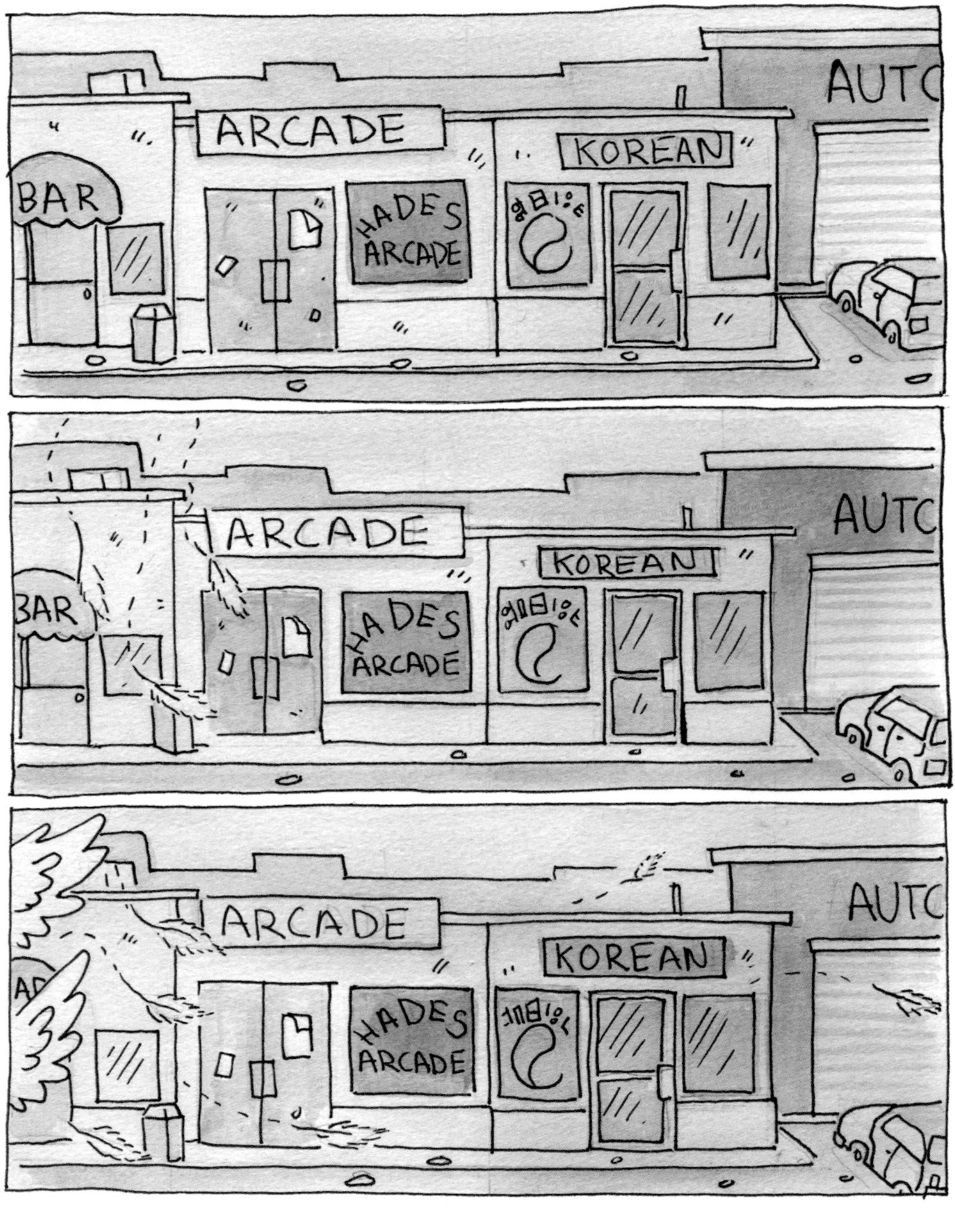
BAR
ARCADE
KOREAN
HADES ARCADE
BAR
ARCADE
KOREAN
HADES ARCADE
ARCADE
KOREAN
HADES ARCADE

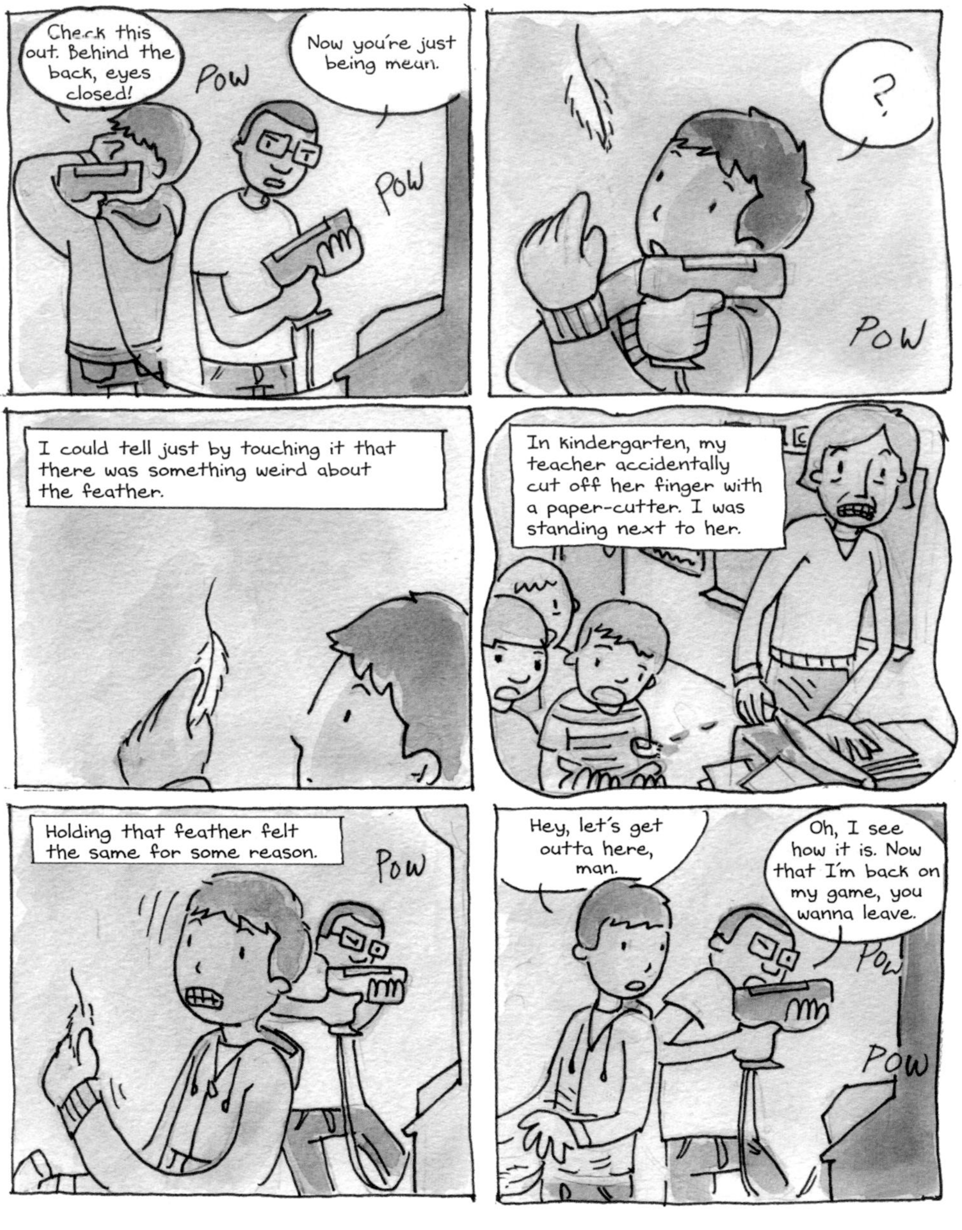
Check this out. Behind the back, eyes closed!
POW
Now you're just being mean.
POW
?
POW
I could tell just by touching it that there was something weird about the feather.
In kindergarten, my teacher accidentally cut off her finger with a paper-cutter. I was standing next to her.
Holding that feather felt the same for some reason.
POW
Hey, let's get outta here, man.
Oh, I see how it is. Now that I'm back on my game, you wanna leave.
POW
POW

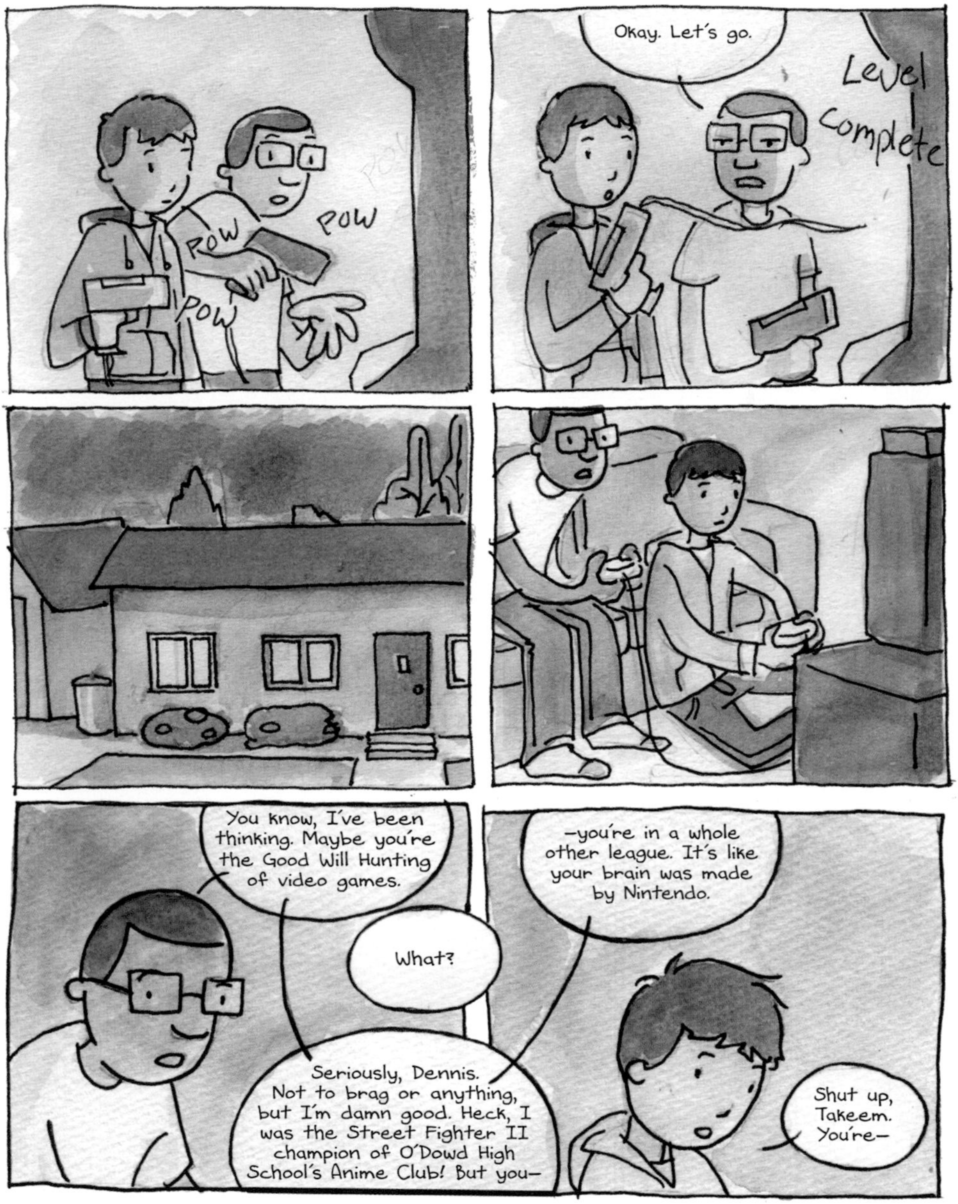
POW
POW
POW
POW
Okay. Let's go.
Level complete
You know, I've been thinking. Maybe you're the Good Will Hunting of video games.
What?
Seriously, Dennis. Not to brag or anything, but I'm damn good. Heck, I was the Street Fighter II champion of O'Dowd High School's Anime Club! But you—
—you're in a whole other league. It's like your brain was made by Nintendo.
Shut up, Takeem. You're—

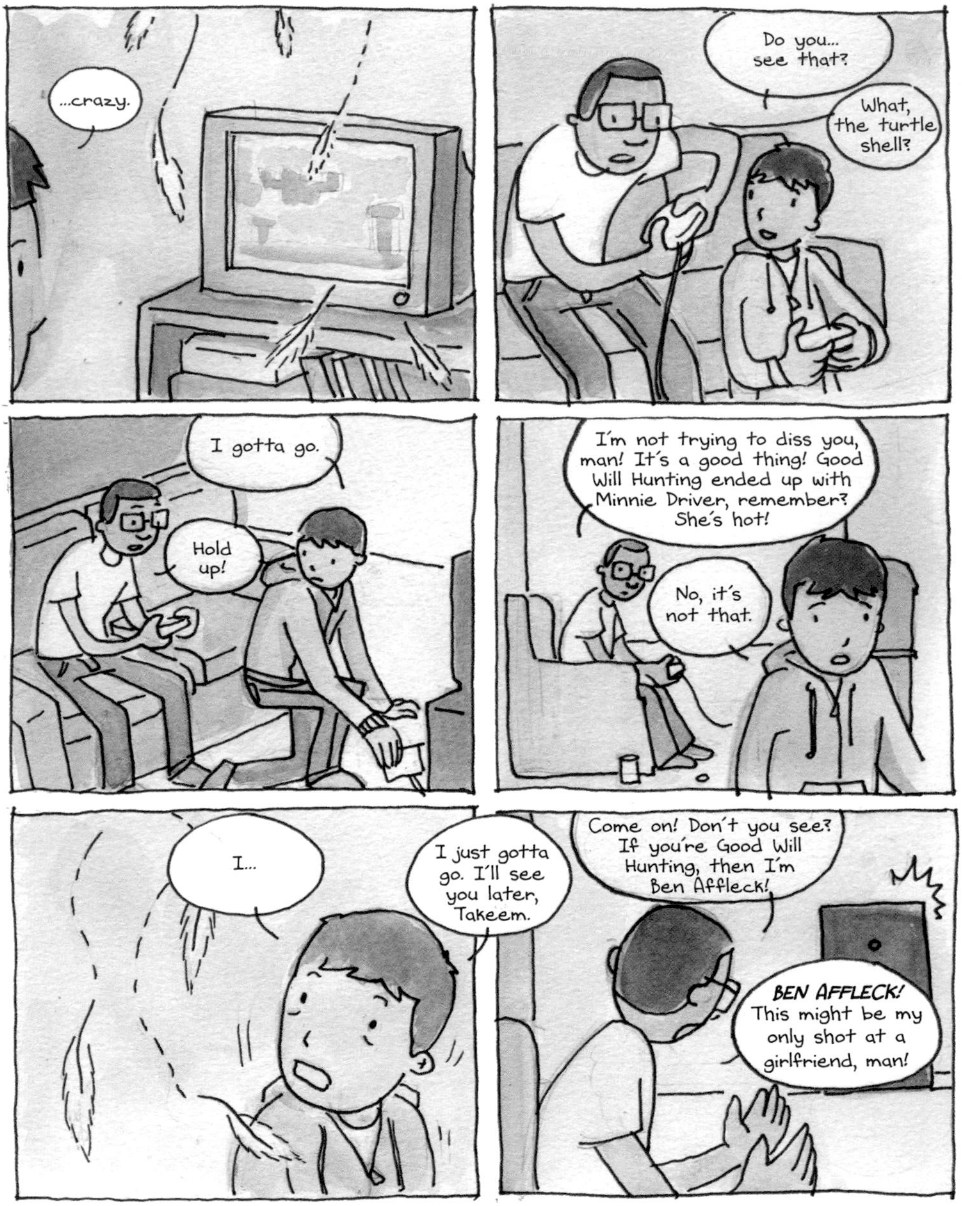
...crazy.
Do you... see that?
What, the turtle shell?
I gotta go.
Hold up!
I'm not trying to diss you, man! It's a good thing! Good Will Hunting ended up with Minnie Driver, remember? She's hot!
No, it's not that.
I...
I just gotta go. I'll see you later, Takeem.
Come on! Don't you see? If you're Good Will Hunting, then I'm Ben Affleck!
BEN AFFLECK! This might be my only shot at a girlfriend, man!

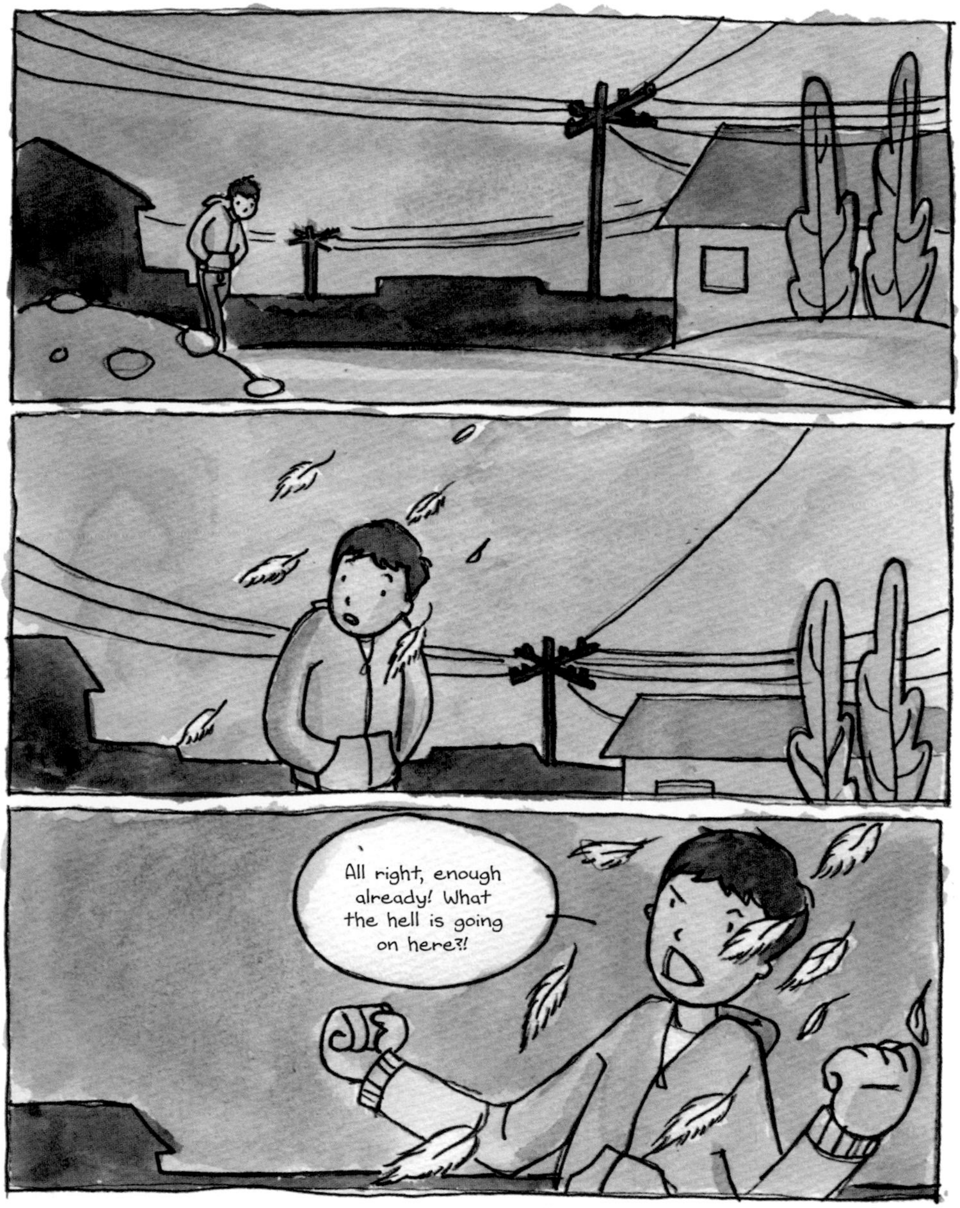
All right, enough already! What the hell is going on here?!

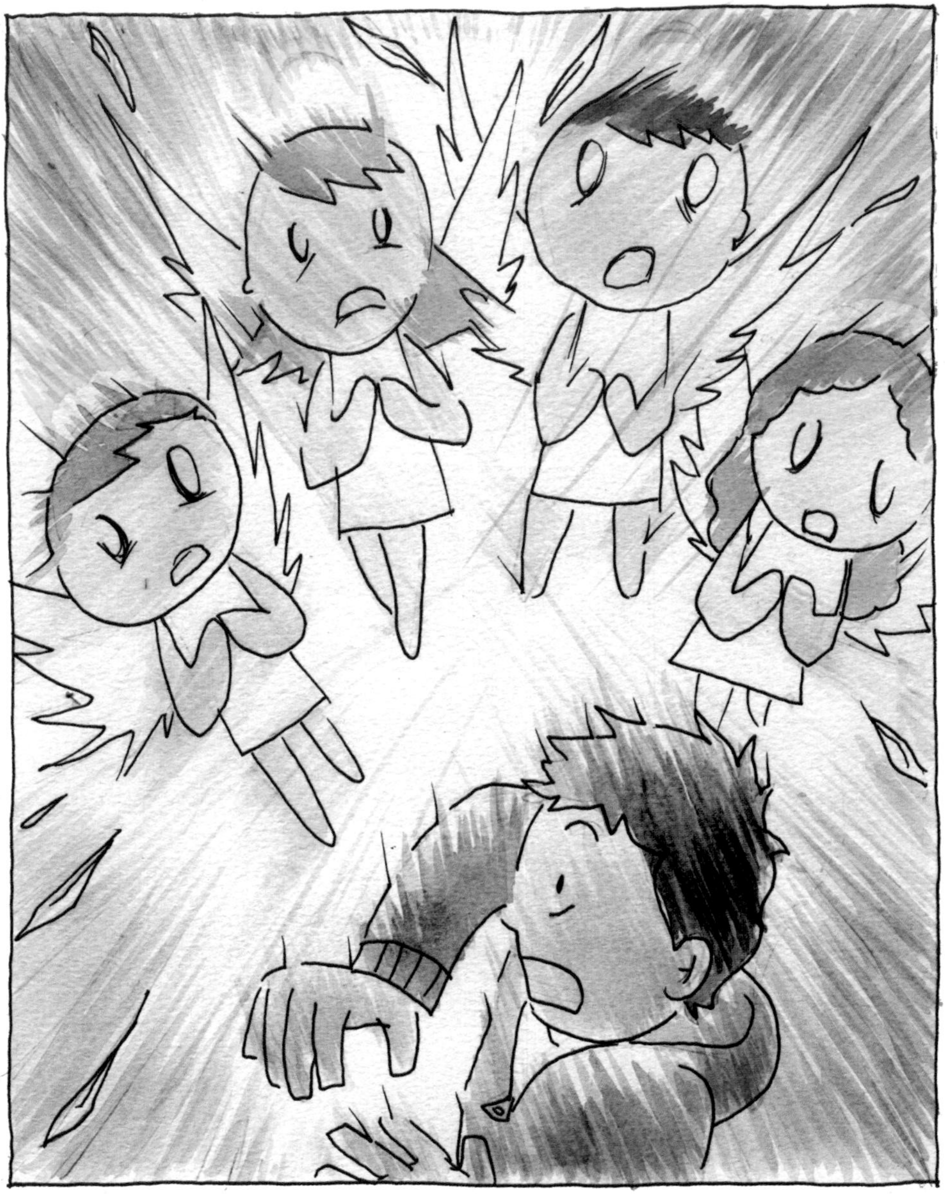

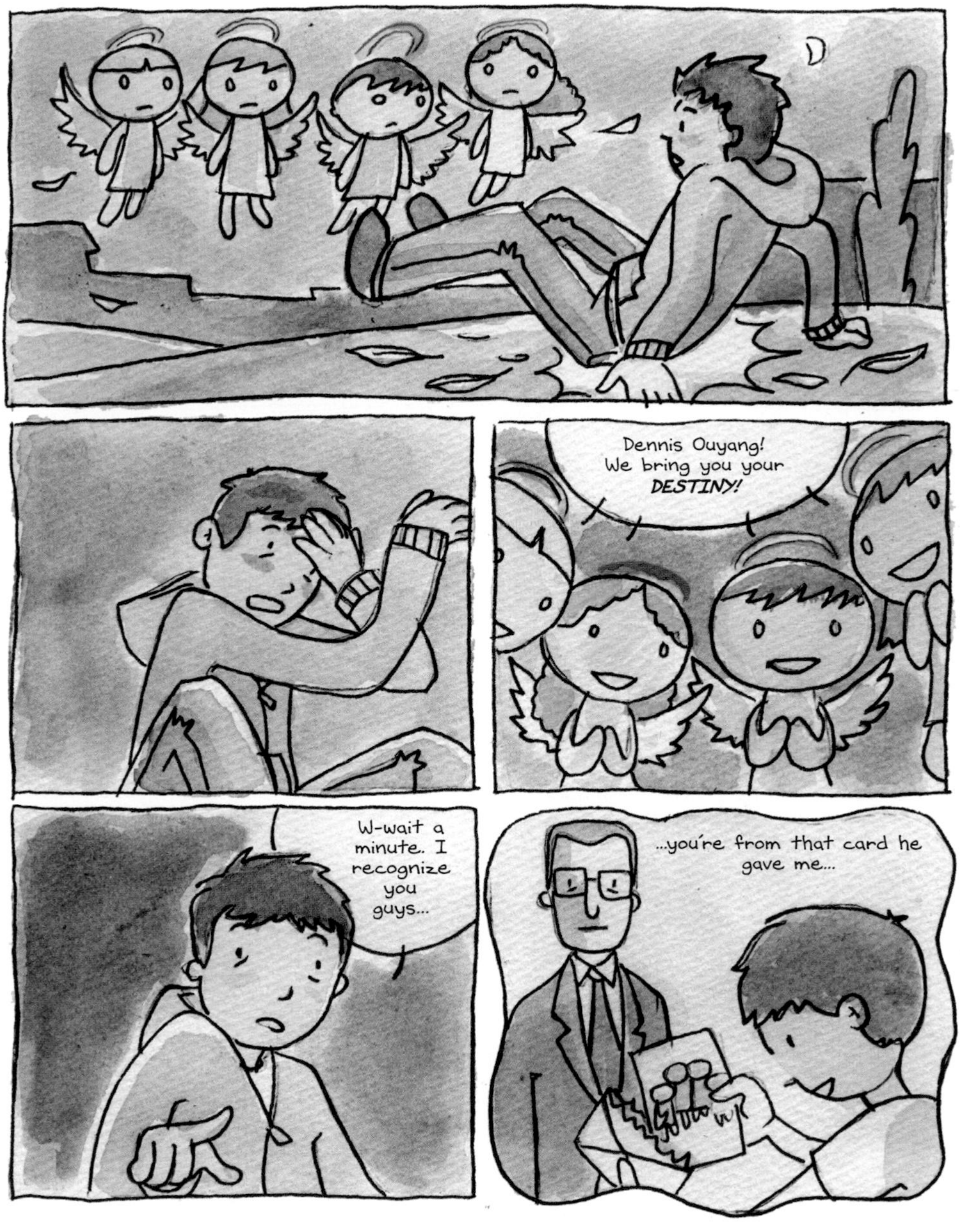
Dennis Ouyang!
We bring you your
DESTINY!
W-wait a
minute. I
recognize
you
guys...
...you're from that card he
gave me...

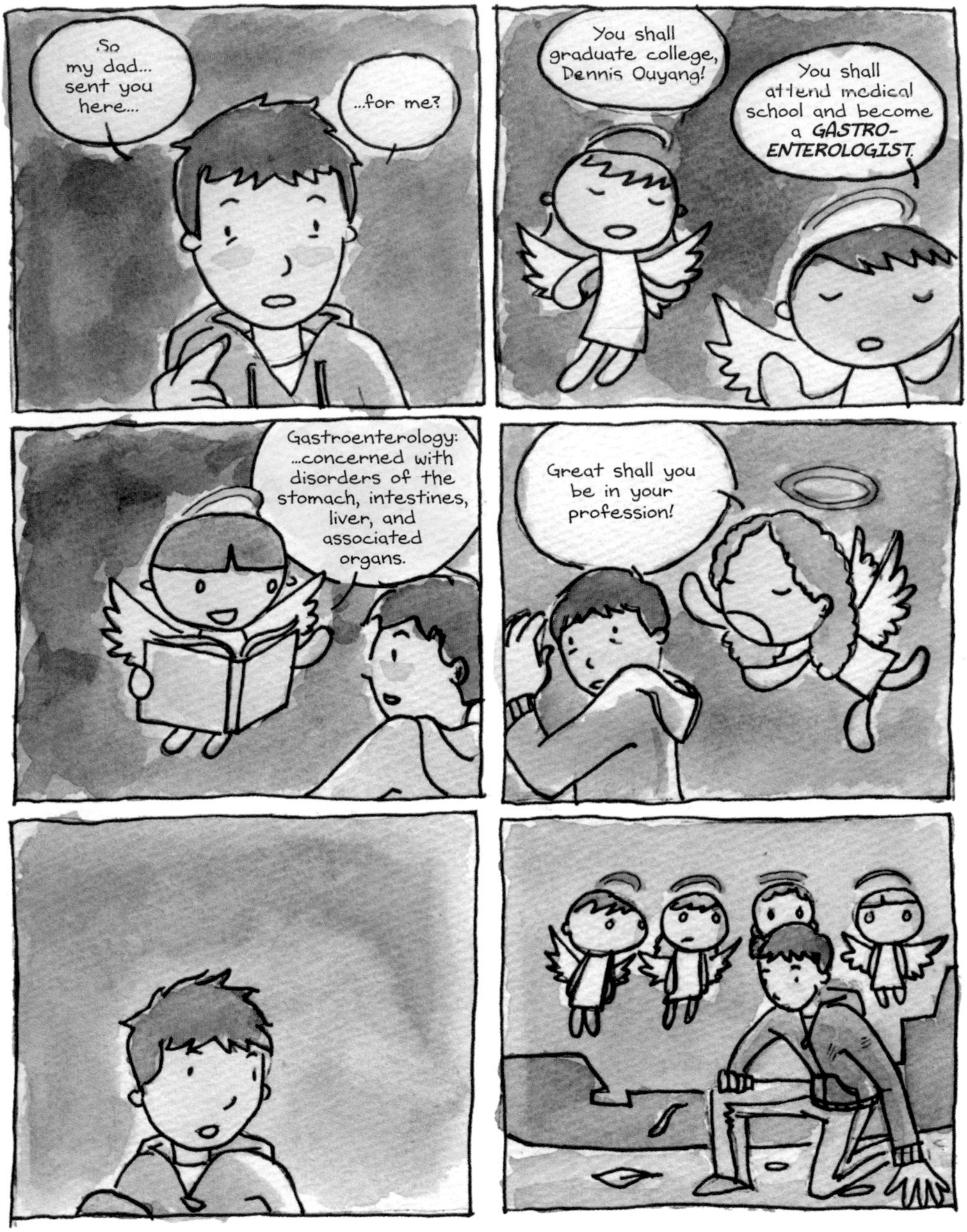
So my dad... sent you here...
...for me?
You shall graduate college, Dennis Ouyang!
You shall attend medical school and become a GASTRO-ENTEROLOGIST.
Gastroenterology: ...concerned with disorders of the stomach, intestines, liver, and associated organs.
Great shall you be in your profession!

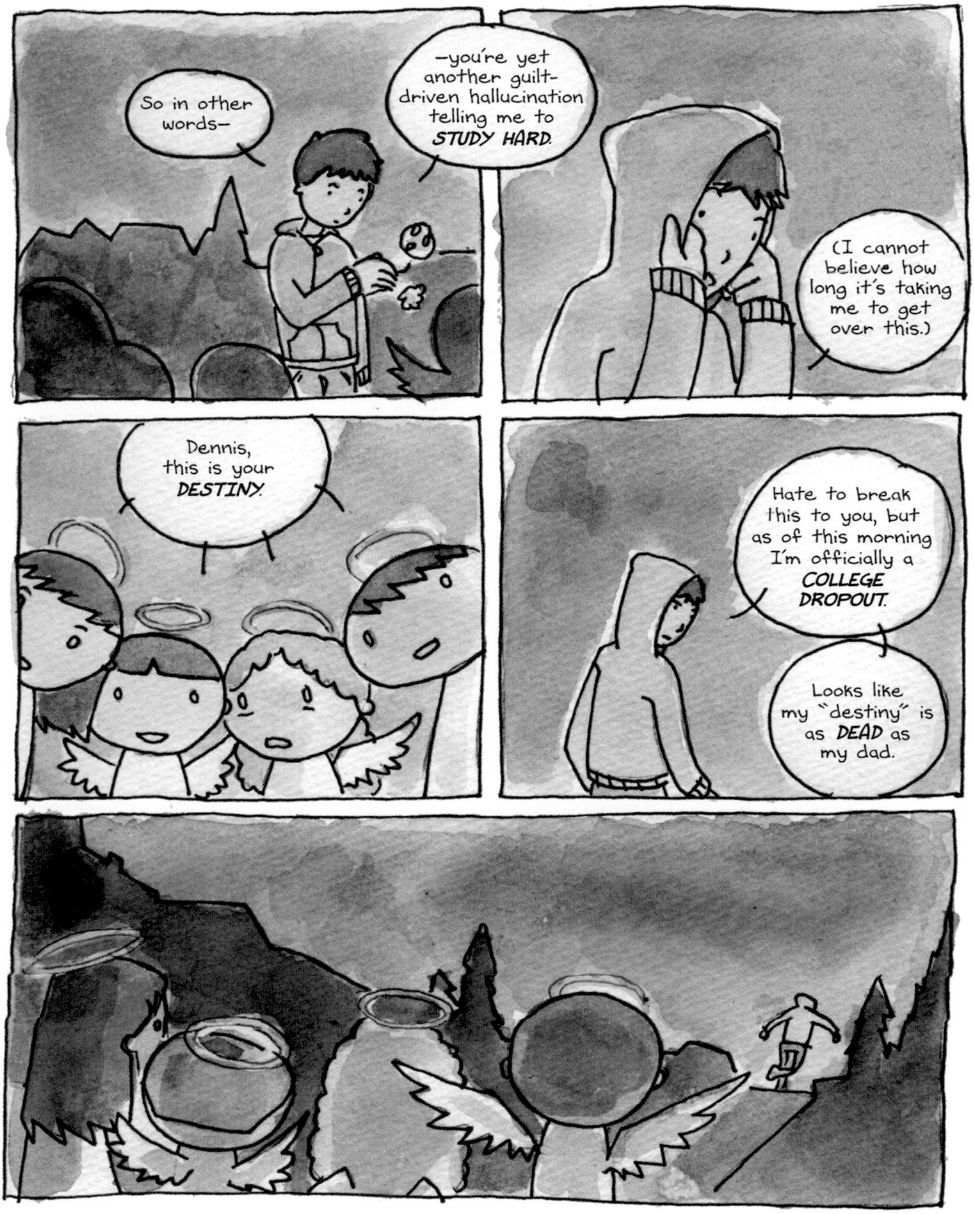
So in other words—
—you're yet another guilt-driven hallucination telling me to STUDY HARD.
(I cannot believe how long it's taking me to get over this.)
Dennis, this is your DESTINY.
Hate to break this to you, but as of this morning I'm officially a COLLEGE DROPOUT.
Looks like my "destiny" is as DEAD as my dad.

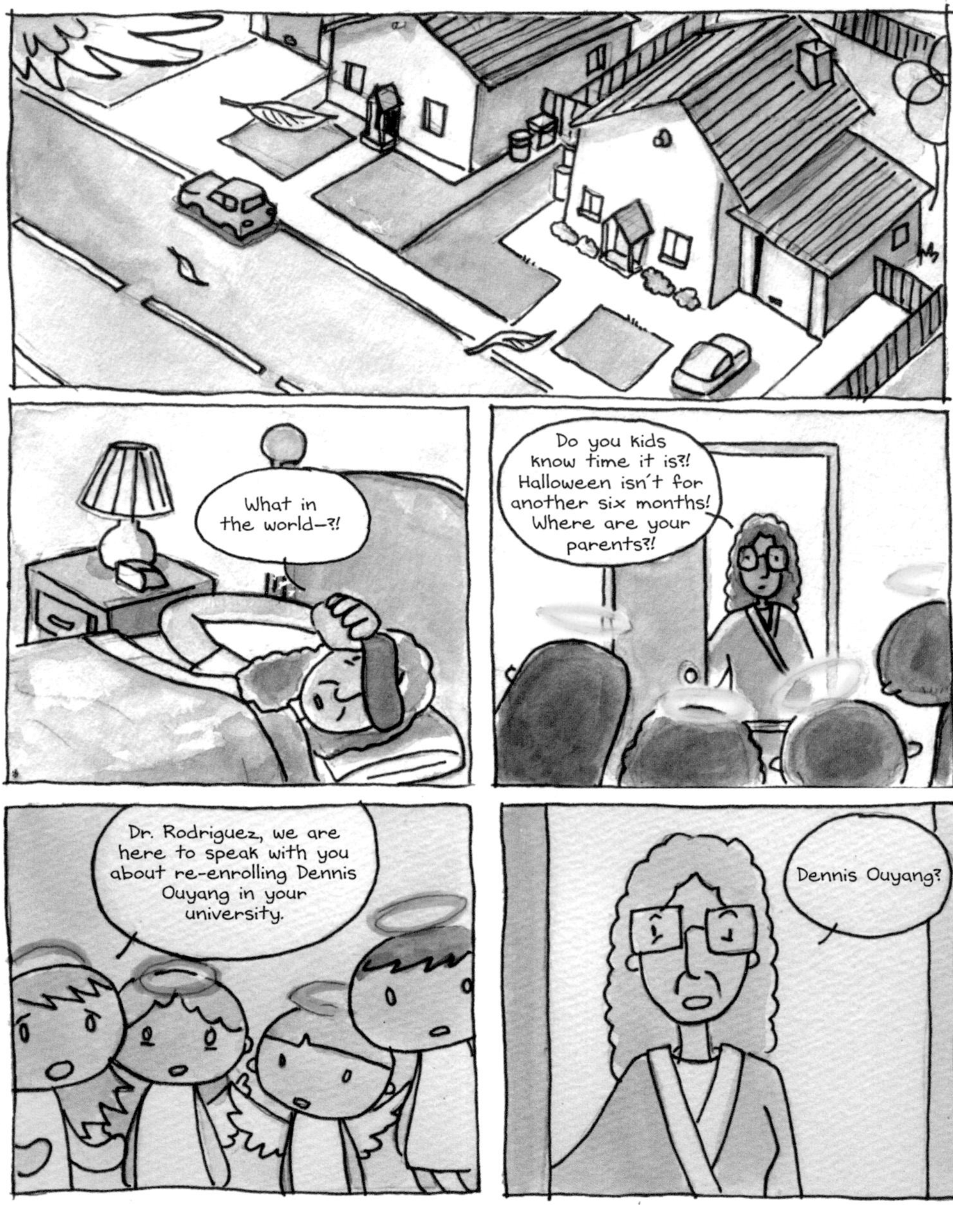
What in the world—?!
Do you kids know time it is?! Halloween isn't for another six months! Where are your parents?!
Dr. Rodriguez, we are here to speak with you about re-enrolling Dennis Ouyang in your university.
Dennis Ouyang?

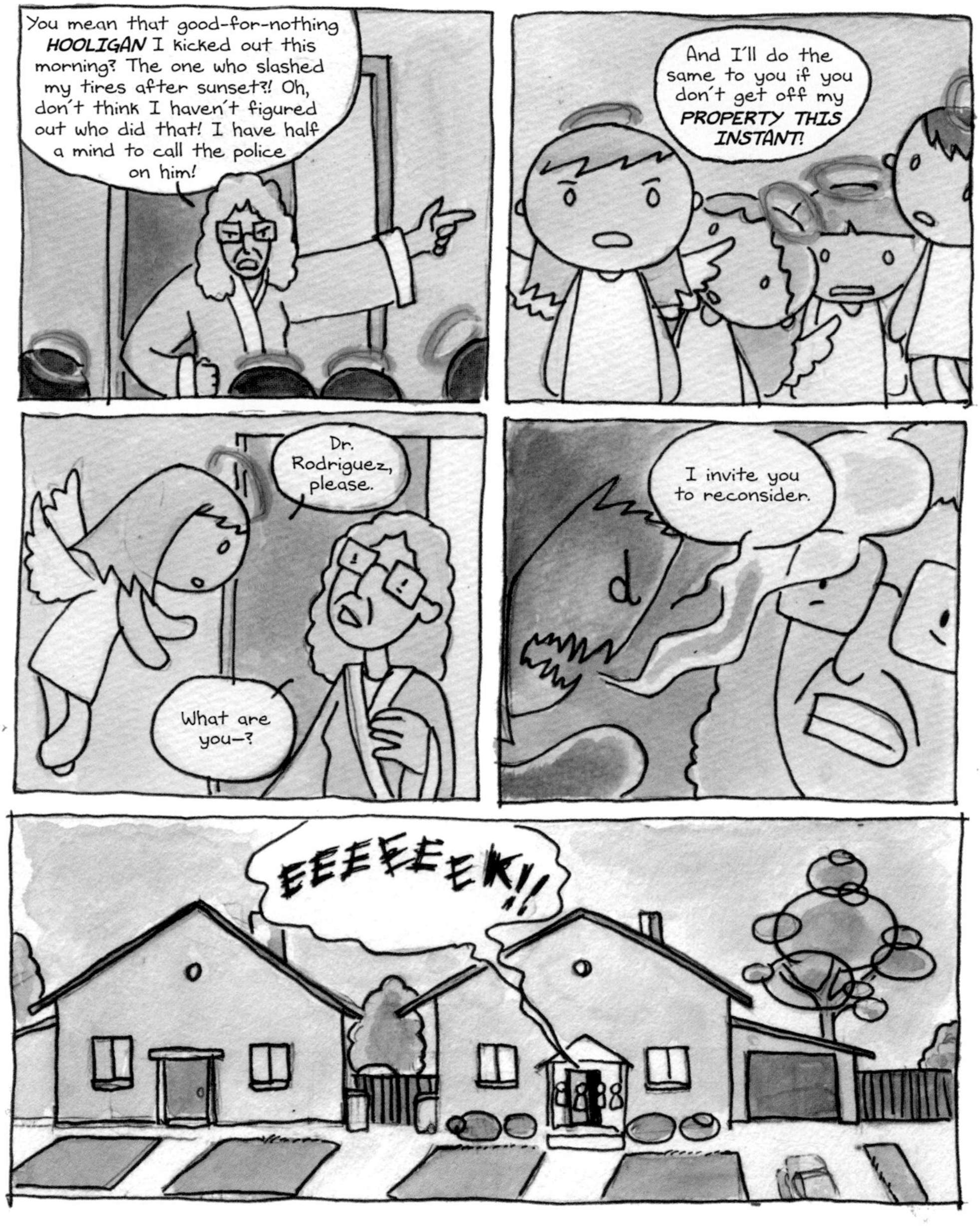
You mean that good-for-nothing **HOOLIGAN** I kicked out this morning? The one who slashed my tires after sunset?! Oh, don't think I haven't figured out who did that! I have half a mind to call the police on him!
And I'll do the same to you if you don't get off my **PROPERTY THIS INSTANT!**
Dr. Rodriguez, please.
What are you—?
I invite you to reconsider.
EEEEEEEK!!

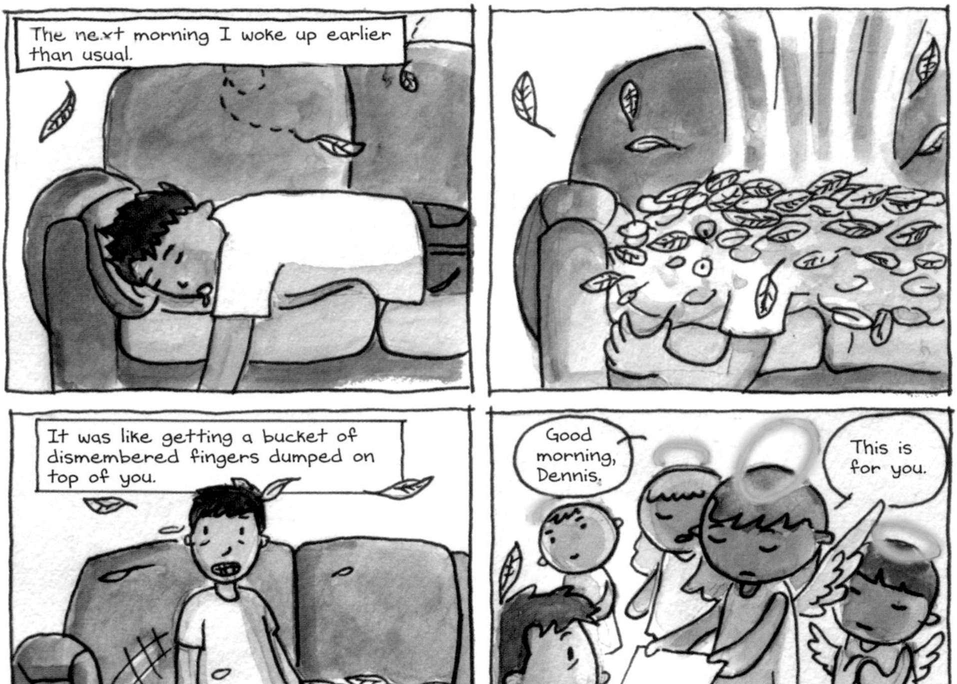
The next morning I woke up earlier than usual.
It was like getting a bucket of dismembered fingers dumped on top of you.
Good morning, Dennis.
This is for you.
A letter from Dr. Rodriguez. This is real?
Yes.
How did you—?
It is done. That's all that matters.
So I'm back in college, then. Back on track.

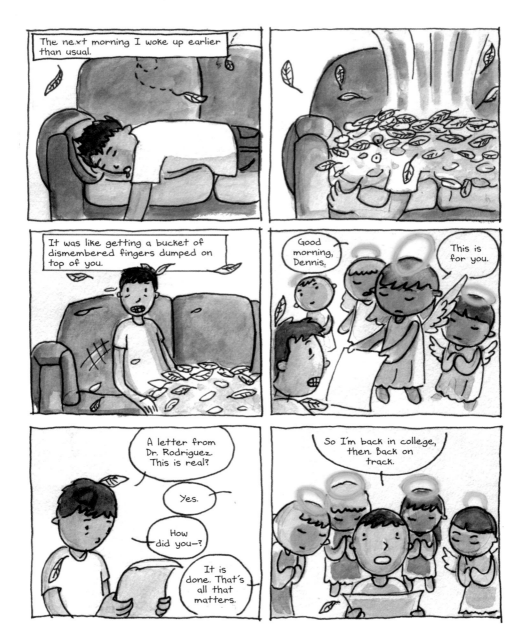

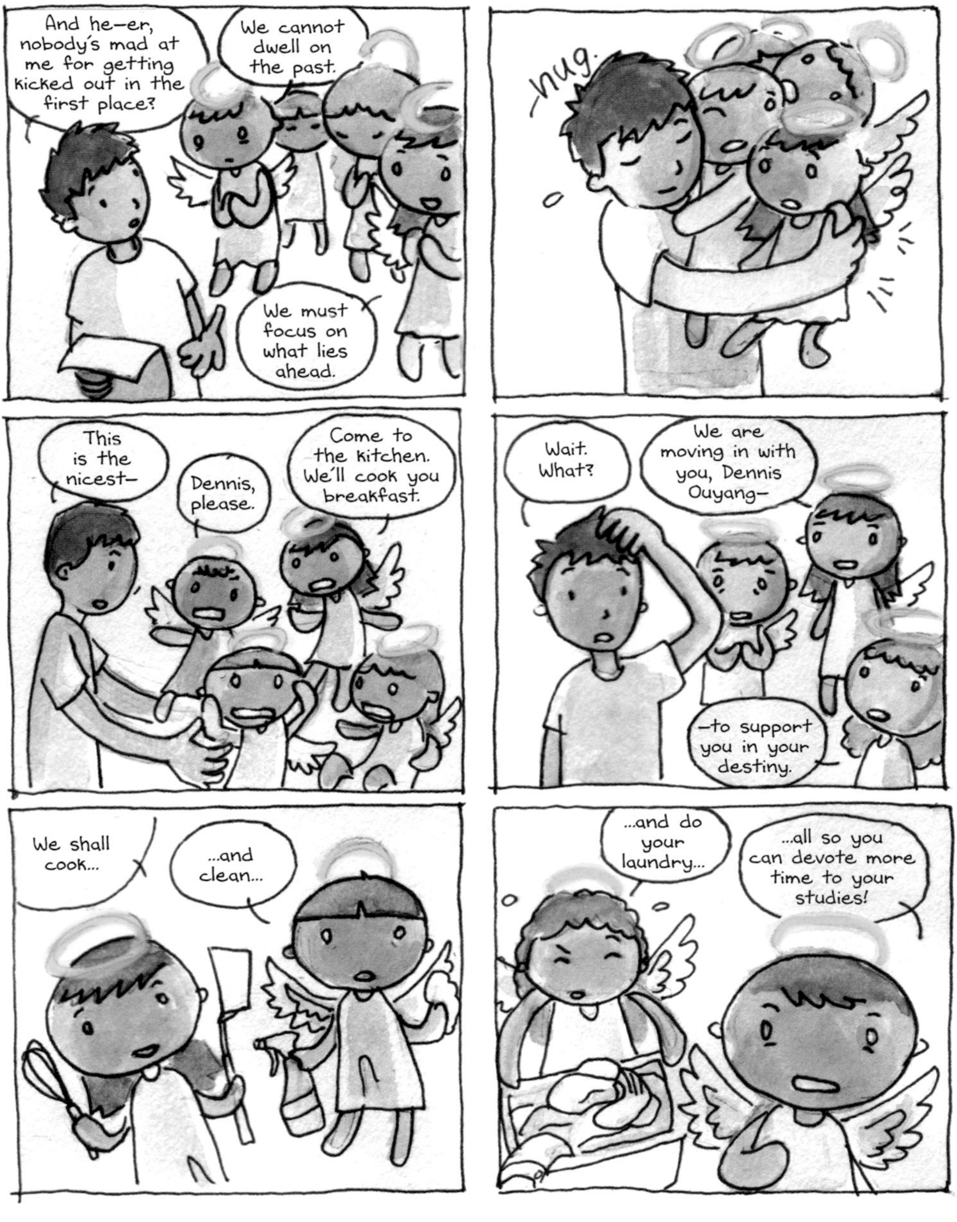
And he—er, nobody's mad at me for getting kicked out in the first place?
We cannot dwell on the past.
We must focus on what lies ahead.
-hug-
This is the nicest—
Dennis, please.
Come to the kitchen. We'll cook you breakfast.
Wait. What?
We are moving in with you, Dennis Ouyang—
—to support you in your destiny.
We shall cook...
...and clean...
...and do your laundry...
...all so you can devote more time to your studies!

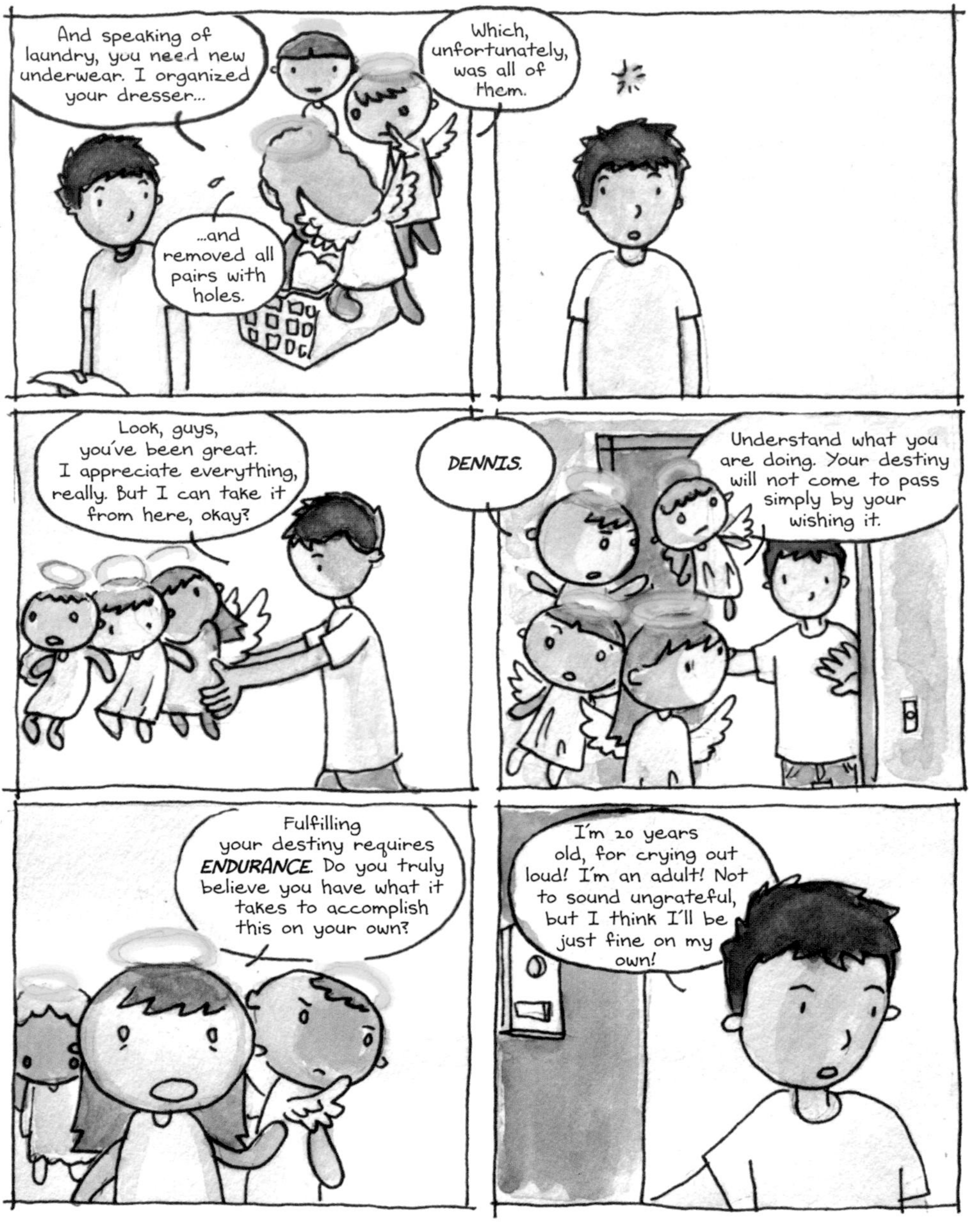

And speaking of laundry, you need new underwear. I organized your dresser...
...and removed all pairs with holes.
Which, unfortunately, was all of them.
Look, guys, you've been great. I appreciate everything, really. But I can take it from here, okay?
DENNIS.
Understand what you are doing. Your destiny will not come to pass simply by your wishing it.
Fulfilling your destiny requires **ENDURANCE**. Do you truly believe you have what it takes to accomplish this on your own?
I'm 20 years old, for crying out loud! I'm an adult! Not to sound ungrateful, but I think I'll be just fine on my own!

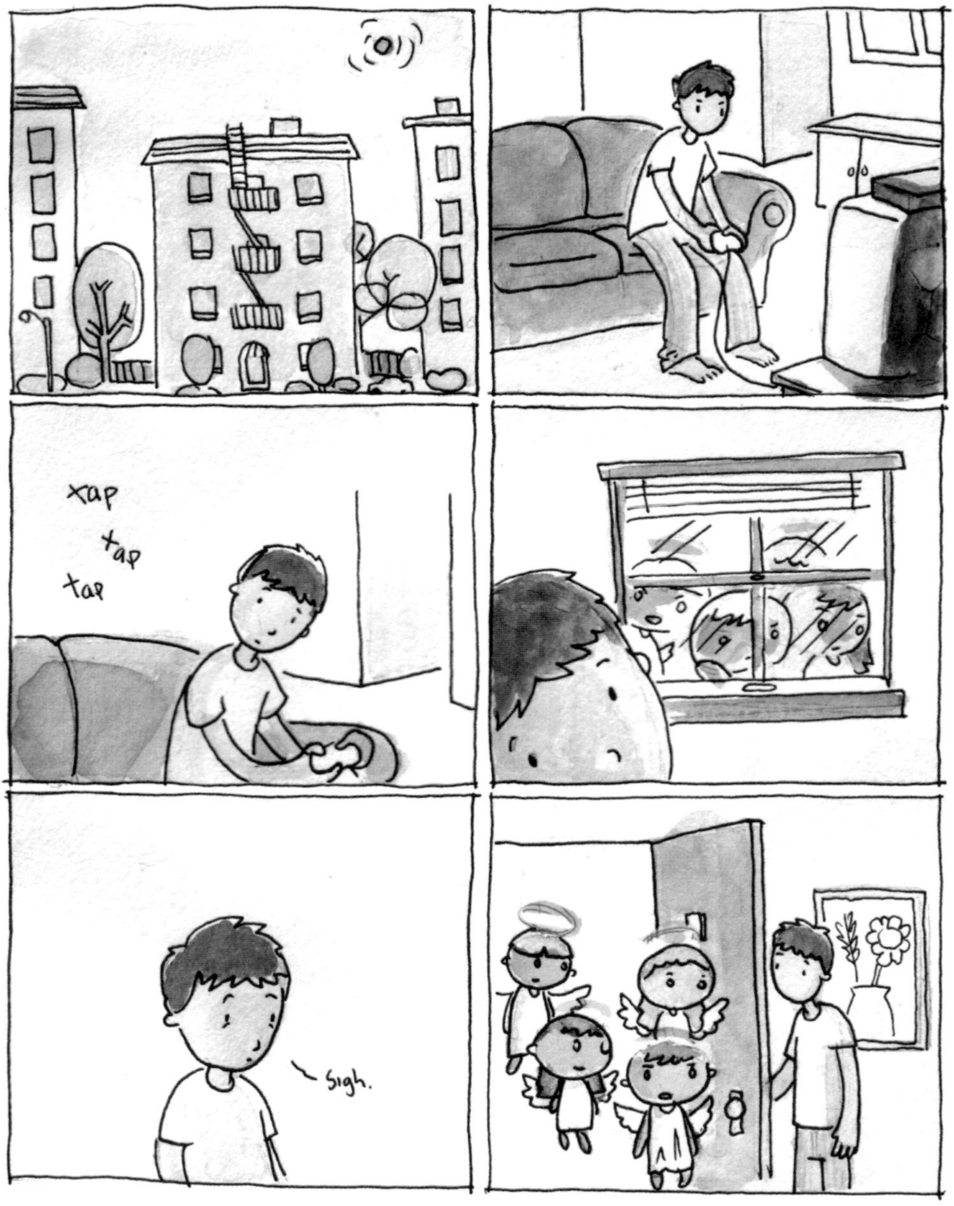
tap
tap
tap
Sigh.

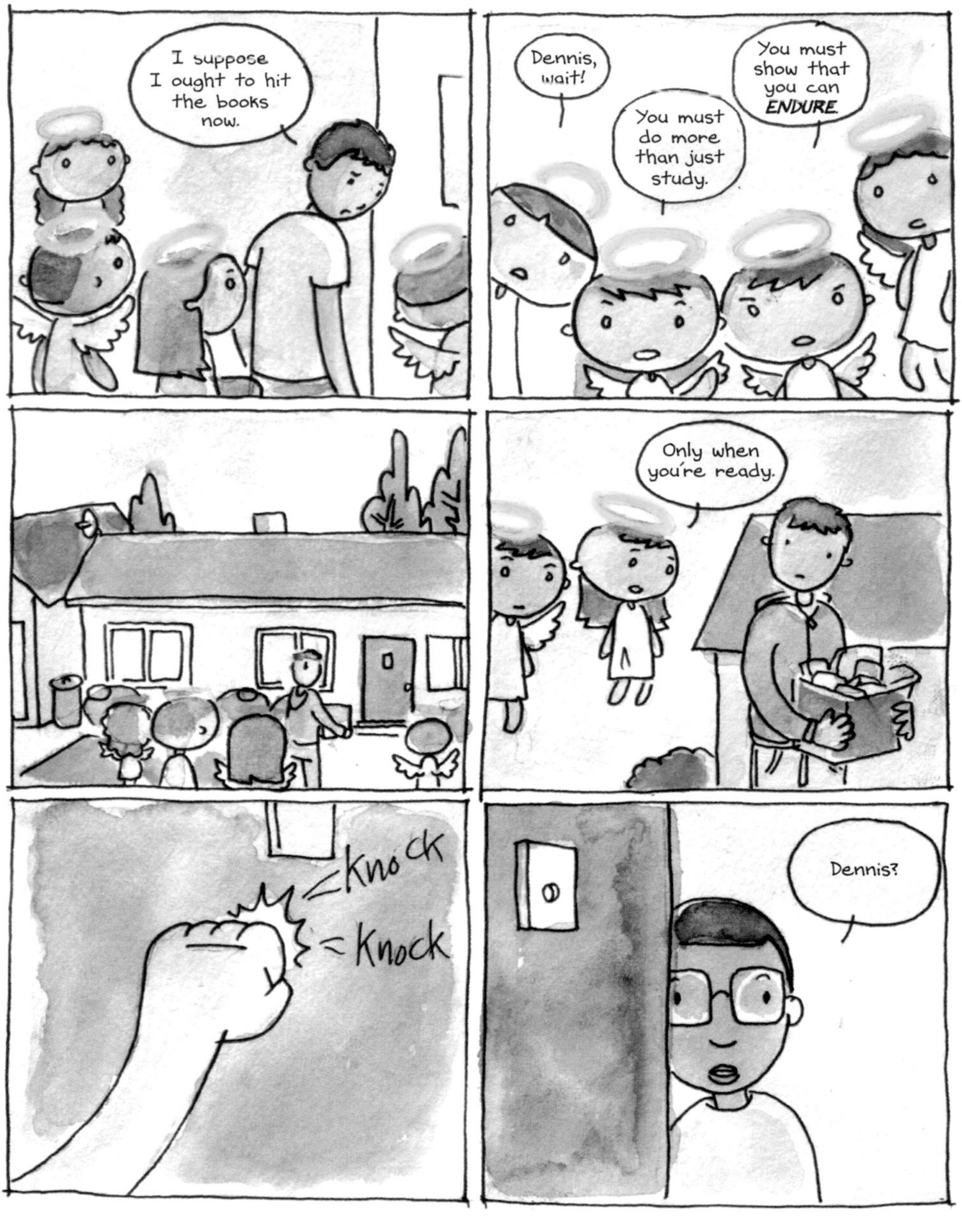
I suppose I ought to hit the books now.
Dennis, wait!
You must do more than just study.
You must show that you can ENDURE.
Only when you're ready.
Knock
Knock
Dennis?

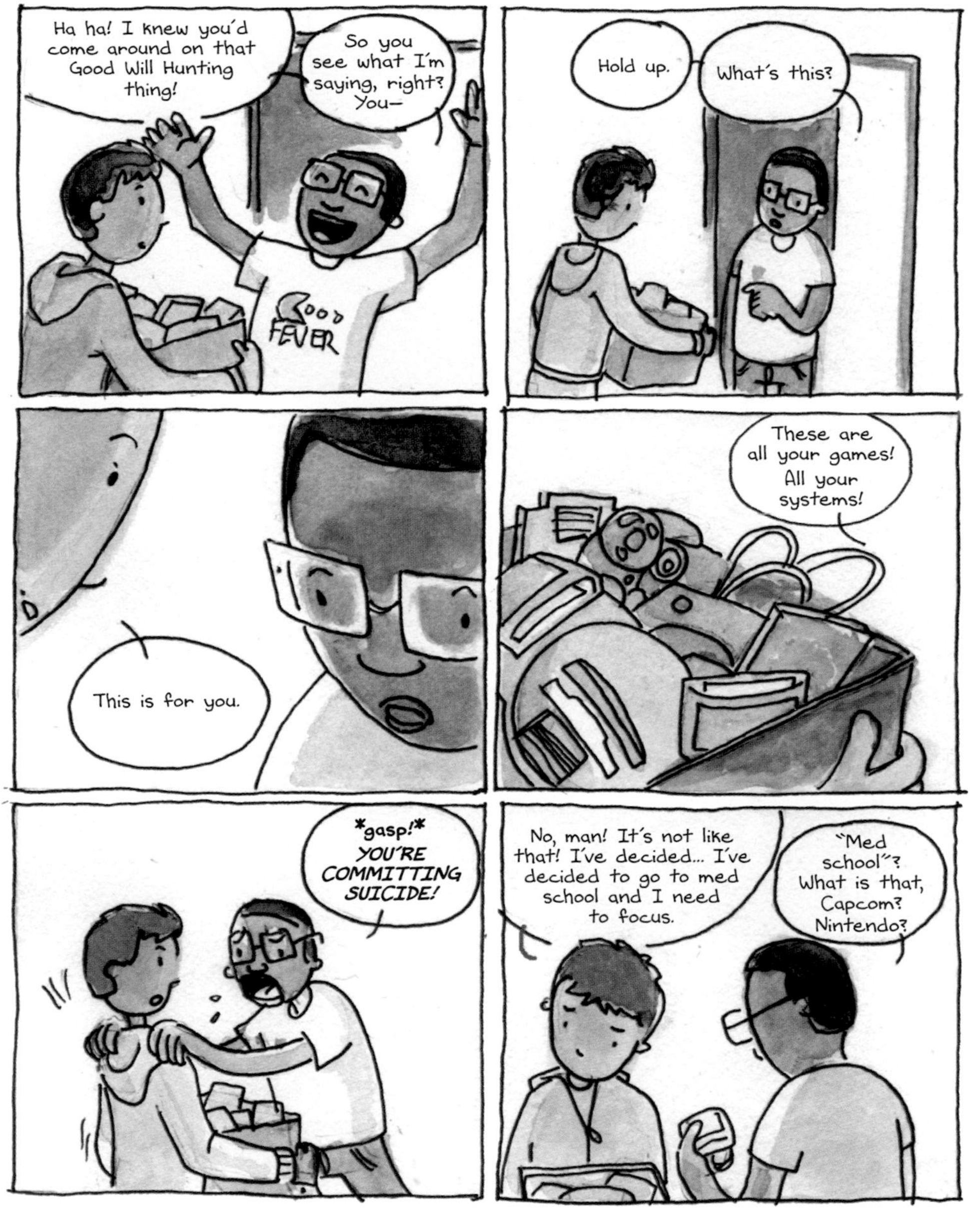
Ha ha! I knew you'd come around on that Good Will Hunting thing!
So you see what I'm saying, right? You—
GOOD FEVER
Hold up.
What's this?
This is for you.
These are all your games! All your systems!
gasp! YOU'RE COMMITTING SUICIDE!
No, man! It's not like that! I've decided... I've decided to go to med school and I need to focus.
"Med school"? What is that, Capcom? Nintendo?

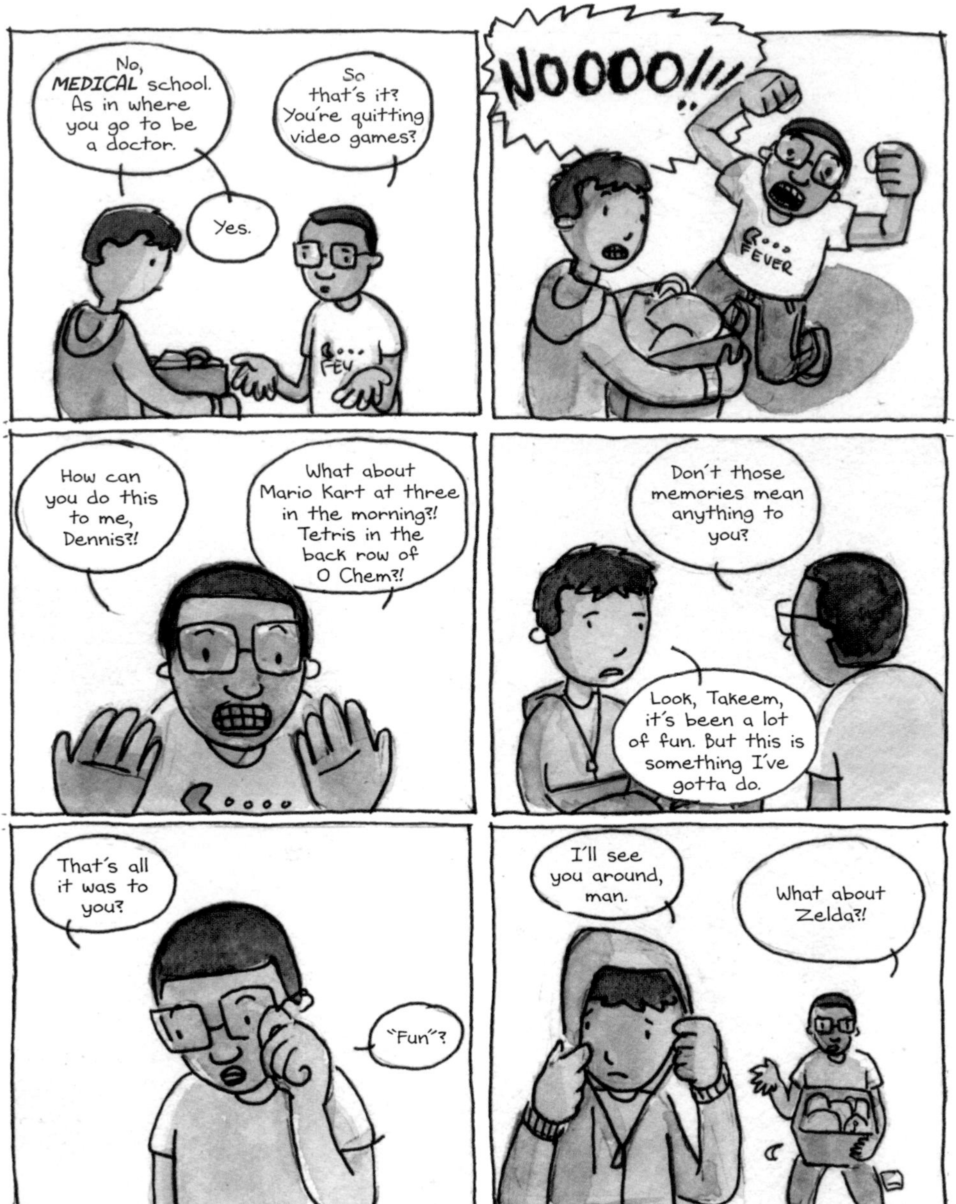
No, MEDICAL school. As in where you go to be a doctor.
Yes.
So that's it? You're quitting video games?
NOOOO!!!
How can you do this to me, Dennis?!
What about Mario Kart at three in the morning?! Tetris in the back row of O Chem?!
Don't those memories mean anything to you?
Look, Takeem, it's been a lot of fun. But this is something I've gotta do.
That's all it was to you?
"Fun"?
I'll see you around, man.
What about Zelda?!

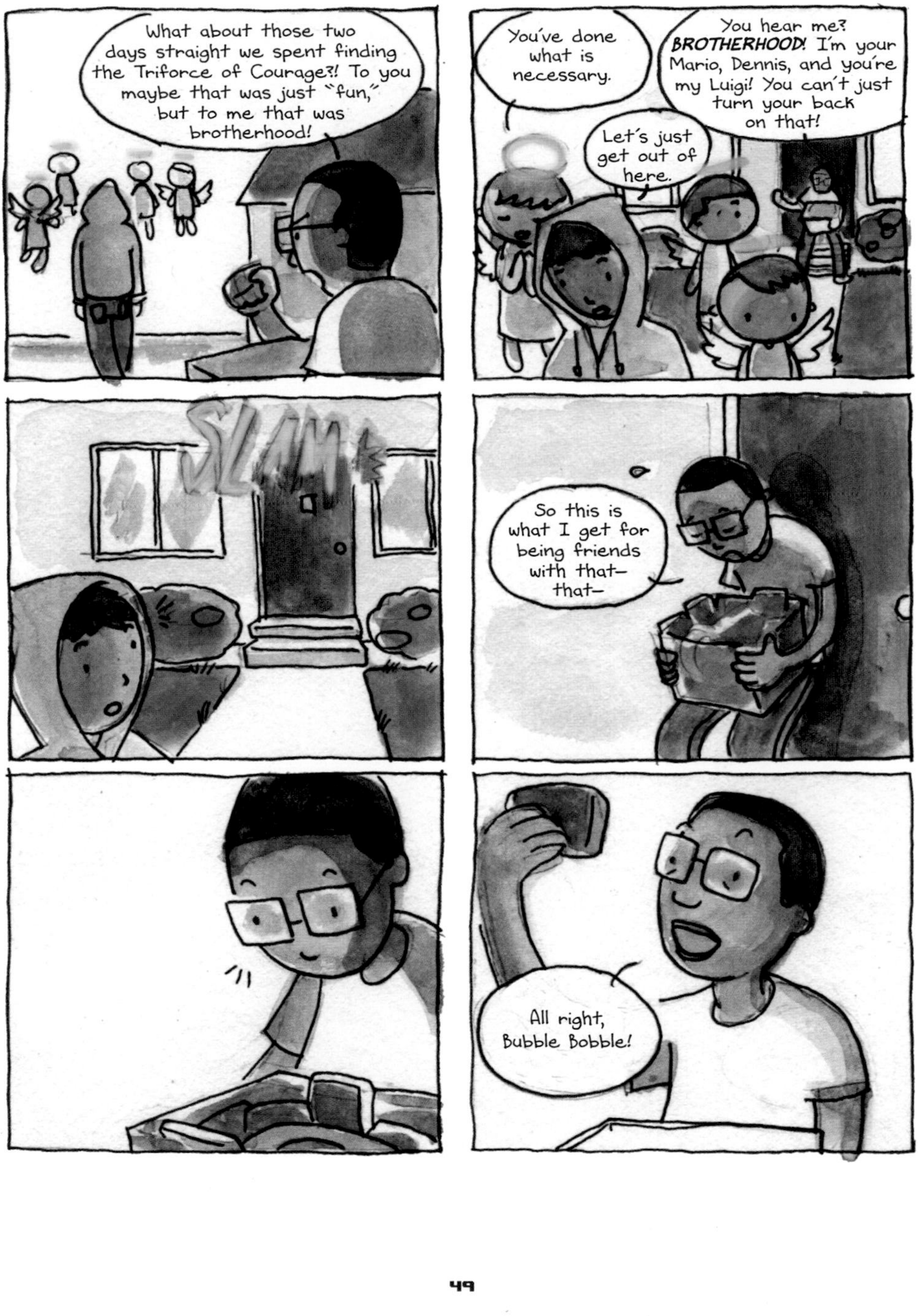
What about those two days straight we spent finding the Triforce of Courage?! To you maybe that was just "fun," but to me that was brotherhood!
You've done what is necessary.
You hear me? BROTHERHOOD! I'm your Mario, Dennis, and you're my Luigi! You can't just turn your back on that!
Let's just get out of here.
SLAM
So this is what I get for being friends with that— that—
All right, Bubble Bobble!

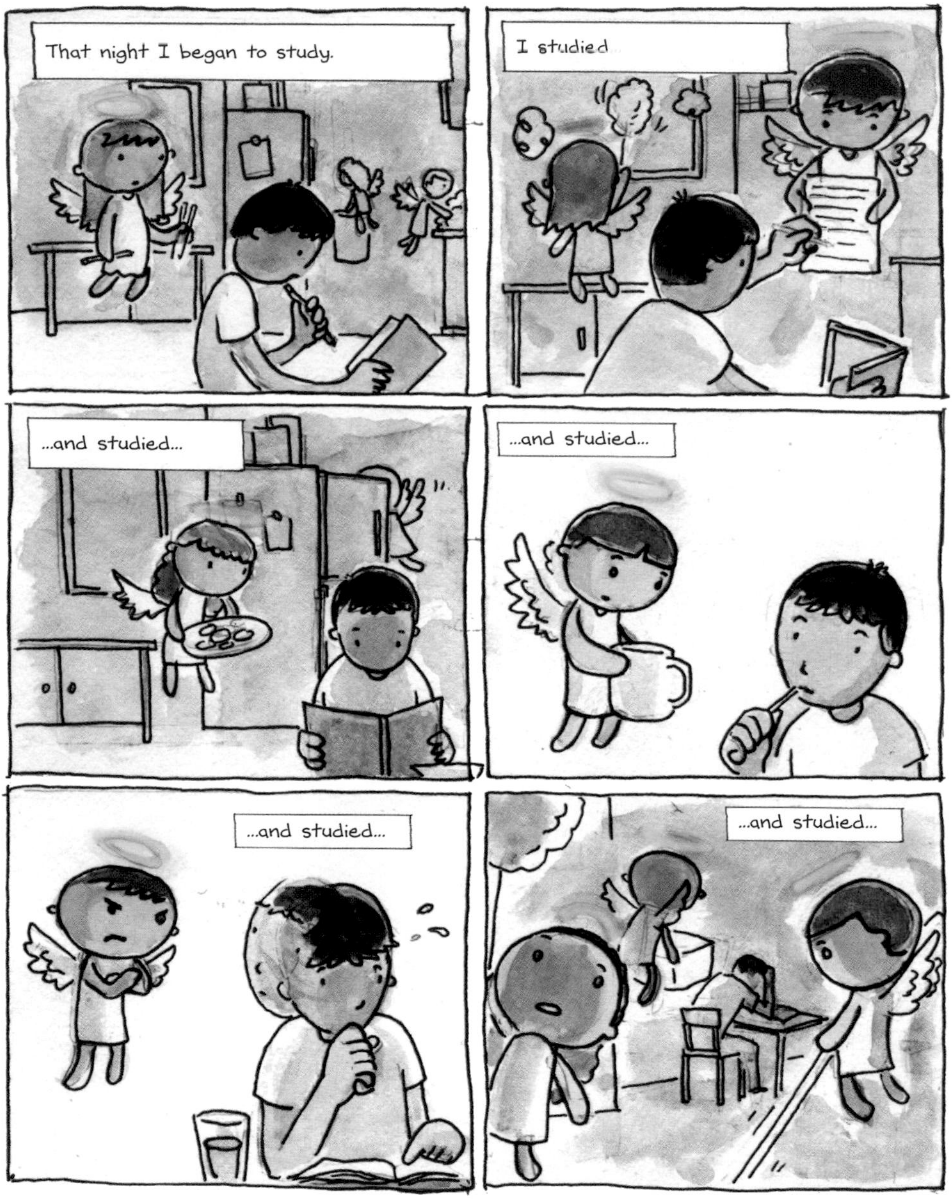
That night I began to study.
I studied...
...and studied...
...and studied...
...and studied...
...and studied...

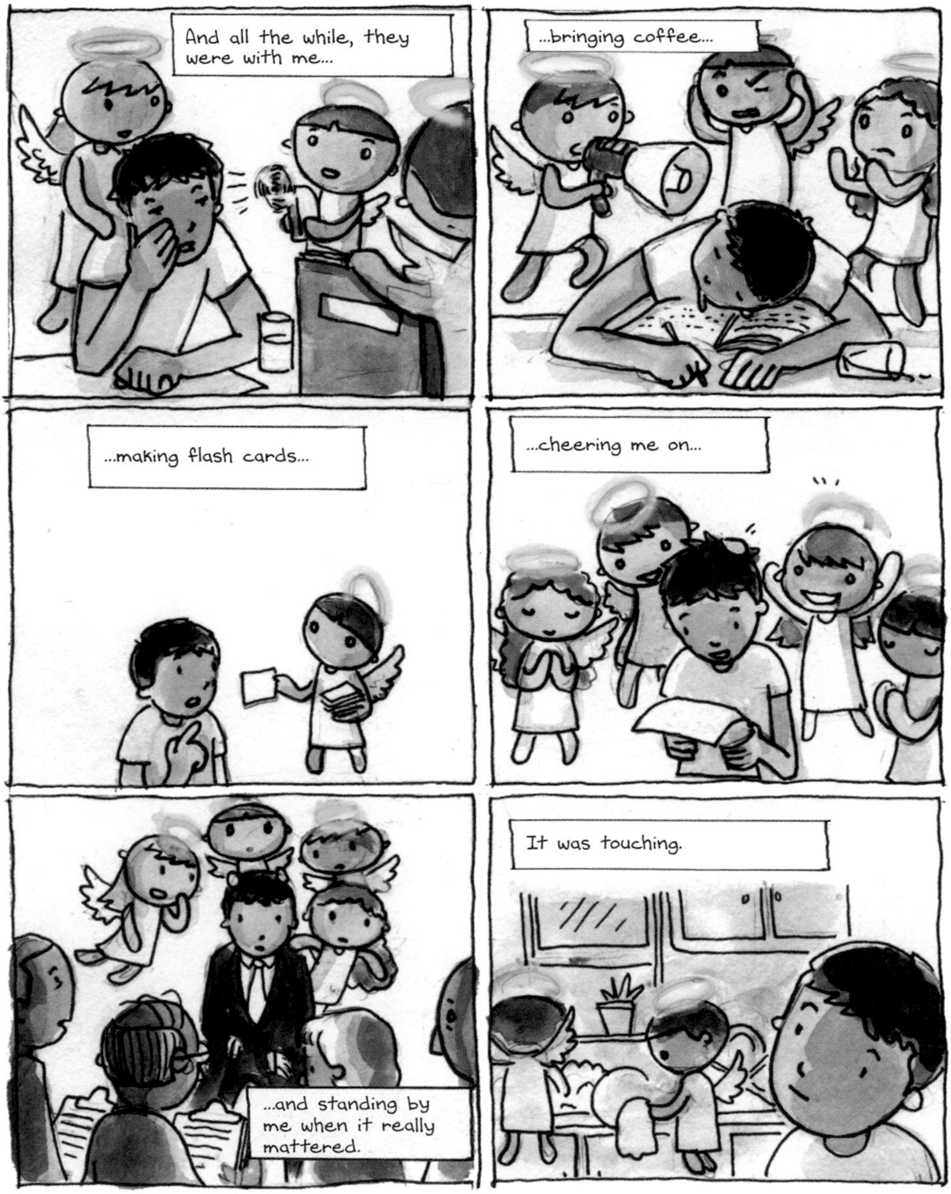
And all the while, they were with me...
...bringing coffee...
...making flash cards...
...cheering me on...
...and standing by me when it really mattered.
It was touching.

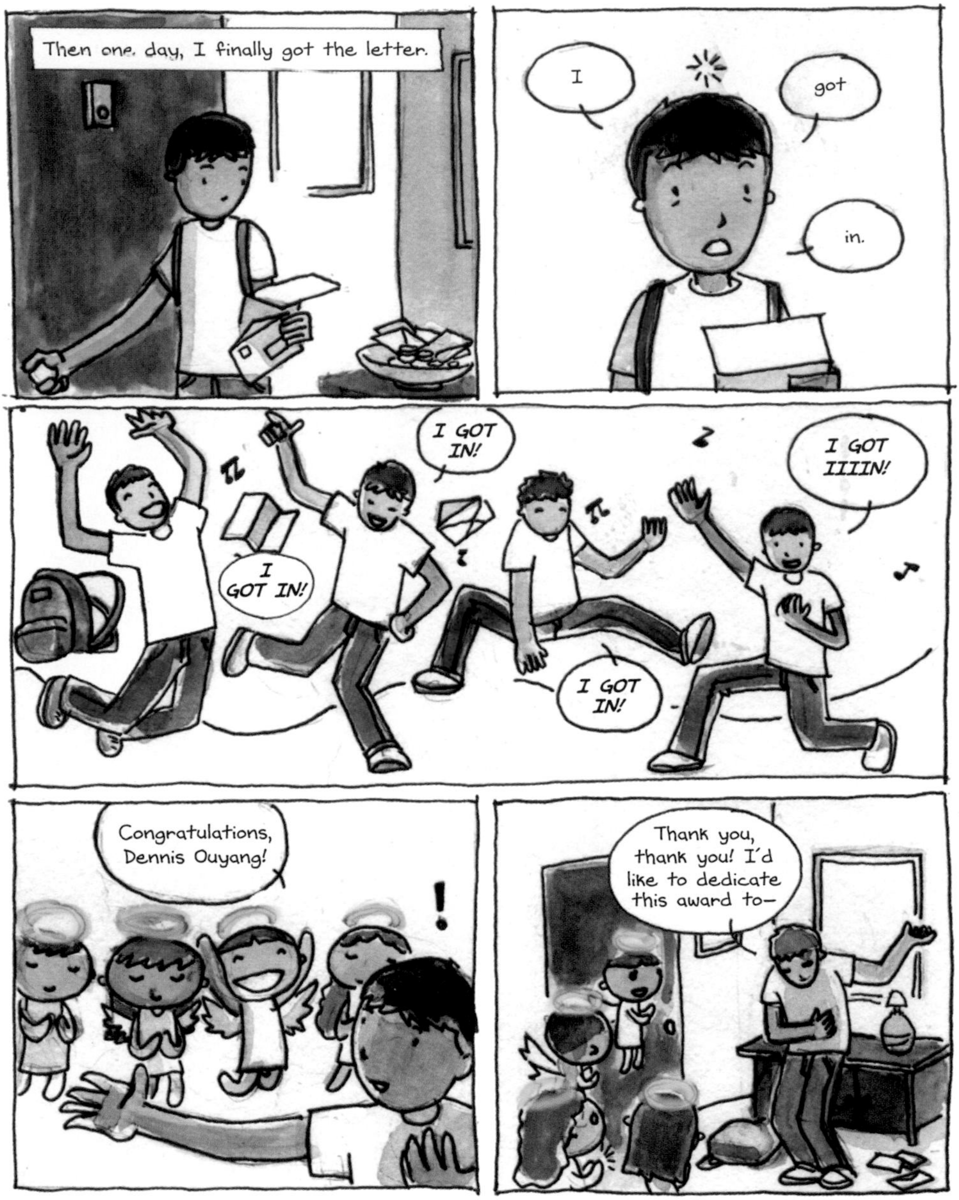
Then one day, I finally got the letter.
I
got
in.
I GOT IN!
I GOT IN!
I GOT IN!
I GOT IIIIN!
Congratulations, Dennis Ouyang!
!
Thank you, thank you! I'd like to dedicate this award to—

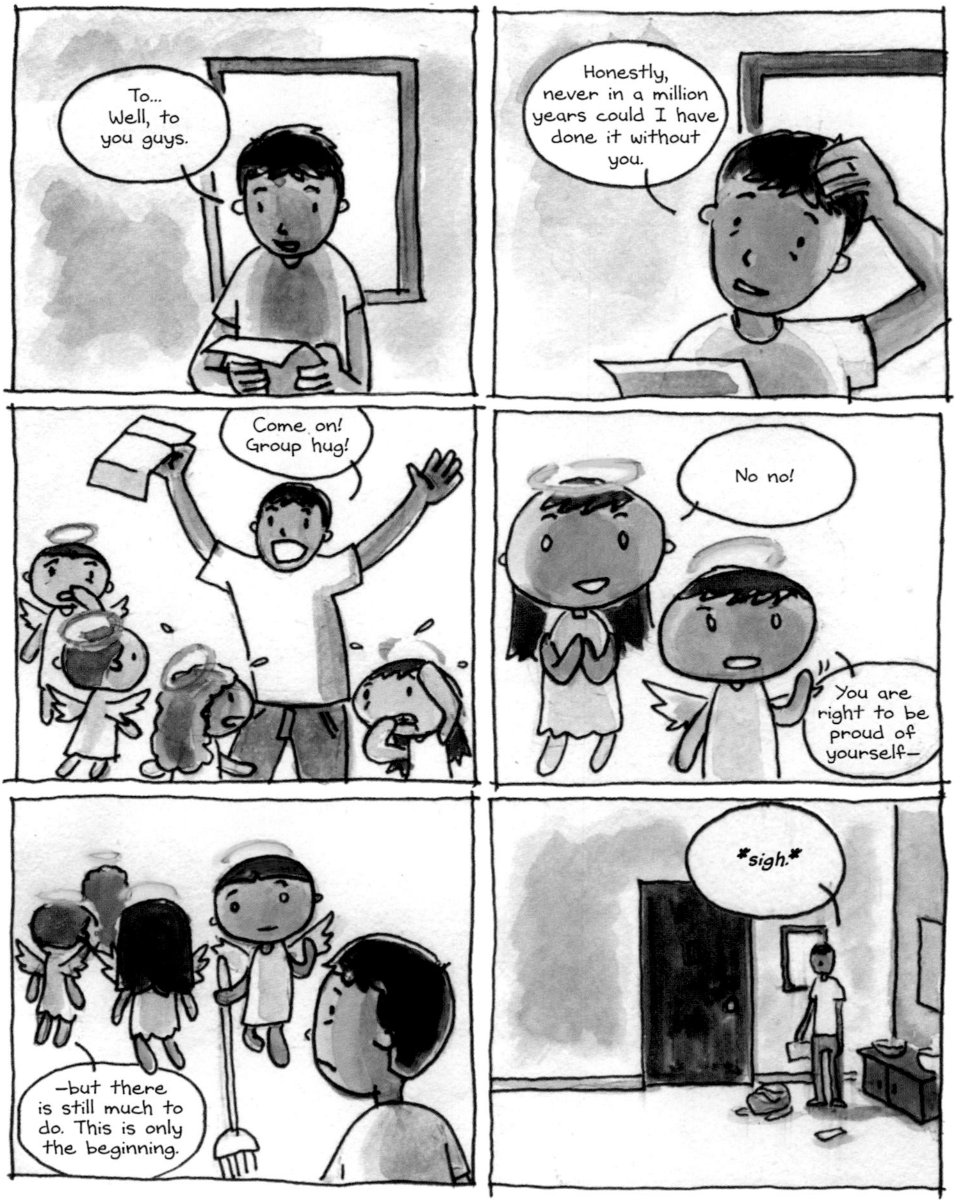
To...
Well, to you guys.
Honestly, never in a million years could I have done it without you.
Come on! Group hug!
No no!
You are right to be proud of yourself—
—but there is still much to do. This is only the beginning.
sigh.

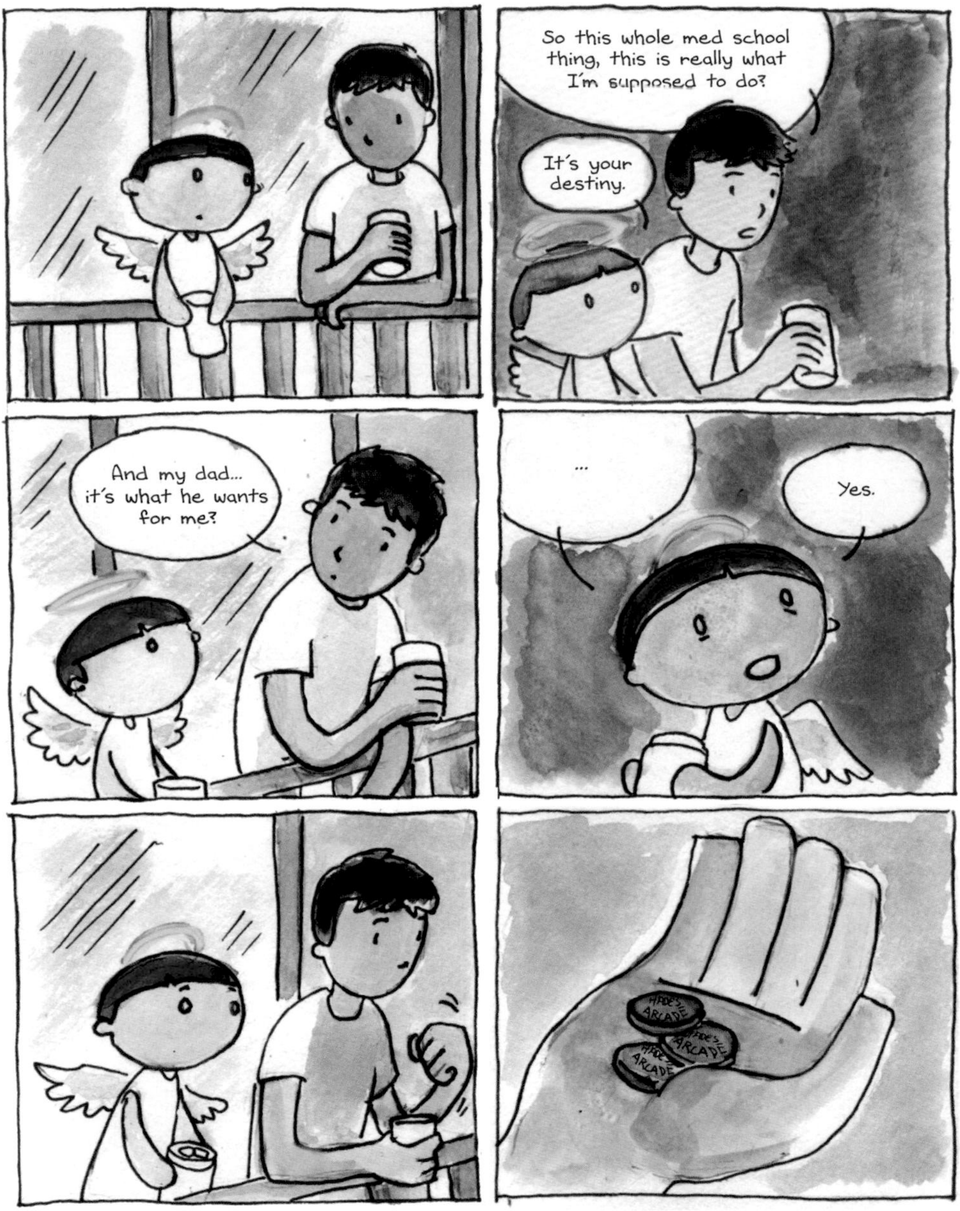
So this whole med school thing, this is really what I'm supposed to do?
It's your destiny.
And my dad... it's what he wants for me?
...
Yes.

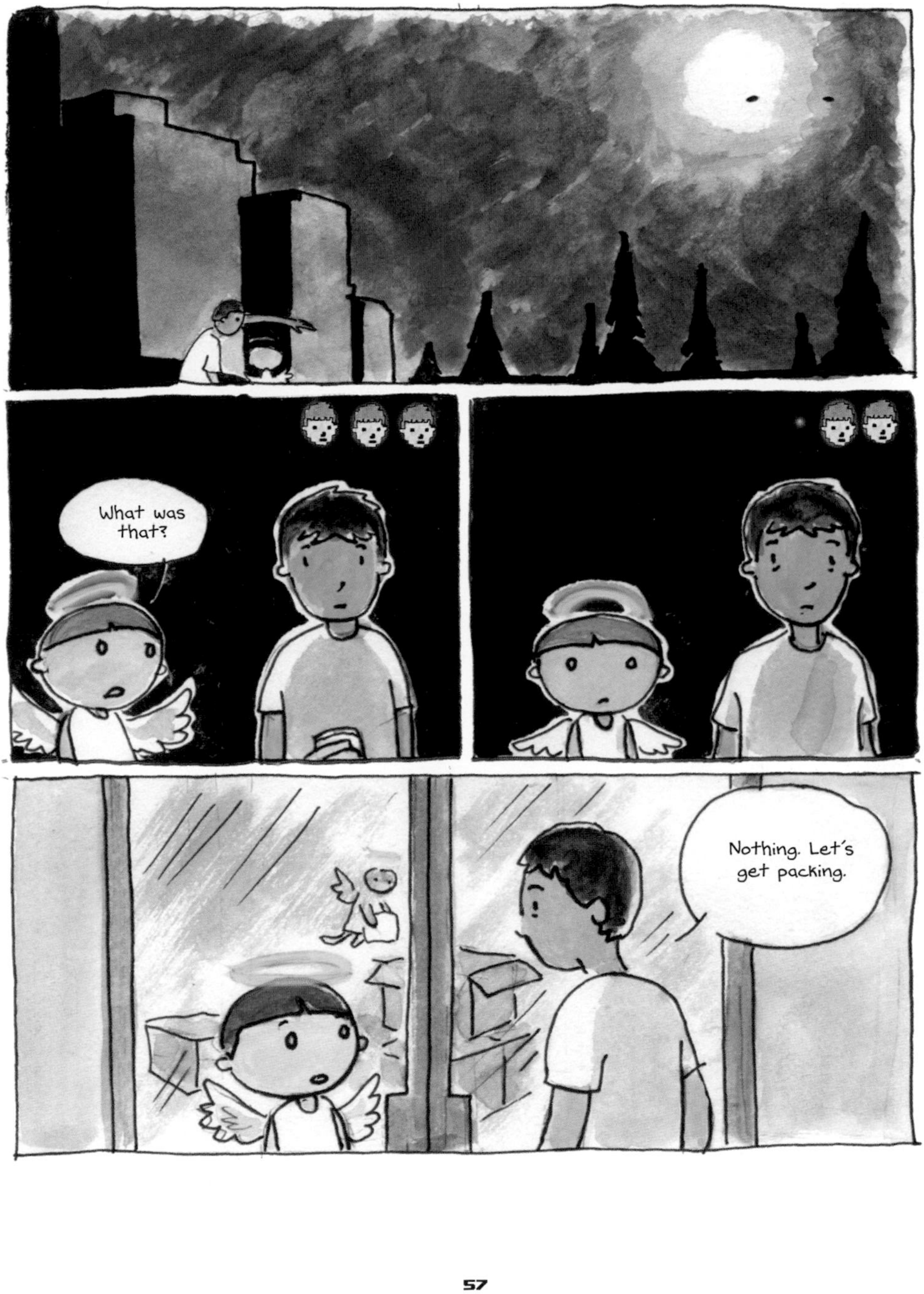
What was that?
Nothing. Let's get packing.

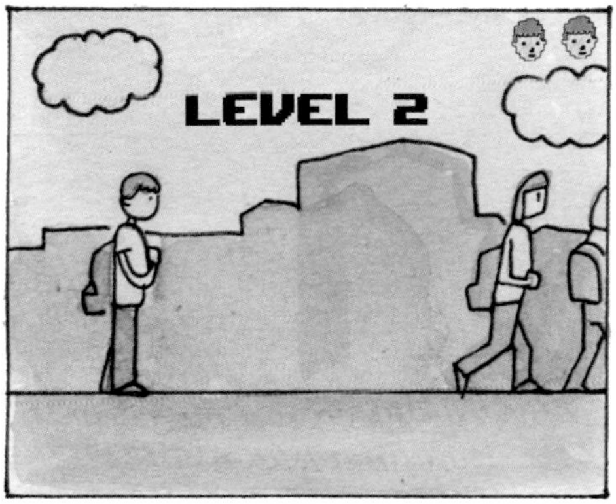
LEVEL 2

On the morning of my first day of med school, everything was *BEAUTIFUL*.

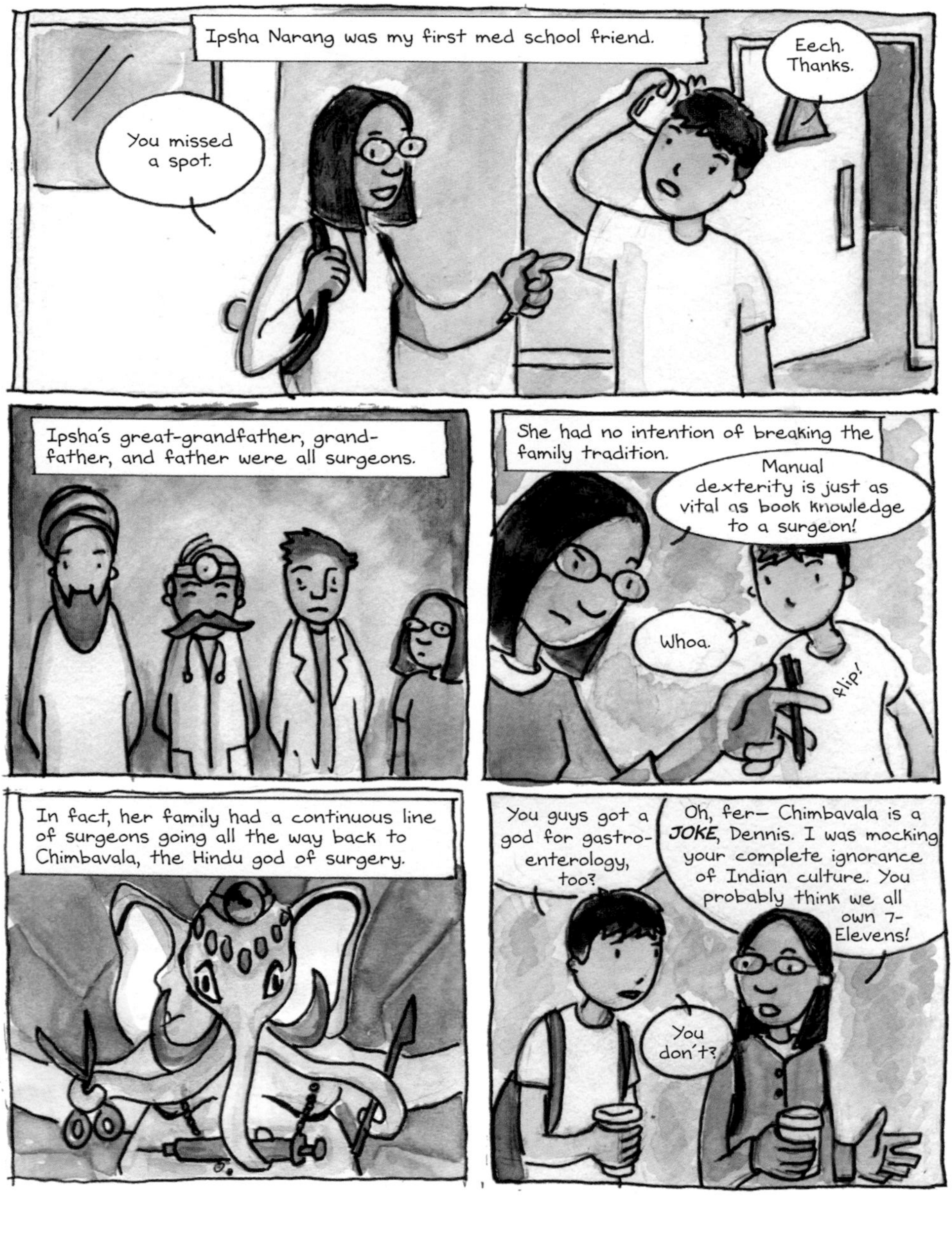
Ipsha Narang was my first med school friend.
You missed a spot.
Eech. Thanks.
Ipsha's great-grandfather, grandfather, and father were all surgeons.
She had no intention of breaking the family tradition.
Manual dexterity is just as vital as book knowledge to a surgeon!
Whoa.
flip!
In fact, her family had a continuous line of surgeons going all the way back to Chimbavala, the Hindu god of surgery.
You guys got a god for gastroenterology, too?
Oh, fer— Chimbavala is a *JOKE*, Dennis. I was mocking your complete ignorance of Indian culture. You probably think we all own 7-Elevens!
You don't?

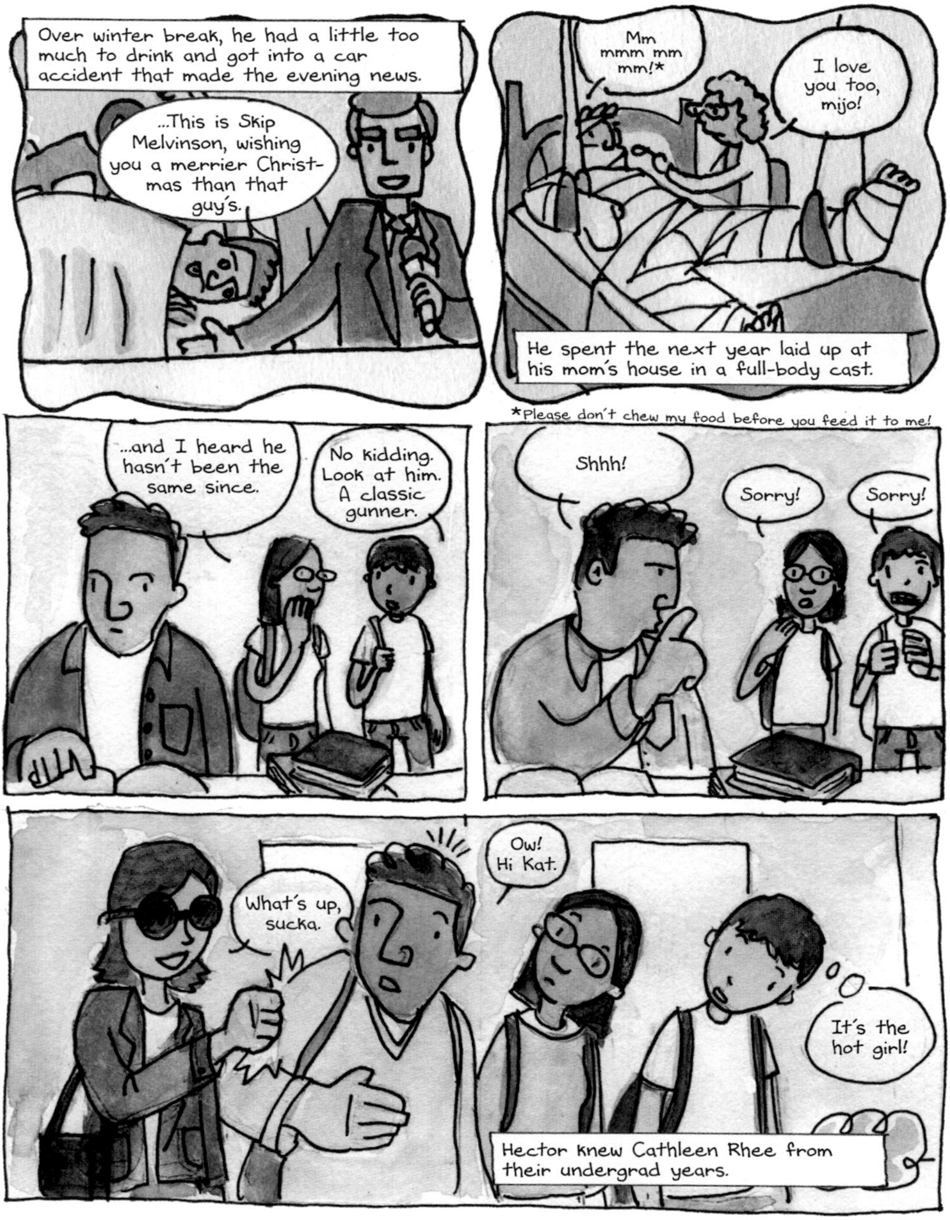
Over winter break, he had a little too much to drink and got into a car accident that made the evening news.
...This is Skip Melvinson, wishing you a merrier Christmas than that guy's.
Mm mmm mm mm!*
I love you too, mijo!
He spent the next year laid up at his mom's house in a full-body cast.
*Please don't chew my food before you feed it to me!
...and I heard he hasn't been the same since.
No kidding. Look at him. A classic gunner.
Shhh!
Sorry!
Sorry!
What's up, sucka.
Ow! Hi Kat.
It's the hot girl!
Hector knew Cathleen Rhee from their undergrad years.

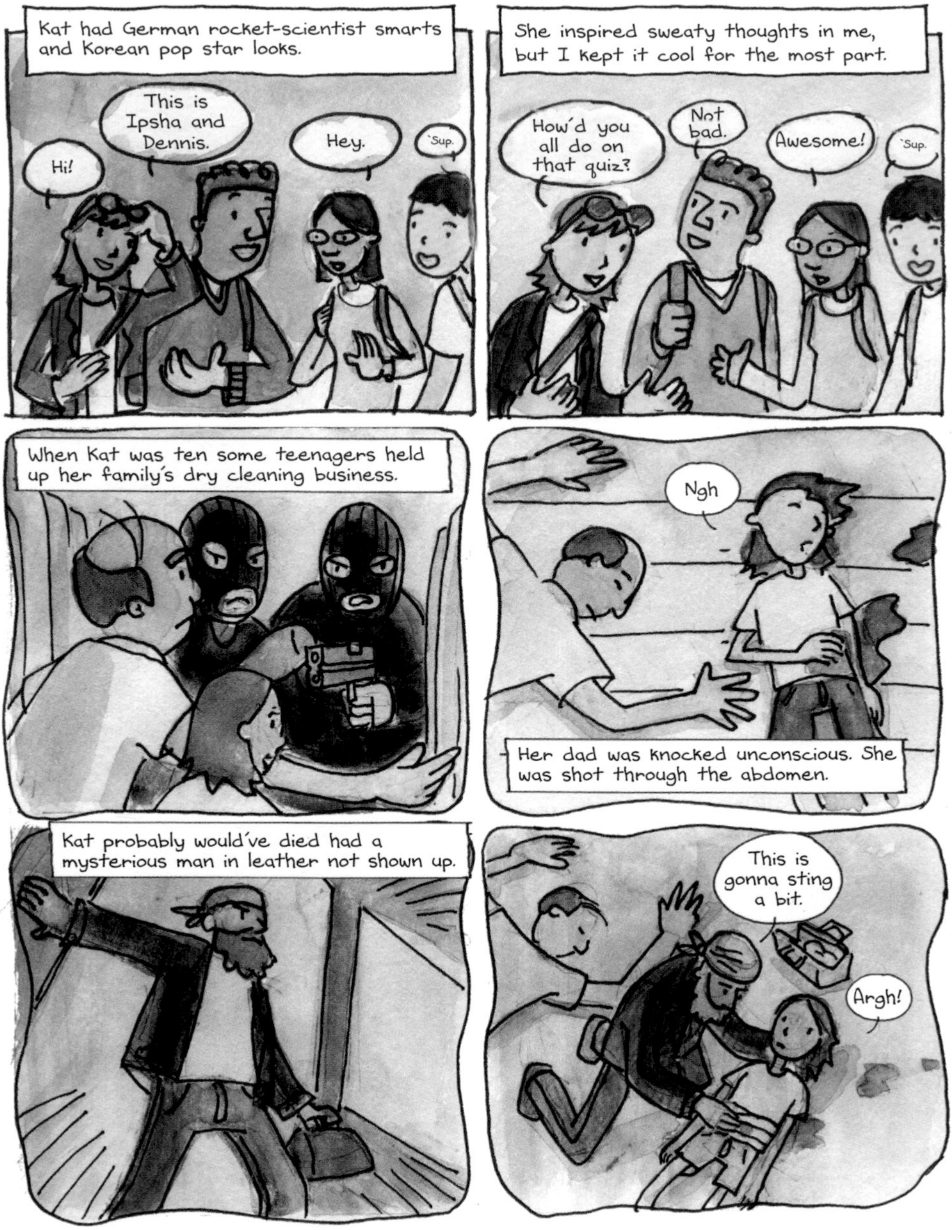
Kat had German rocket-scientist smarts and Korean pop star looks.
Hi!
This is Ipsha and Dennis.
Hey.
`Sup.
She inspired sweaty thoughts in me, but I kept it cool for the most part.
How'd you all do on that quiz?
Not bad.
Awesome!
`Sup.
When Kat was ten some teenagers held up her family's dry cleaning business.
Ngh
Her dad was knocked unconscious. She was shot through the abdomen.
Kat probably would've died had a mysterious man in leather not shown up.
This is gonna sting a bit.
Argh!

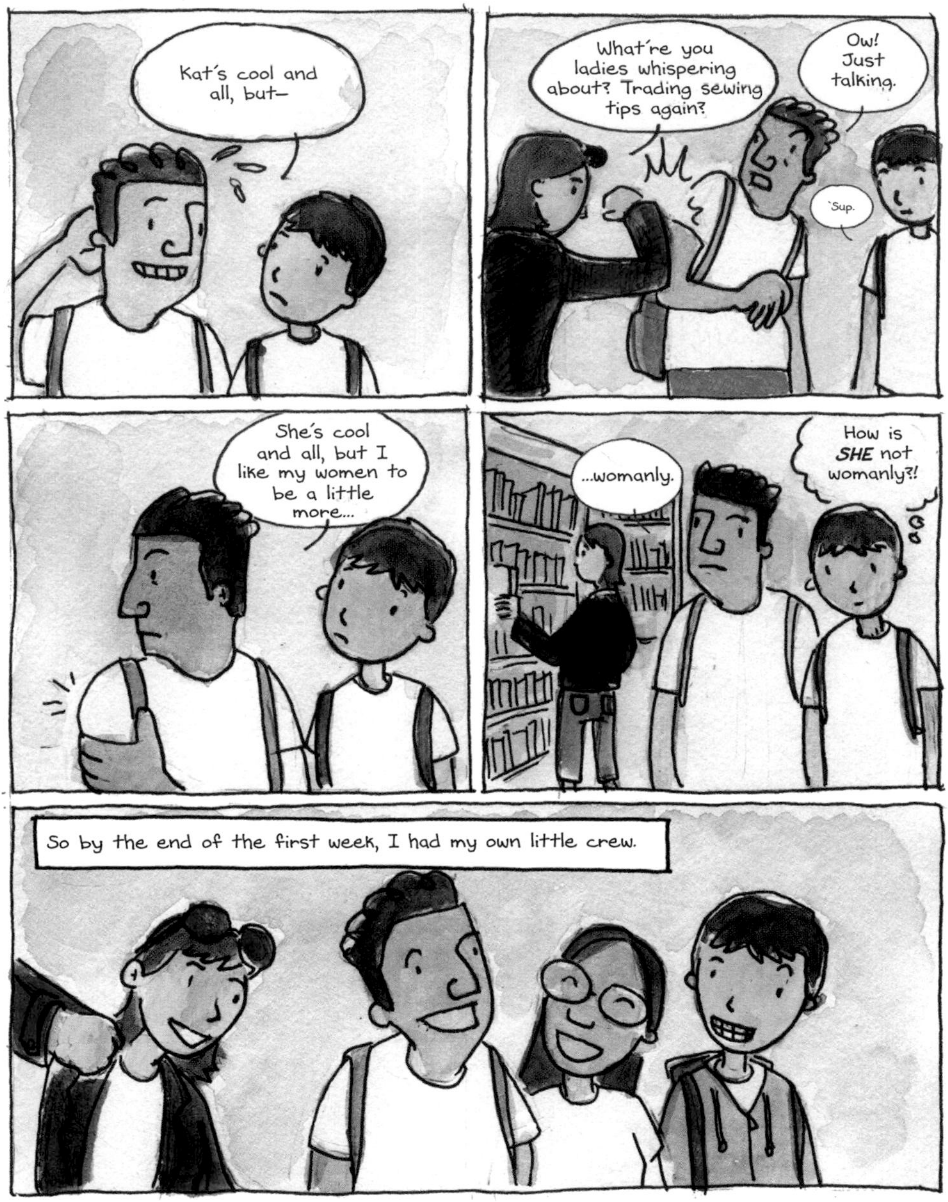
Kat's cool and all, but—
What're you ladies whispering about? Trading sewing tips again?
Ow! Just talking.
`Sup.
She's cool and all, but I like my women to be a little more...
...womanly.
How is SHE not womanly?!
So by the end of the first week, I had my own little crew.

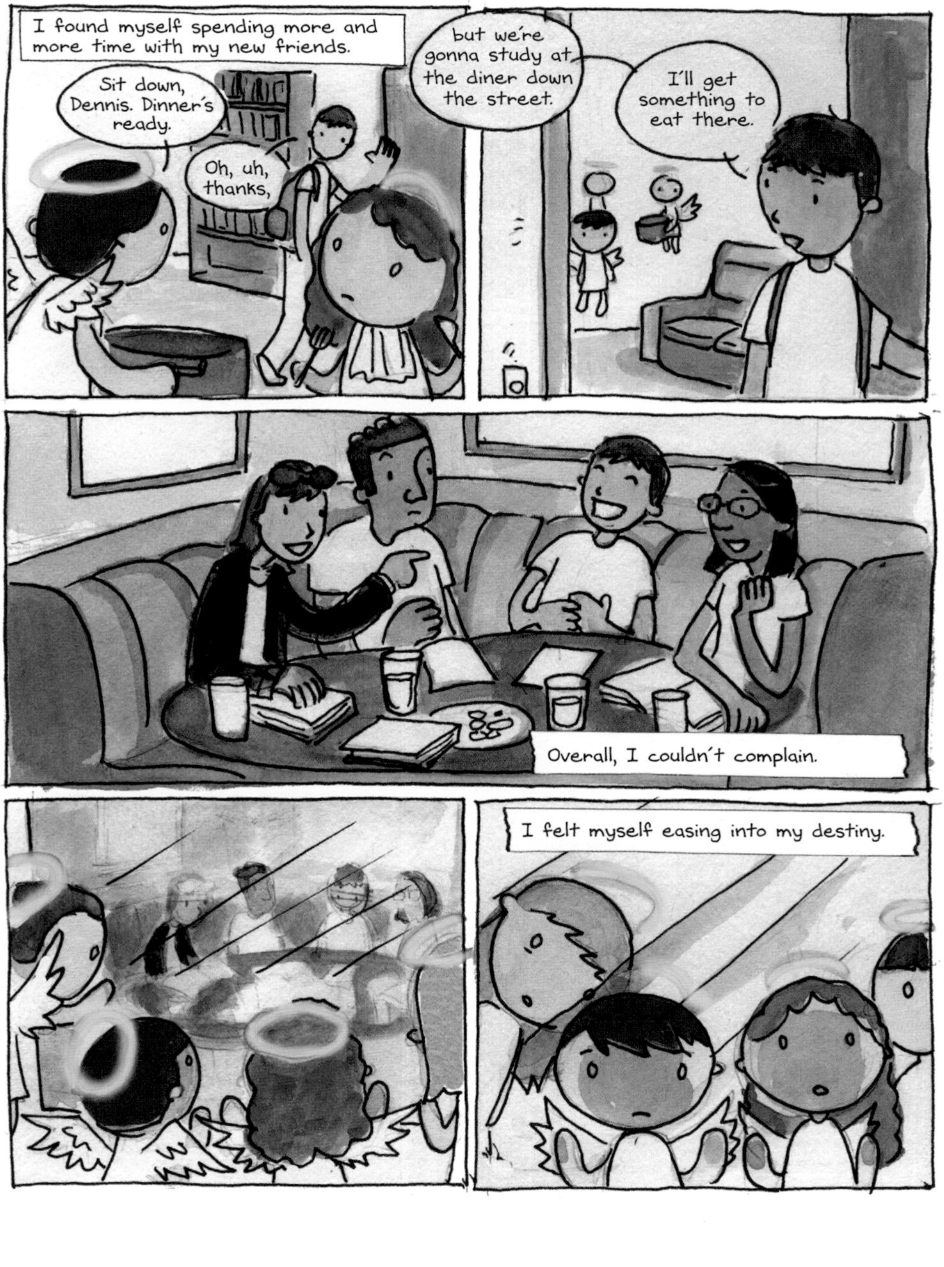
I found myself spending more and more time with my new friends.
Sit down, Dennis. Dinner's ready.
Oh, uh, thanks,
but we're gonna study at the diner down the street.
I'll get something to eat there.
Overall, I couldn't complain.
I felt myself easing into my destiny.

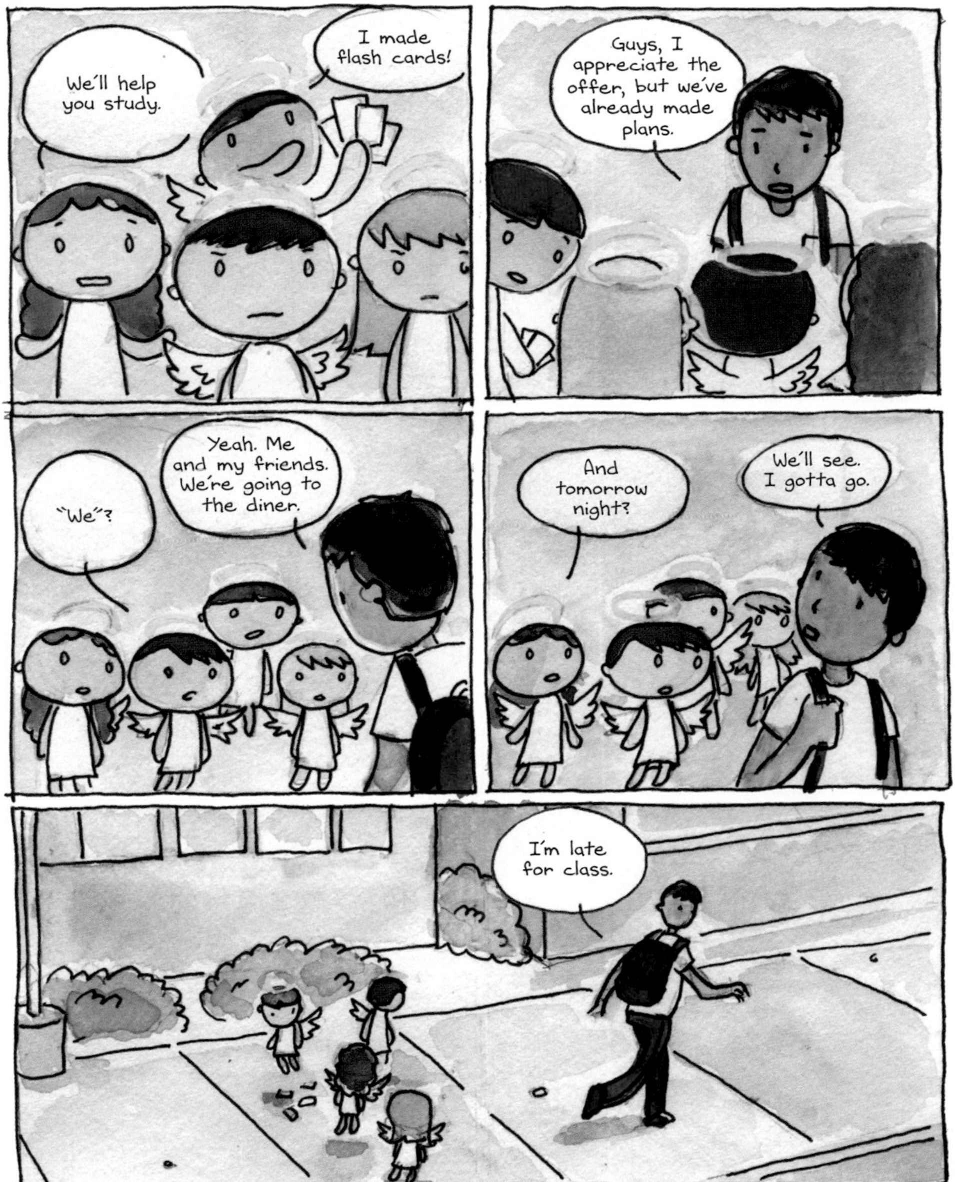
We'll help you study.
I made flash cards!
Guys, I appreciate the offer, but we've already made plans.
"We"?
Yeah. Me and my friends. We're going to the diner.
And tomorrow night?
We'll see. I gotta go.
I'm late for class.

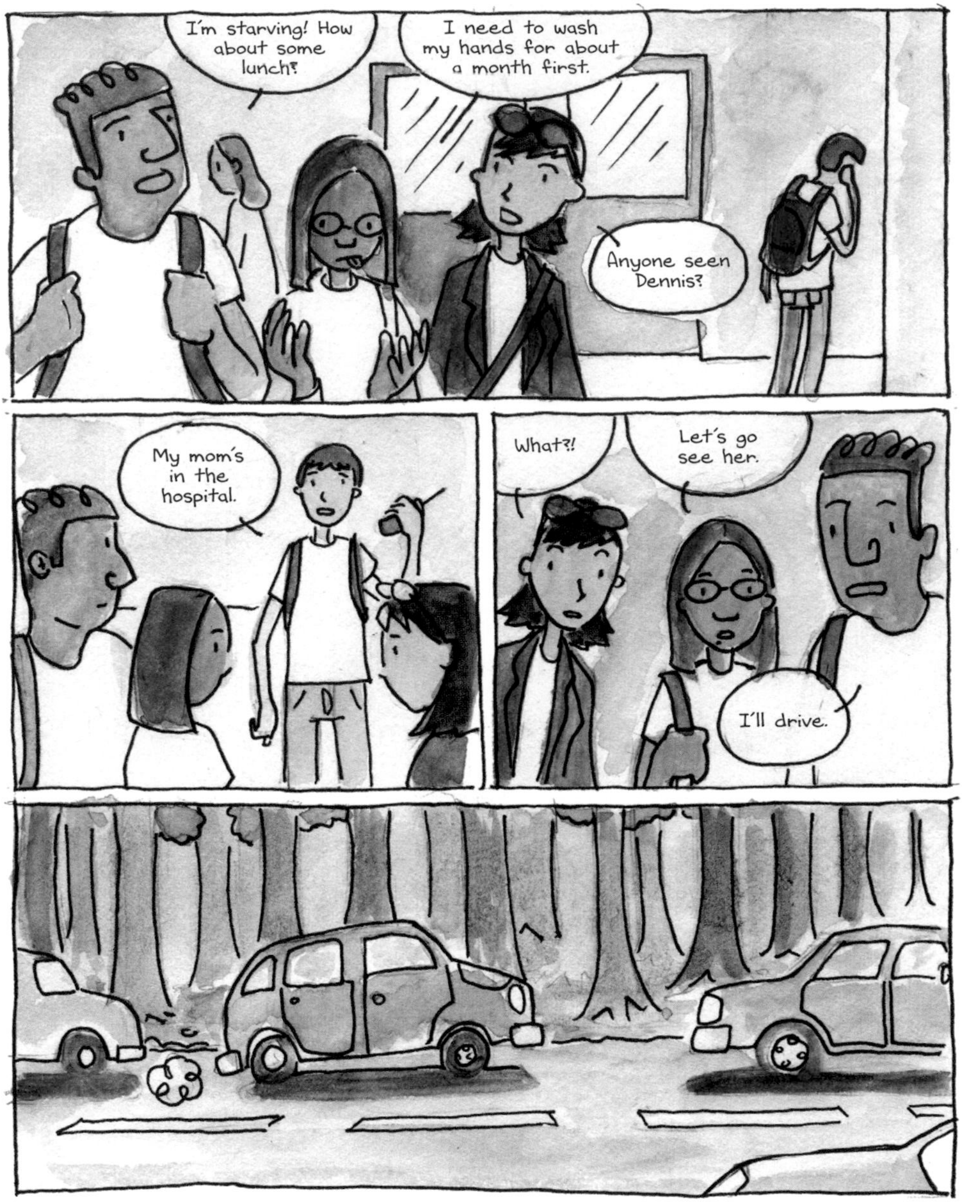
I'm starving! How about some lunch?
I need to wash my hands for about a month first.
Anyone seen Dennis?
My mom's in the hospital.
What?!
Let's go see her.
I'll drive.

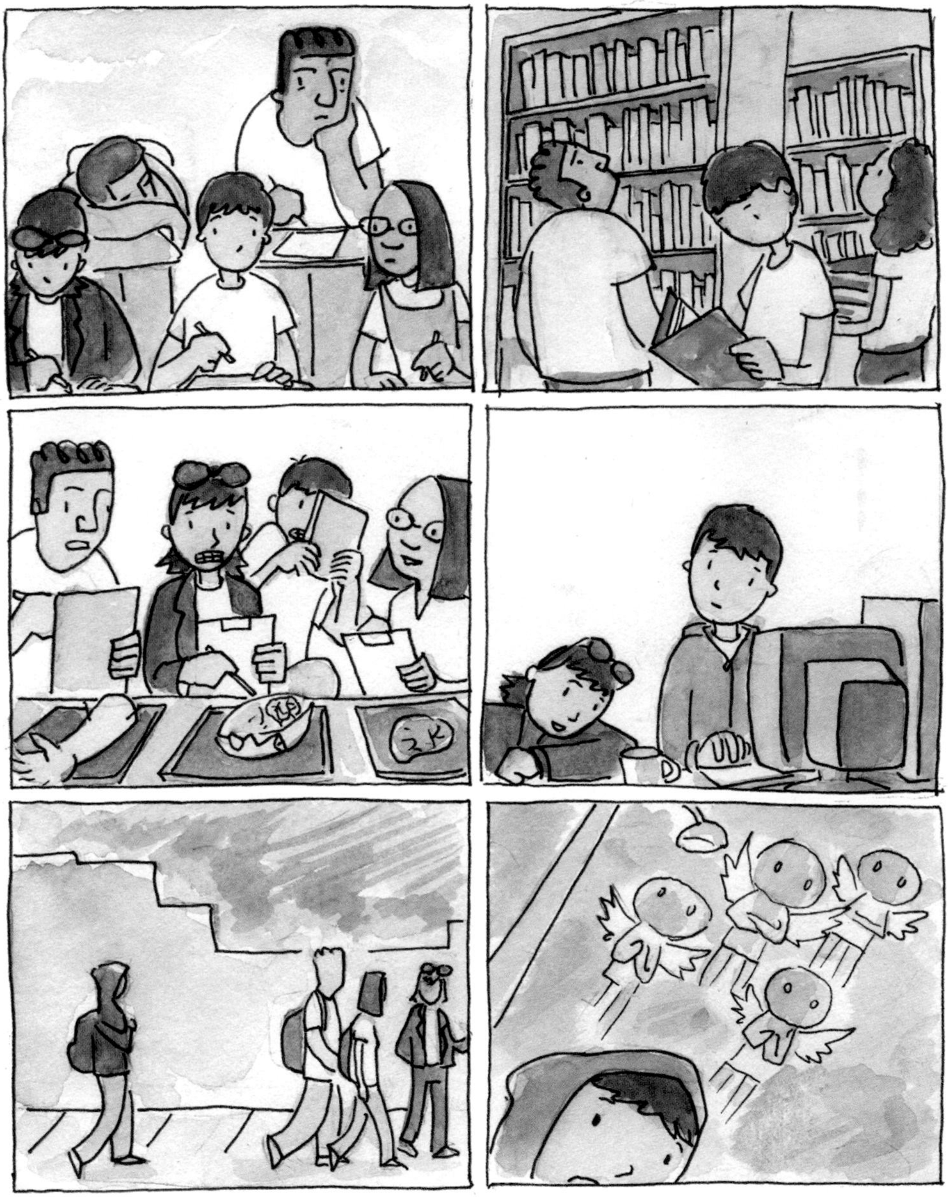

YOU'RE SO good

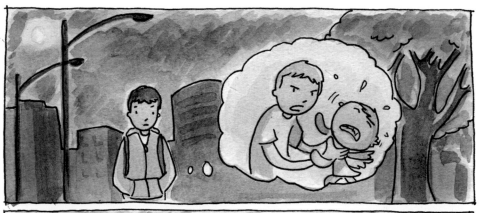

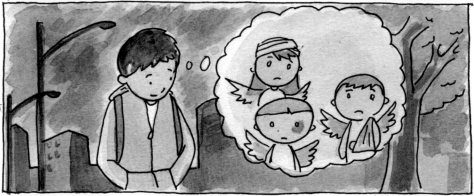

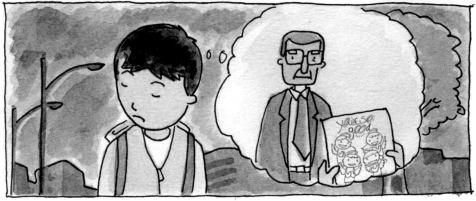

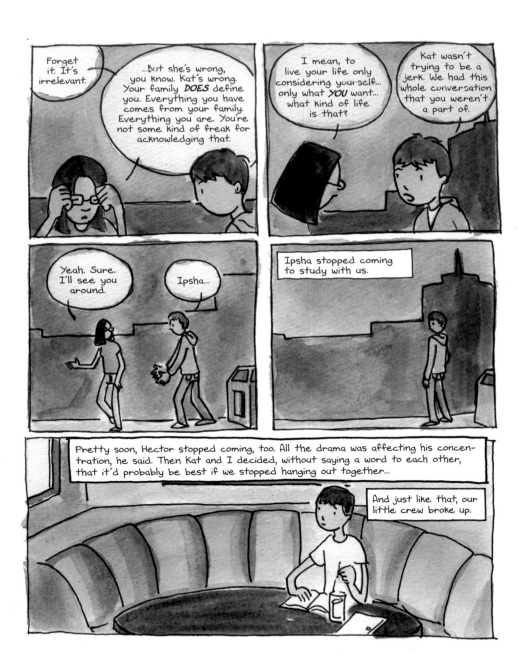

98

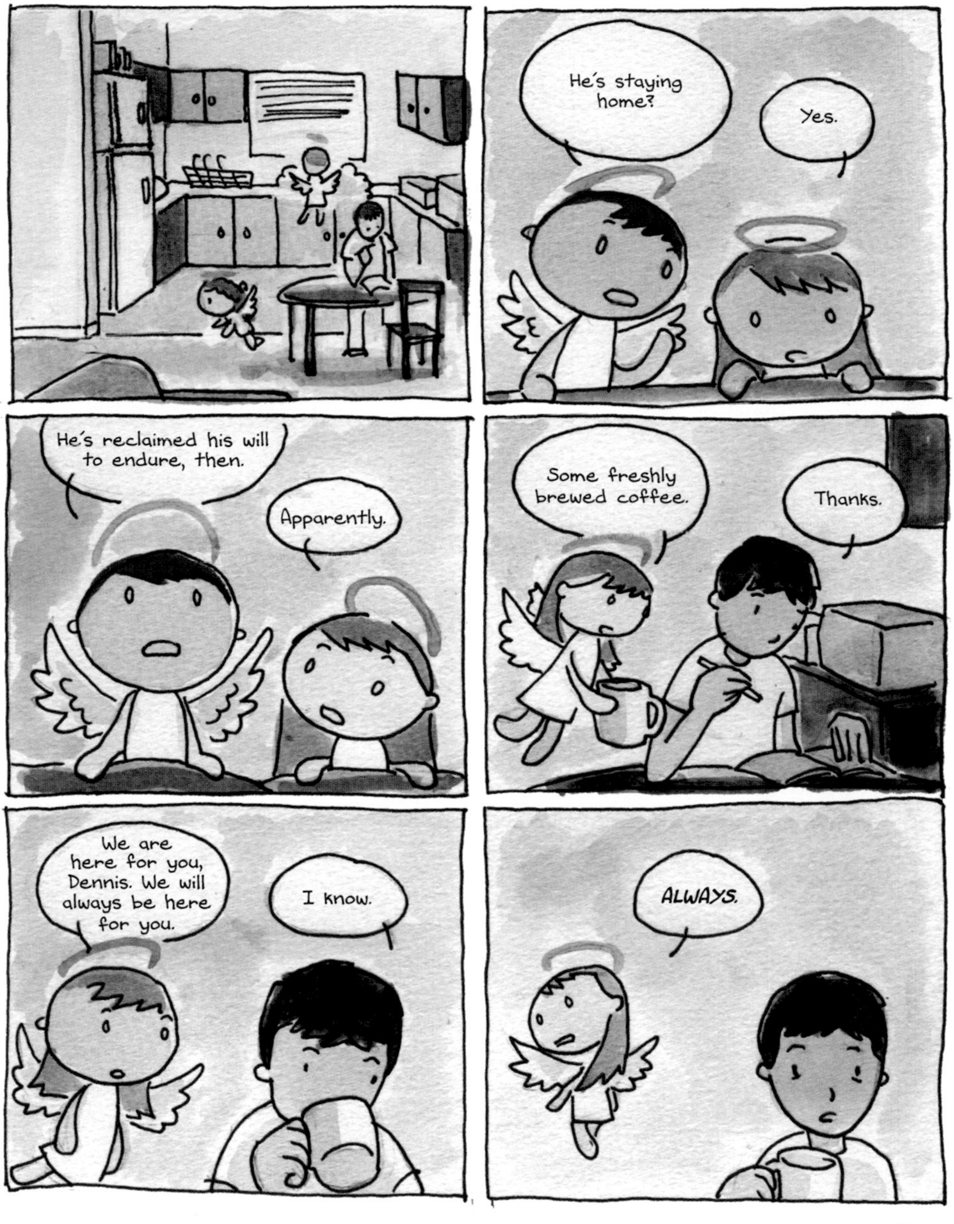
He's staying home?
Yes.
He's reclaimed his will to endure, then.
Apparently.
Some freshly brewed coffee.
Thanks.
We are here for you, Dennis. We will always be here for you.
I know.
ALWAYS.

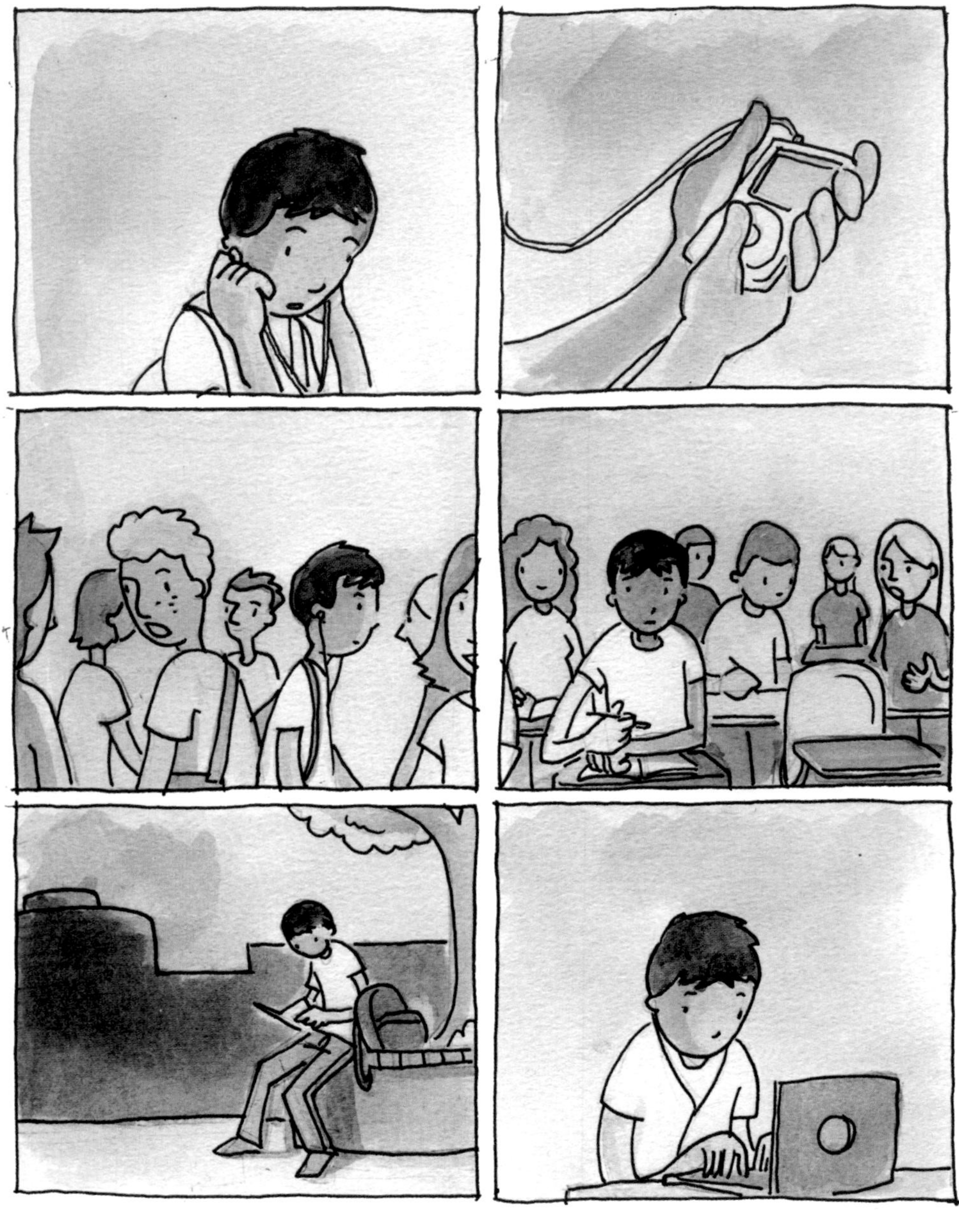

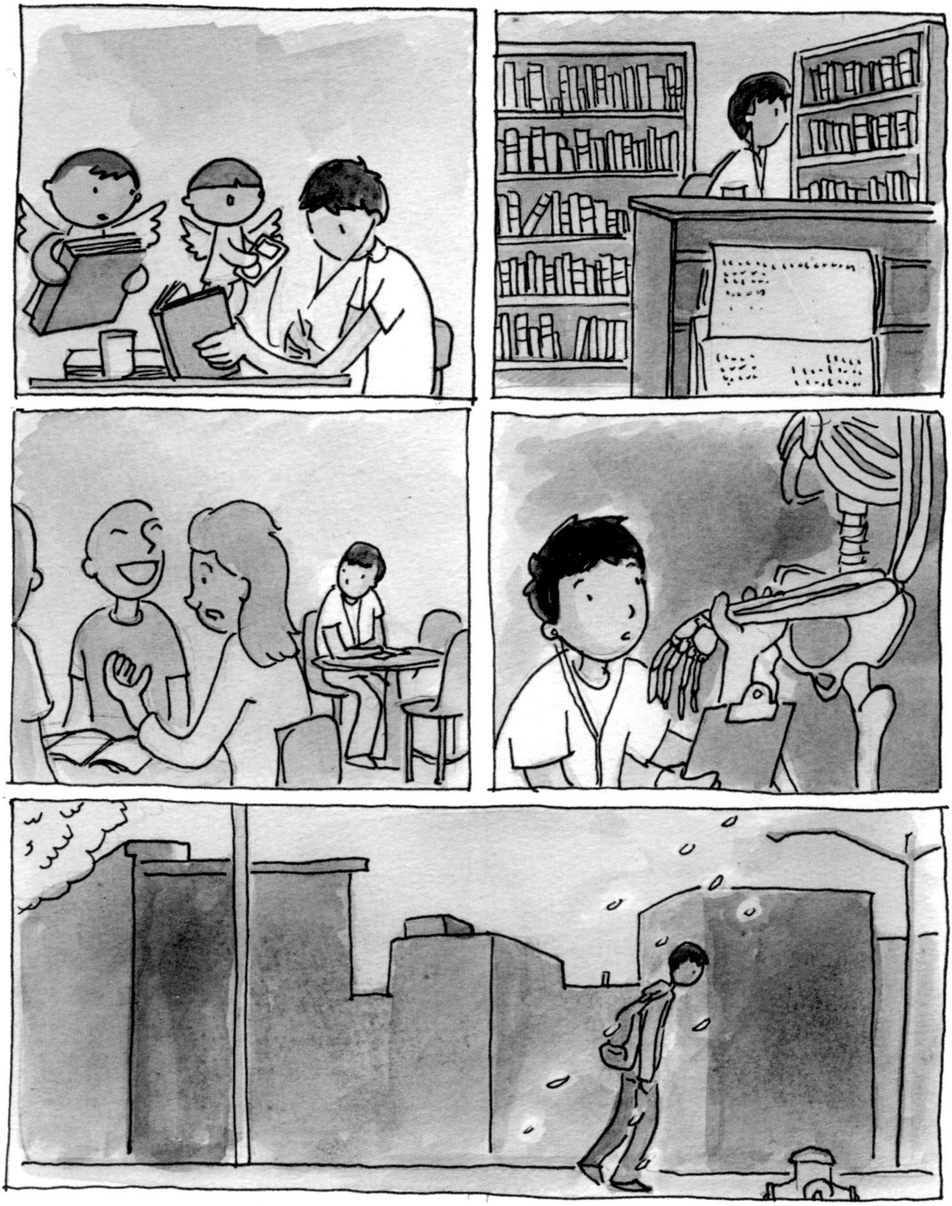

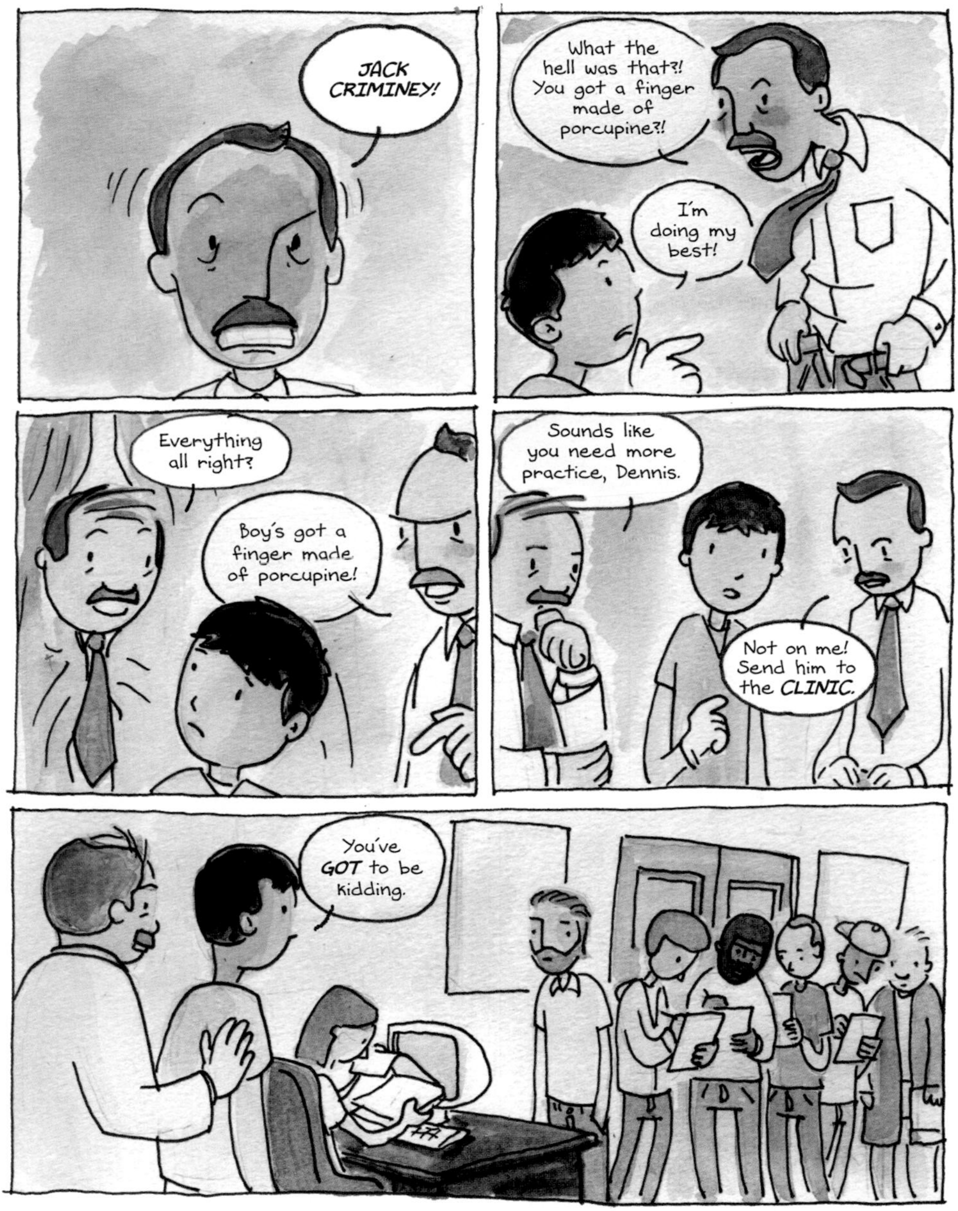
JACK CRIMINEY!
What the hell was that?! You got a finger made of porcupine?!
I'm doing my best!
Everything all right?
Boy's got a finger made of porcupine!
Sounds like you need more practice, Dennis.
Not on me! Send him to the CLINIC.
You've GOT to be kidding.

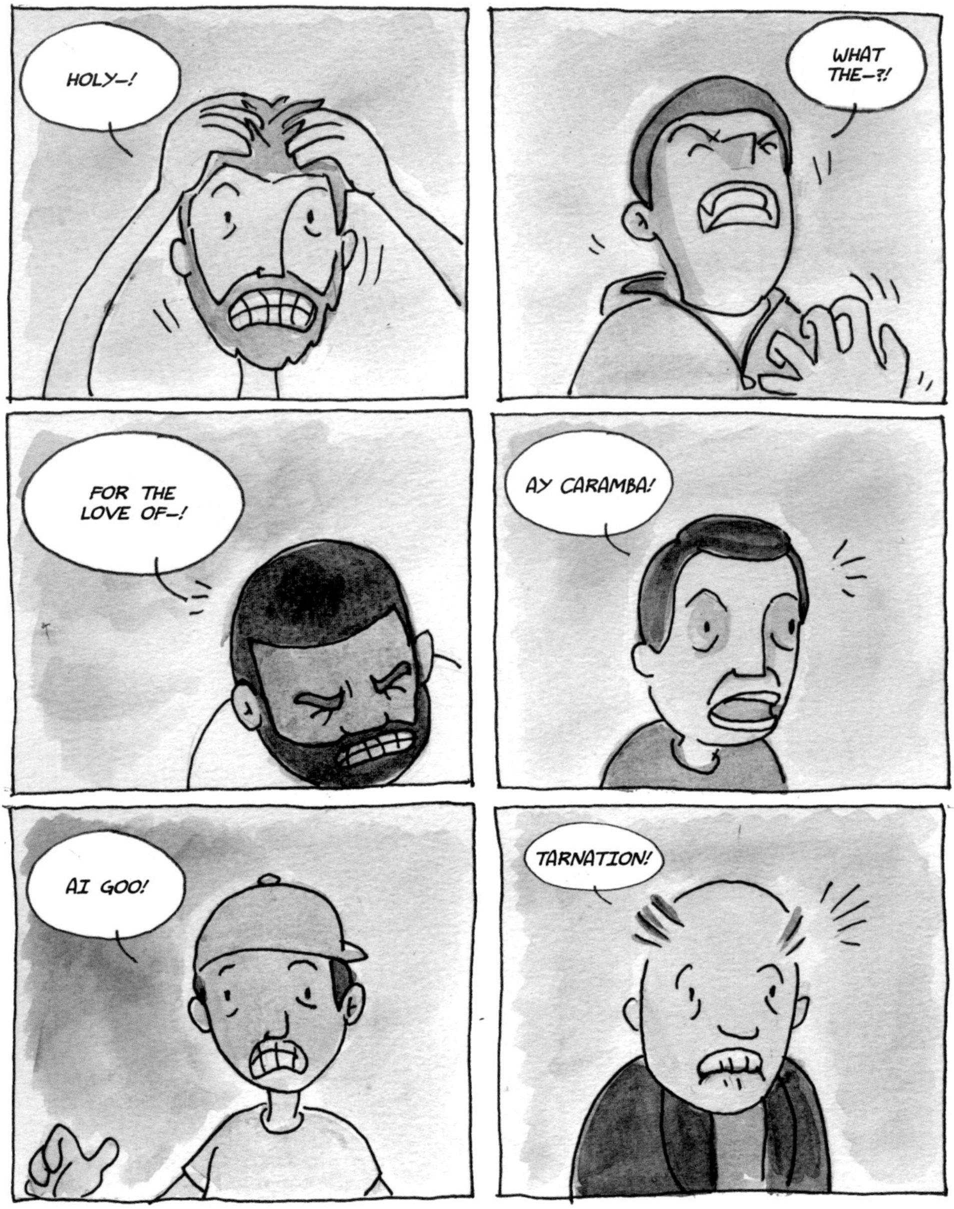
HOLY–!
WHAT THE–?!
FOR THE LOVE OF–!
AY CARAMBA!
AI GOO!
TARNATION!

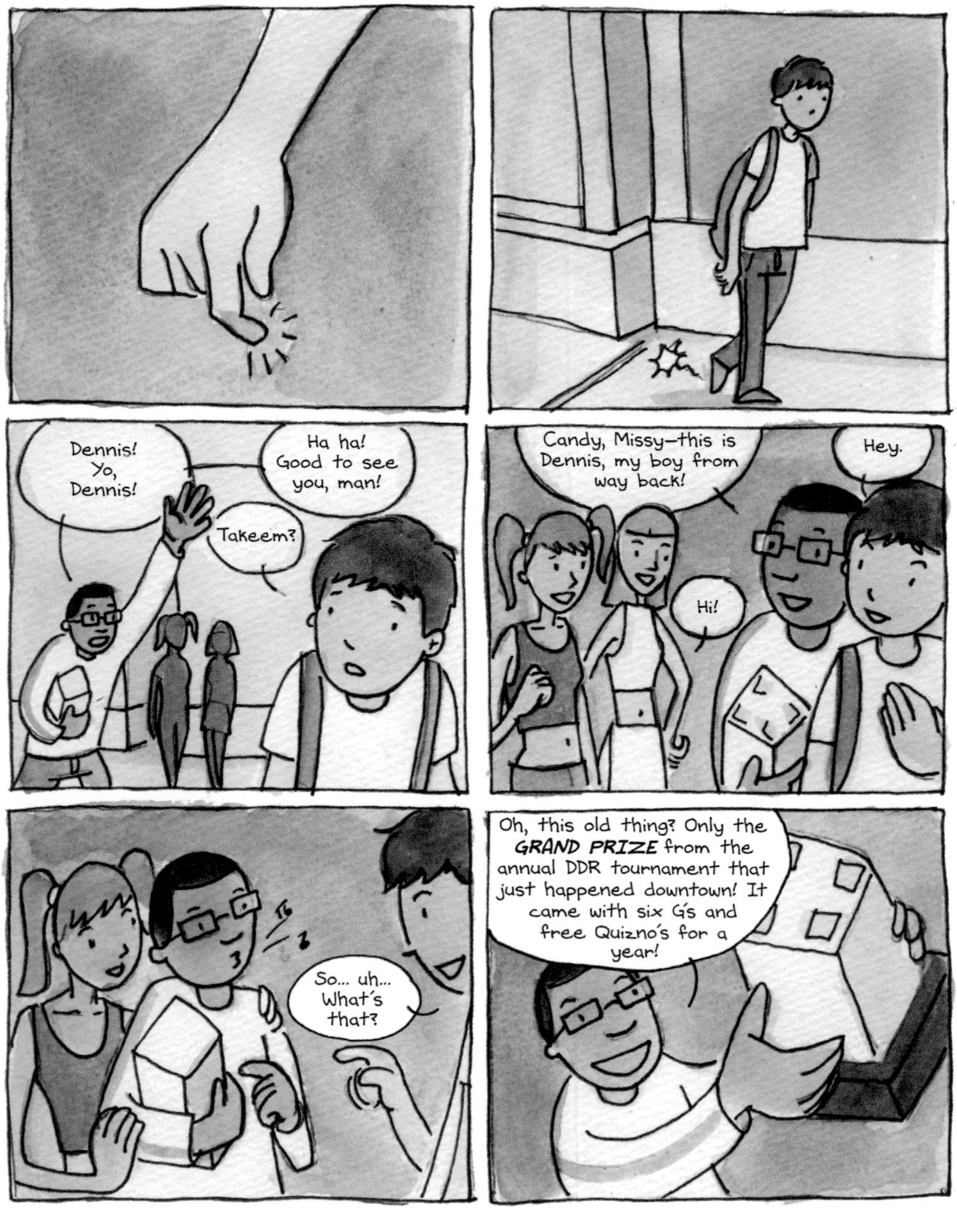
Dennis! Yo, Dennis!
Ha ha! Good to see you, man!
Takeem?
Candy, Missy—this is Dennis, my boy from way back!
Hey.
Hi!
So... uh... What's that?
Oh, this old thing? Only the **GRAND PRIZE** from the annual DDR tournament that just happened downtown! It came with six G's and free Quizno's for a year!

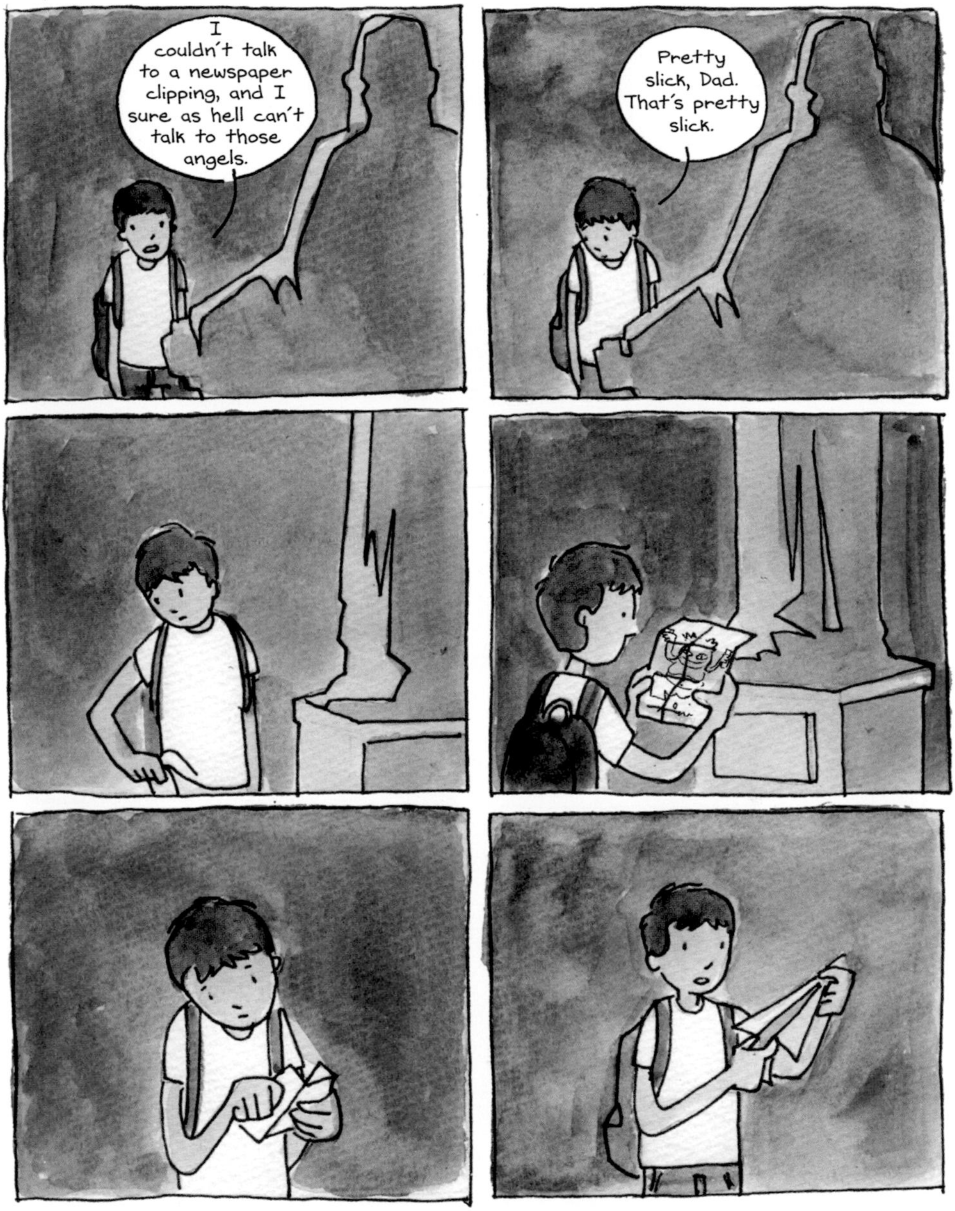
I couldn't talk to a newspaper clipping, and I sure as hell can't talk to those angels.
Pretty slick, Dad. That's pretty slick.

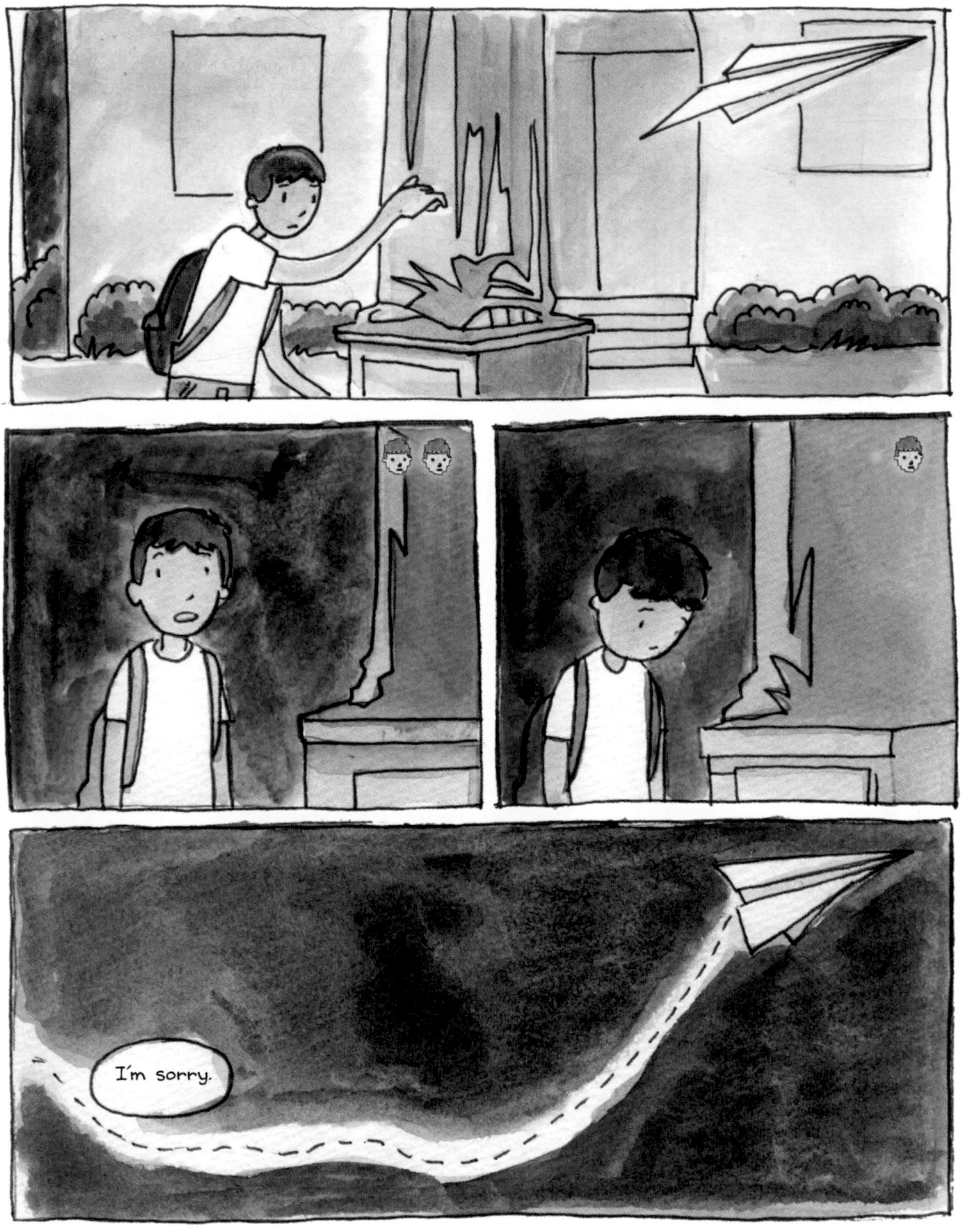
I'm sorry.

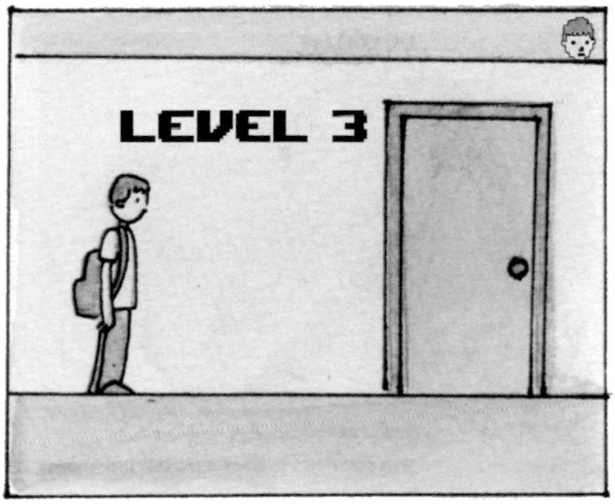
LEVEL 3

I knew exactly what I was going to say and
how I was going to say it. It was my life.
I wanted it back.

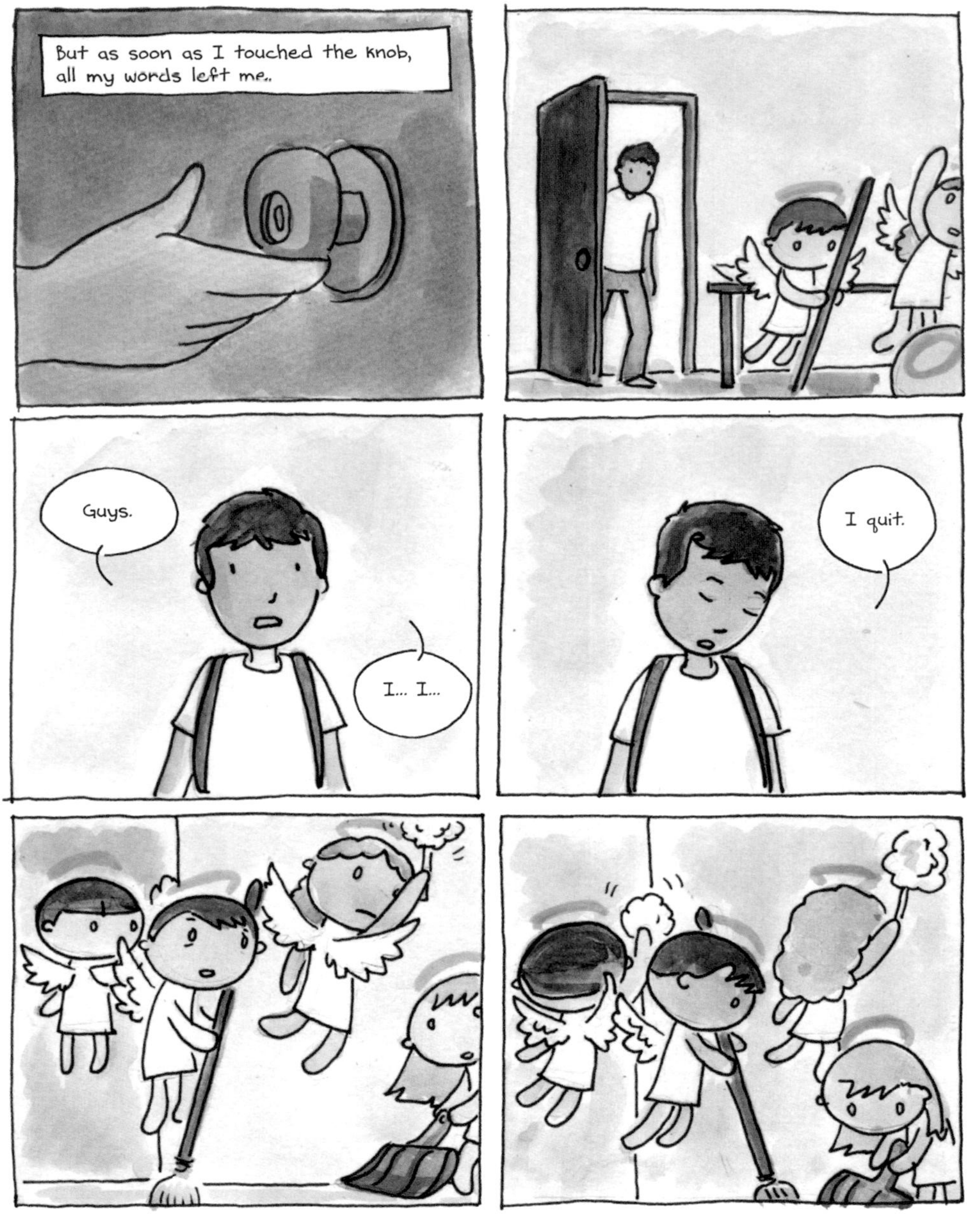
But as soon as I touched the knob, all my words left me..
Guys.
I... I...
I quit.

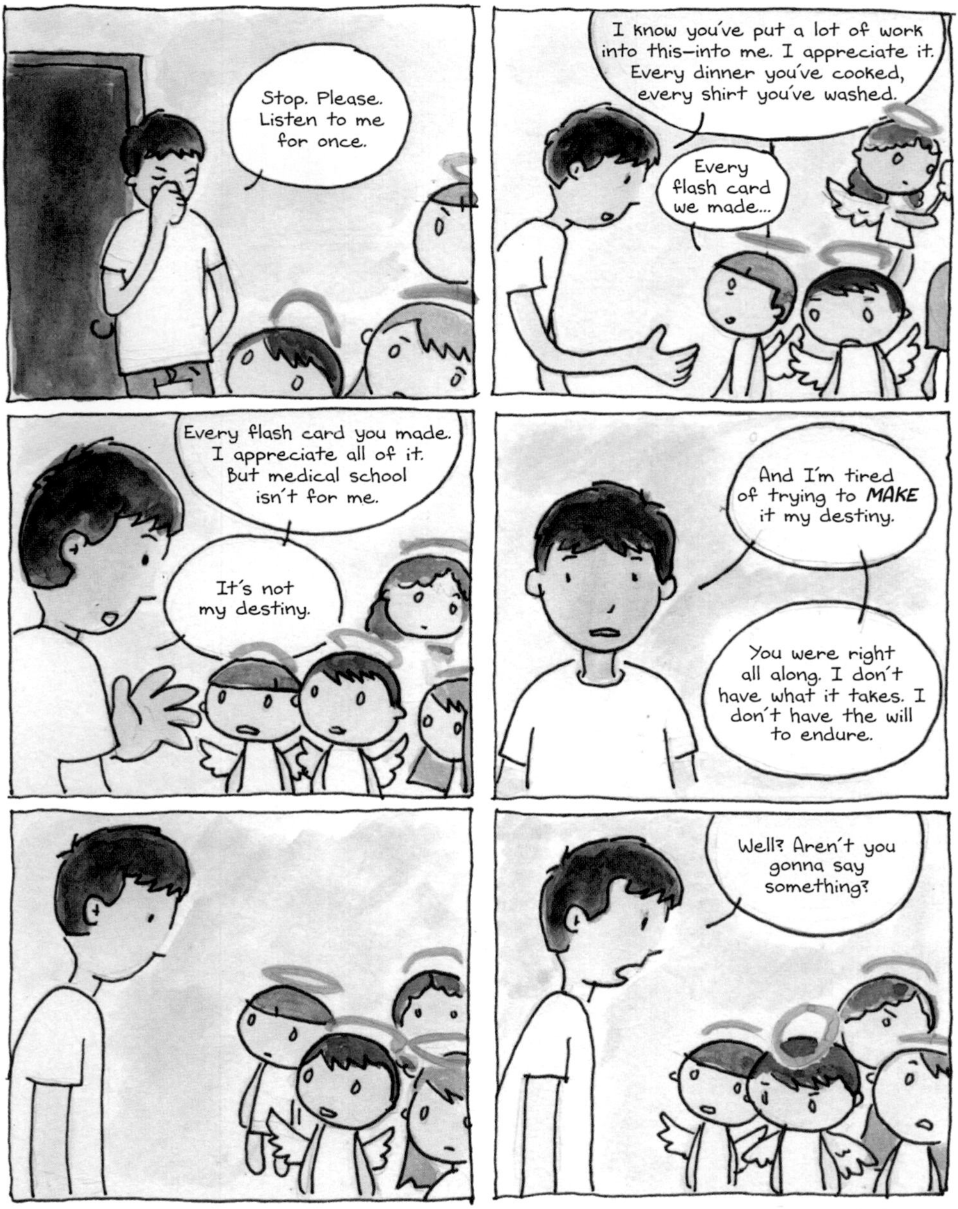
Stop. Please. Listen to me for once.
I know you've put a lot of work into this—into me. I appreciate it. Every dinner you've cooked, every shirt you've washed.
Every flash card we made...
Every flash card you made. I appreciate all of it. But medical school isn't for me.
It's not my destiny.
And I'm tired of trying to MAKE it my destiny.
You were right all along. I don't have what it takes. I don't have the will to endure.
Well? Aren't you gonna say something?

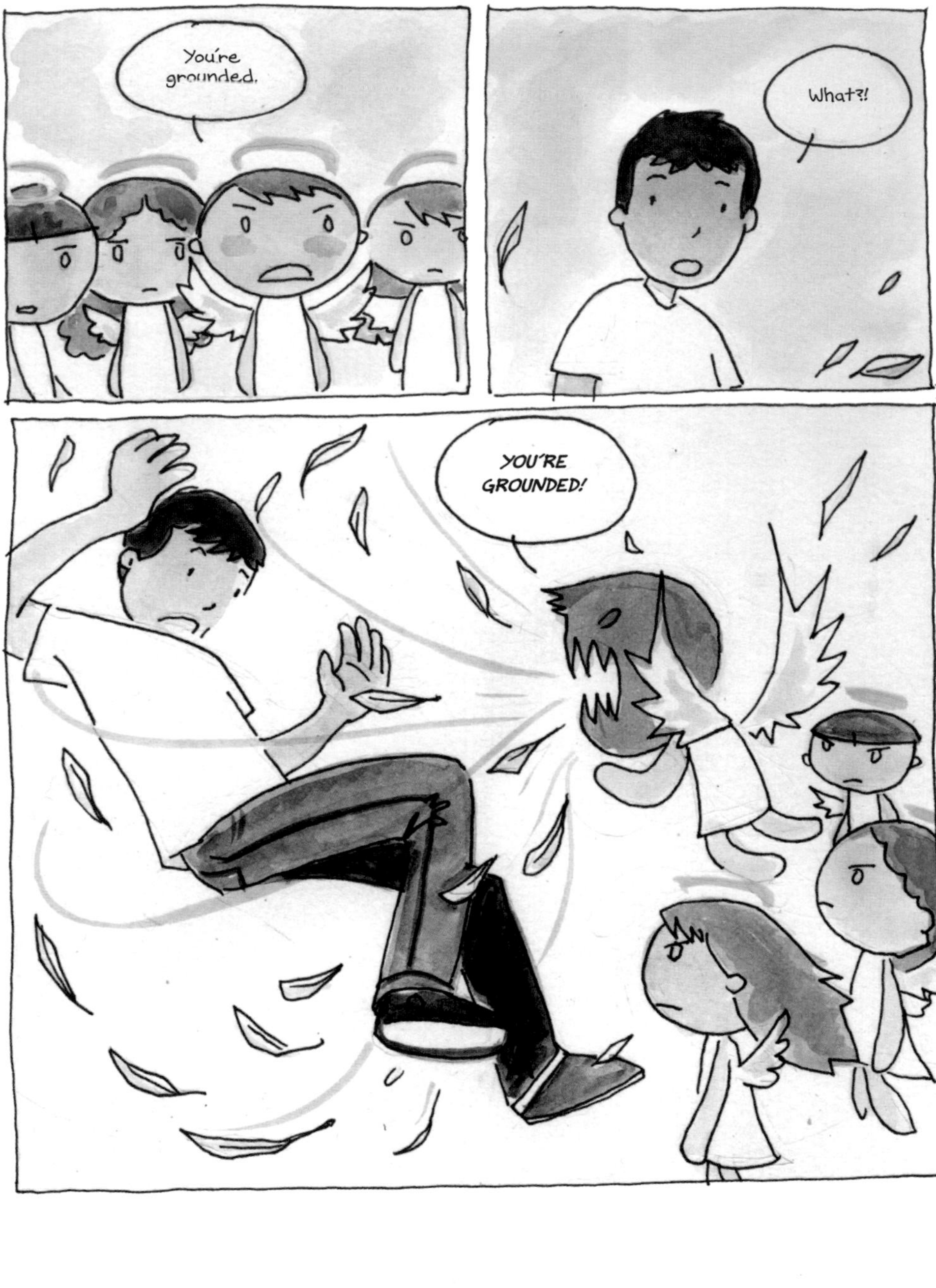
You're grounded.
What?!
YOU'RE GROUNDED!

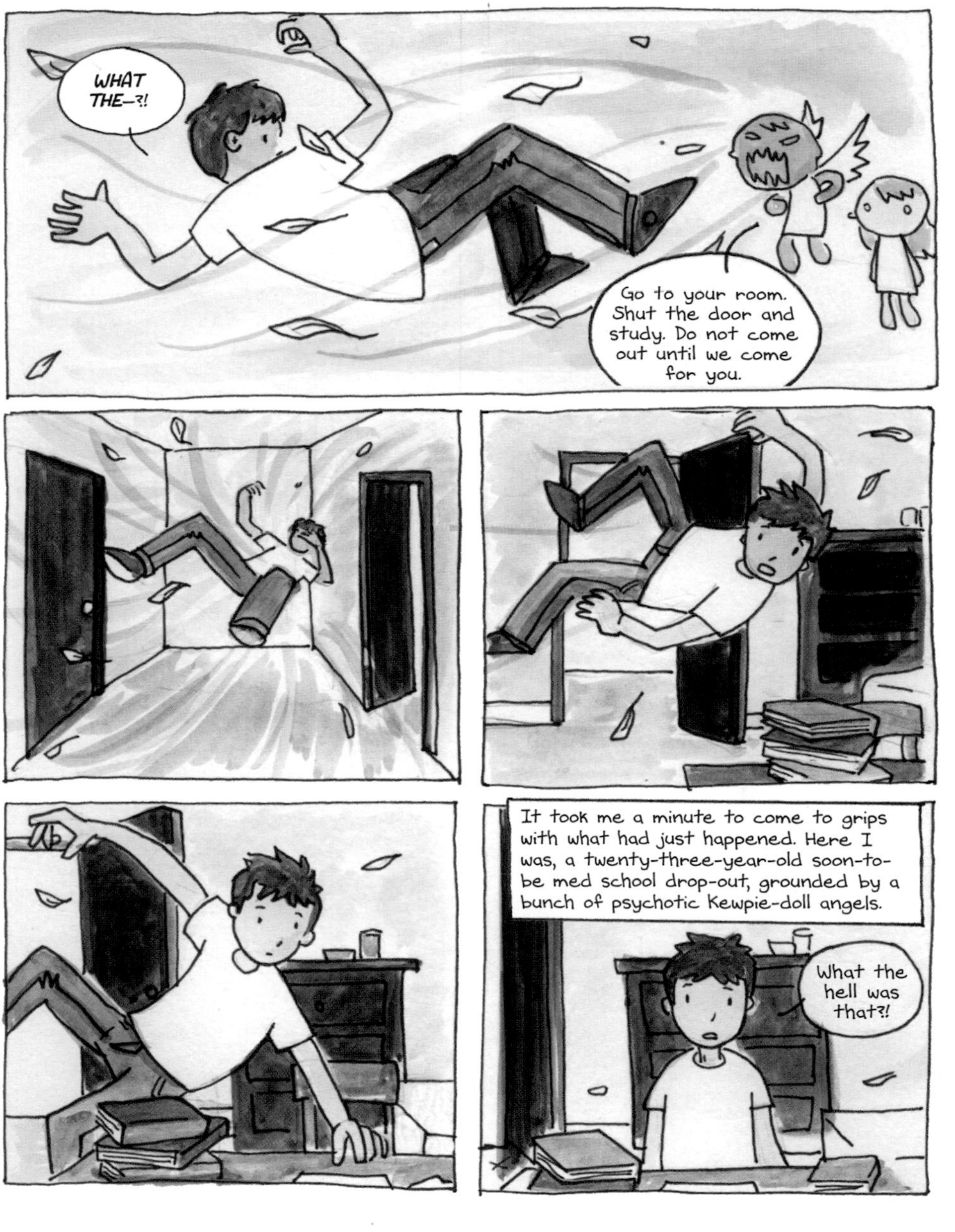
WHAT THE–?!
Go to your room. Shut the door and study. Do not come out until we come for you.
It took me a minute to come to grips with what had just happened. Here I was, a twenty-three-year-old soon-to-be med school drop-out, grounded by a bunch of psychotic Kewpie-doll angels.
What the hell was that?!

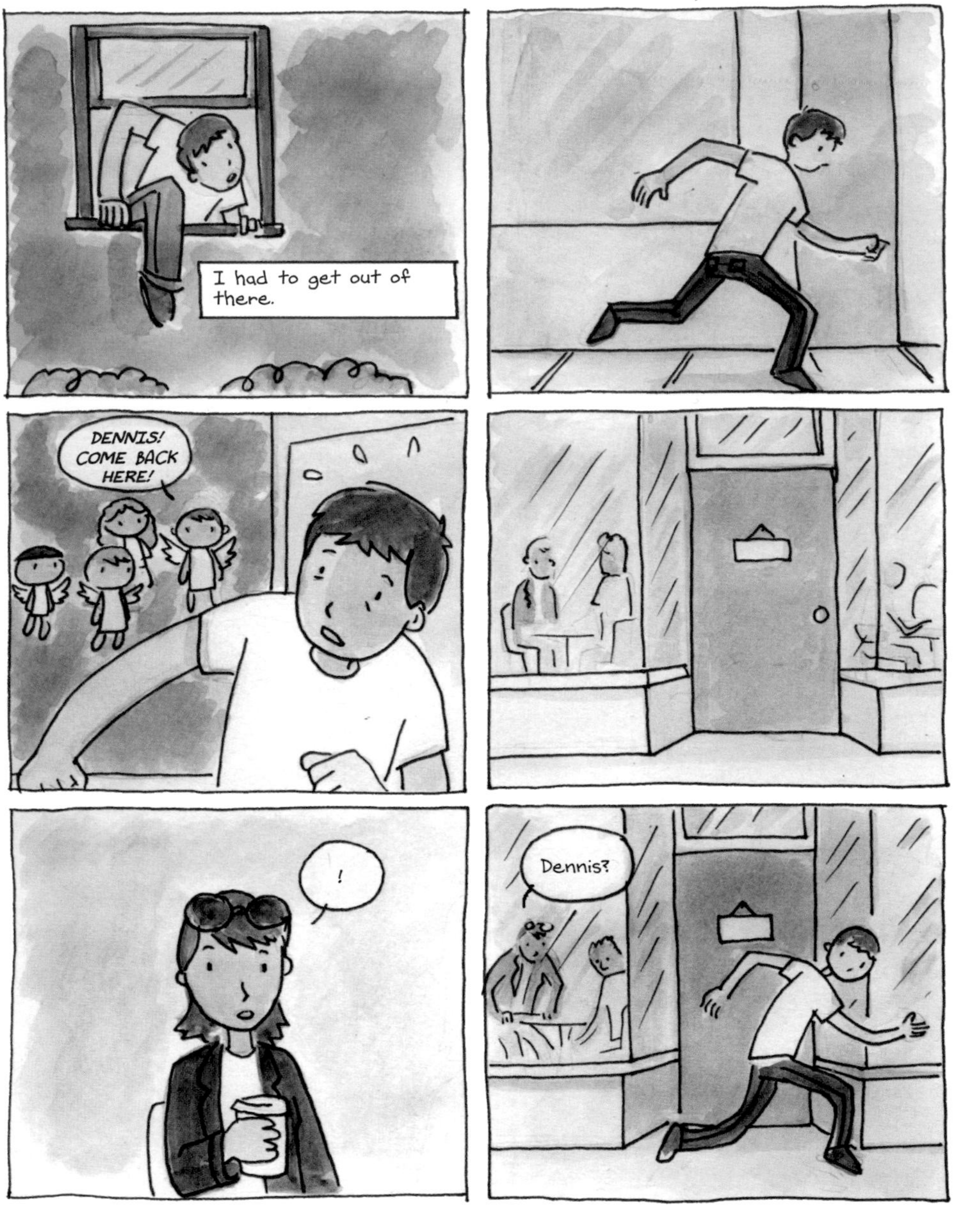
I had to get out of there.
DENNIS! COME BACK HERE!
!
Dennis?

Did you just call me Dennis?
These streets are like a maze...
Wait a minute... I'm running through a maze...

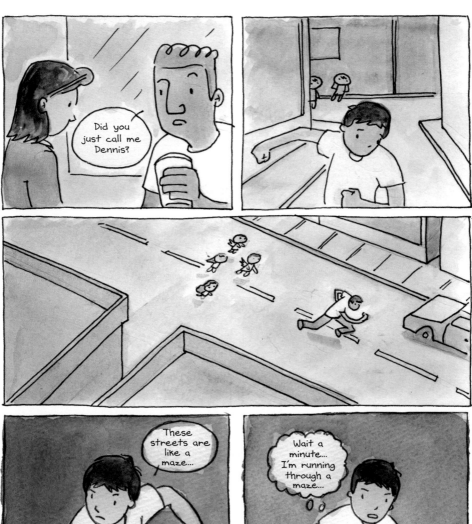

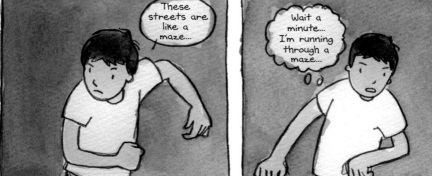

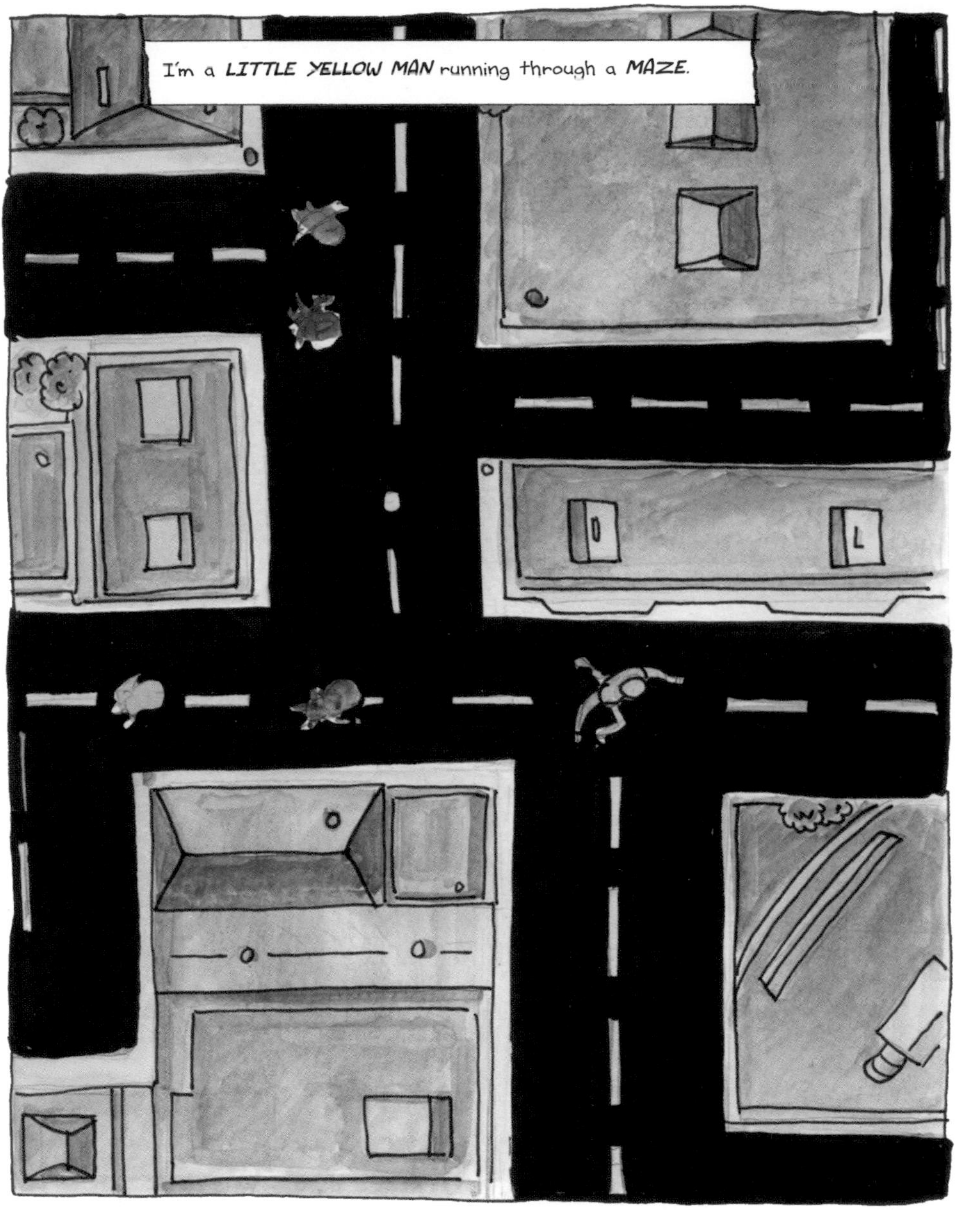
I'm a LITTLE YELLOW MAN running through a MAZE.

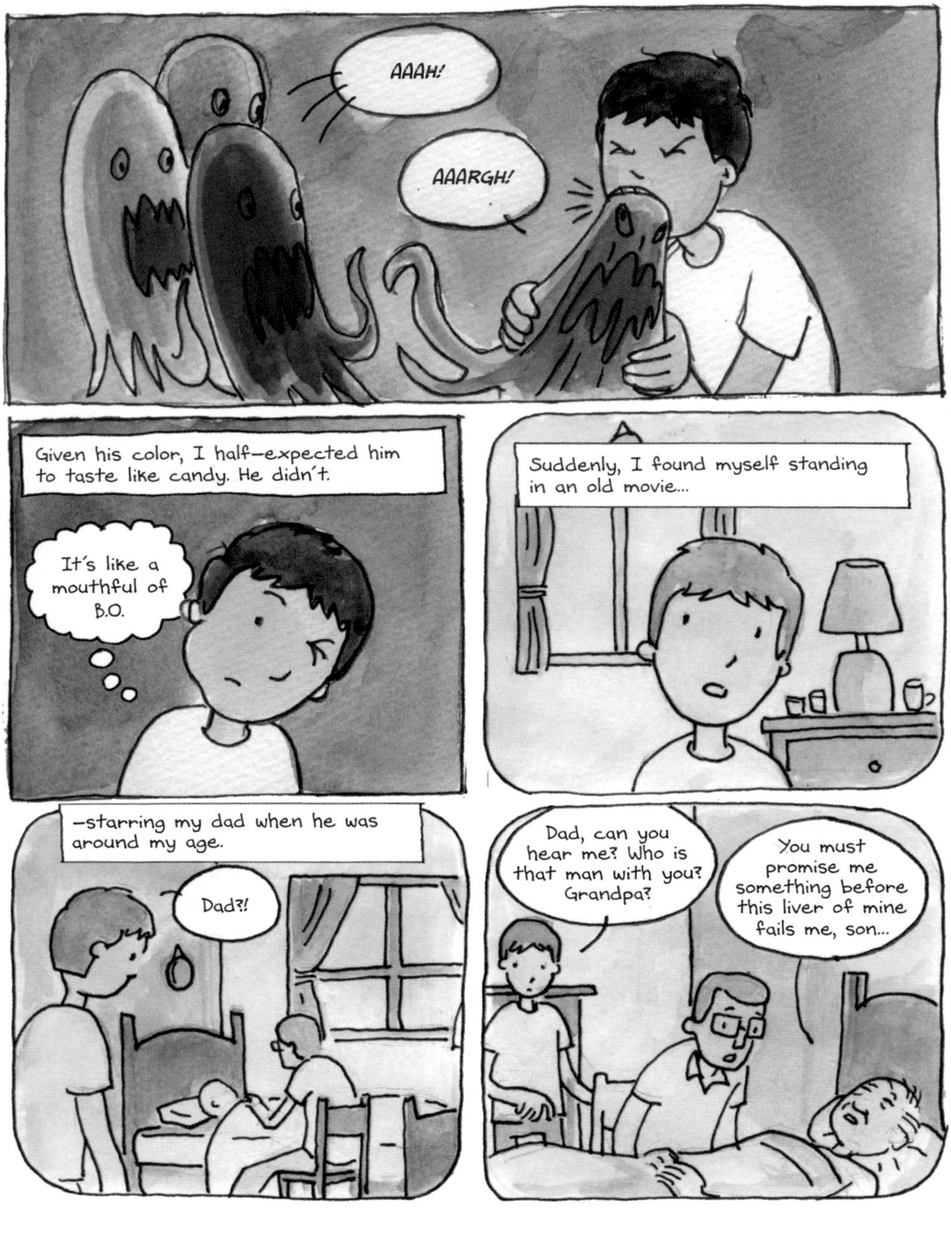
AAAH!
AAARGH!
Given his color, I half-expected him to taste like candy. He didn't.
It's like a mouthful of B.O.
Suddenly, I found myself standing in an old movie...
-starring my dad when he was around my age.
Dad?!
Dad, can you hear me? Who is that man with you? Grandpa?
You must promise me something before this liver of mine fails me, son...

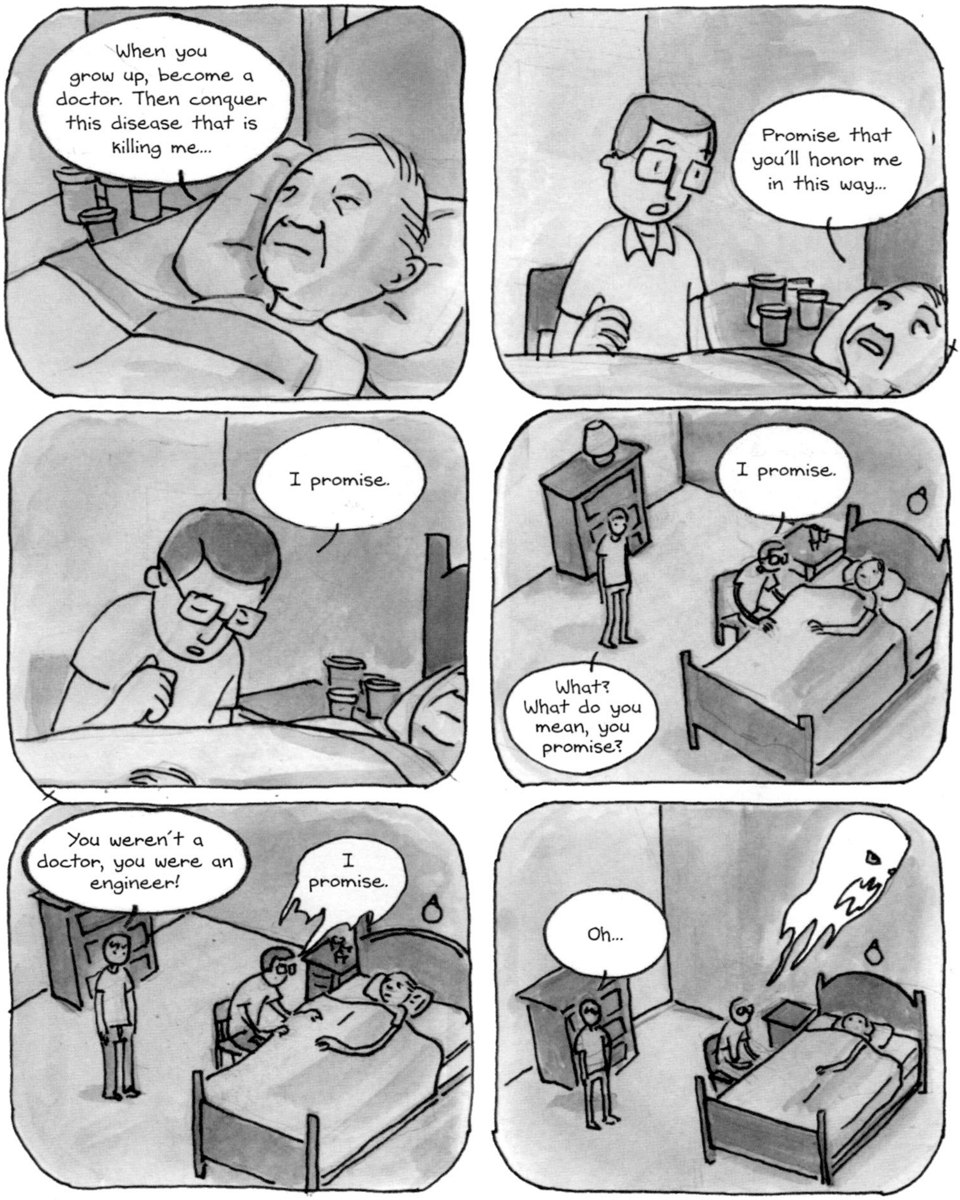
When you grow up, become a doctor. Then conquer this disease that is killing me...
Promise that you'll honor me in this way...
I promise.
I promise.
What? What do you mean, you promise?
You weren't a doctor, you were an engineer!
I promise.
Oh...

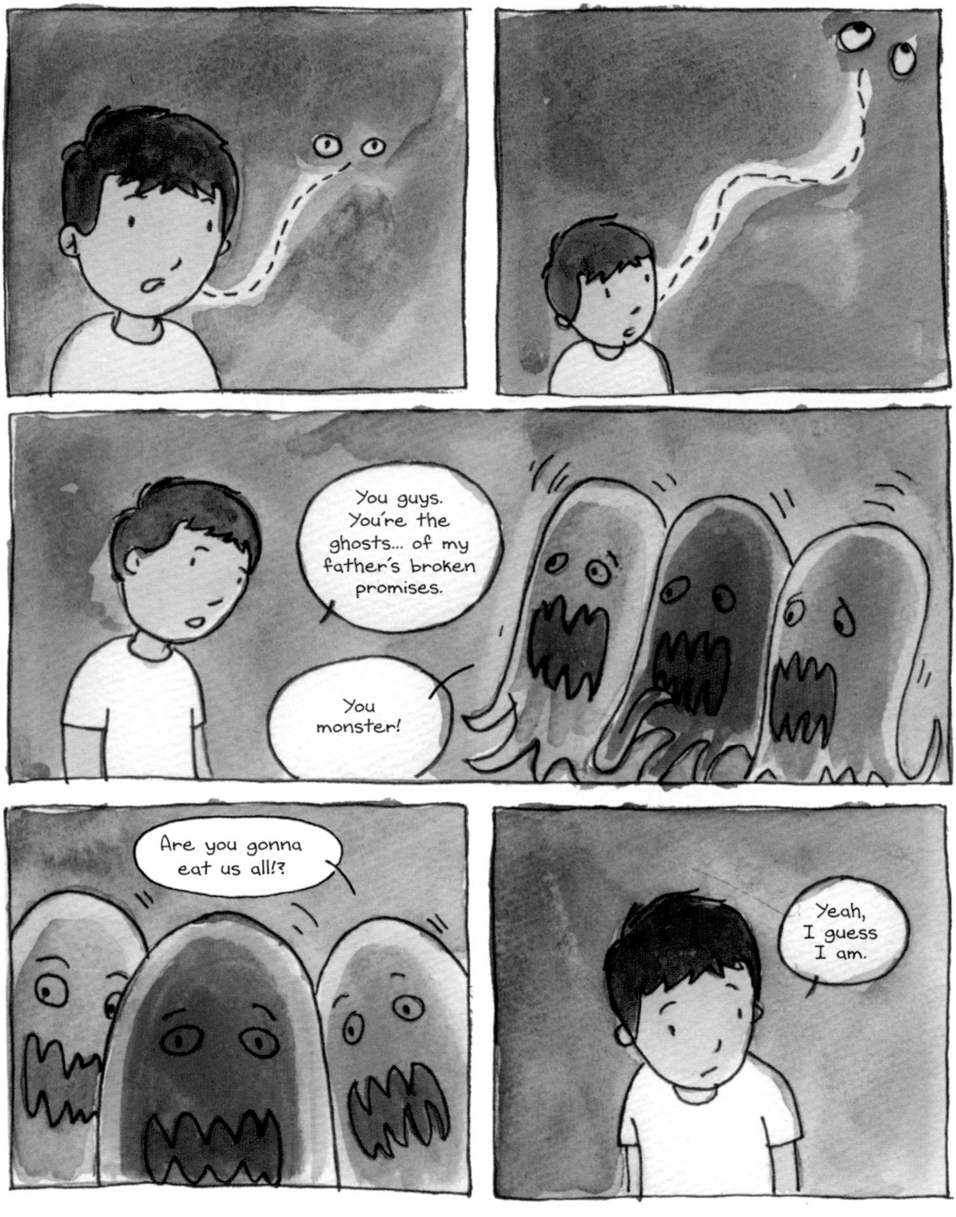
You guys. You're the ghosts... of my father's broken promises.
You monster!
Are you gonna eat us all!?
Yeah, I guess I am.

126

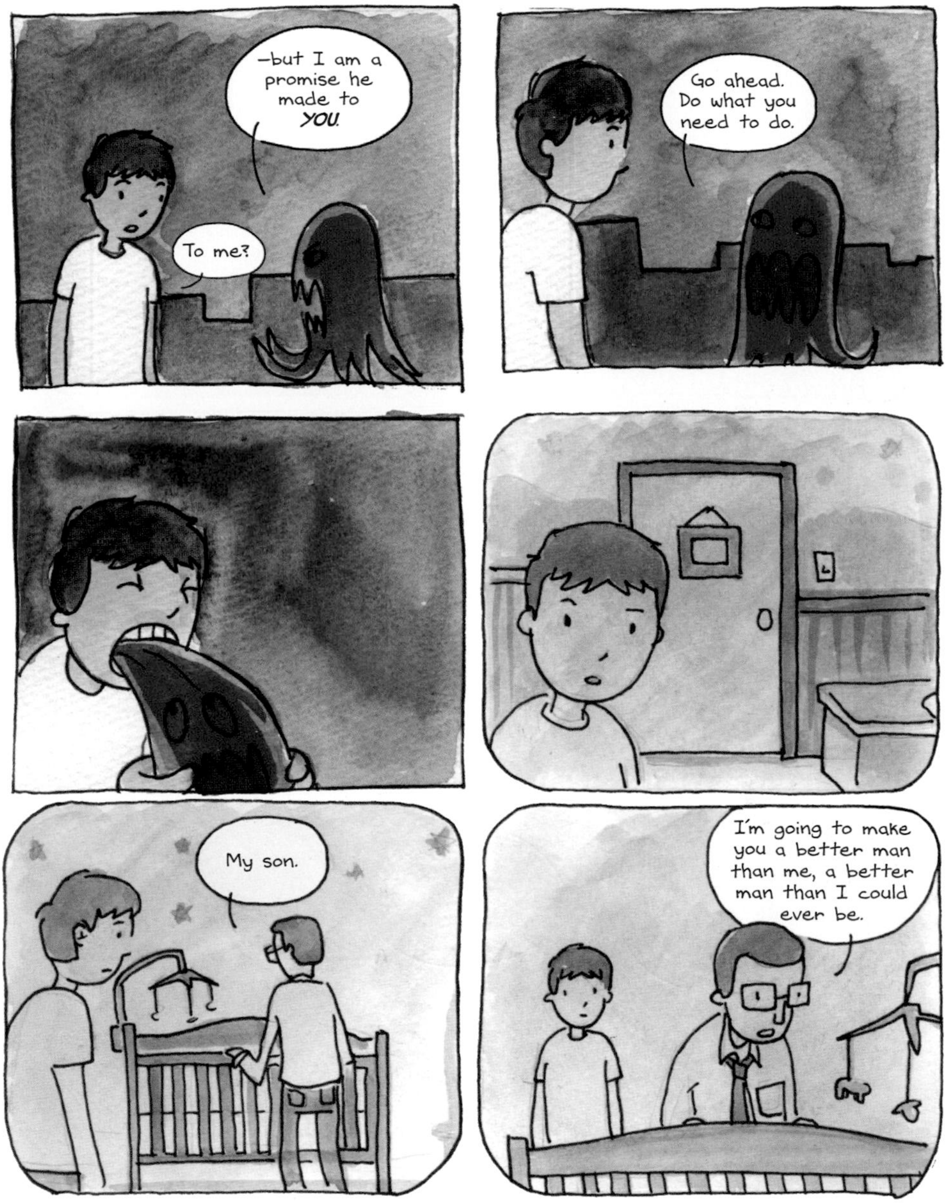
—but I am a promise he made to YOU.
To me?
Go ahead. Do what you need to do.
My son.
I'm going to make you a better man than me, a better man than I could ever be.

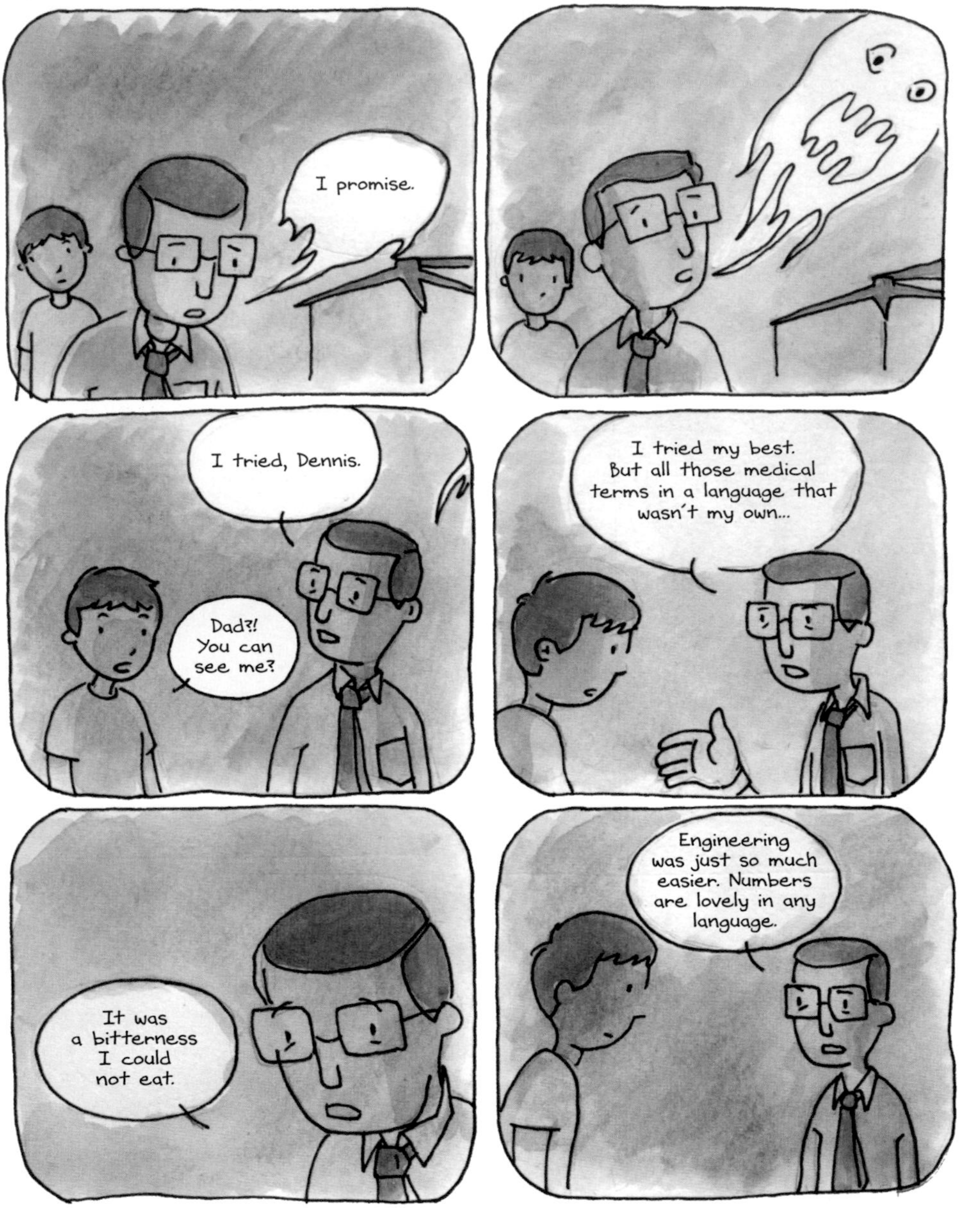
I promise.
I tried, Dennis.
Dad?! You can see me?
I tried my best. But all those medical terms in a language that wasn't my own...
It was a bitterness I could not eat.
Engineering was just so much easier. Numbers are lovely in any language.

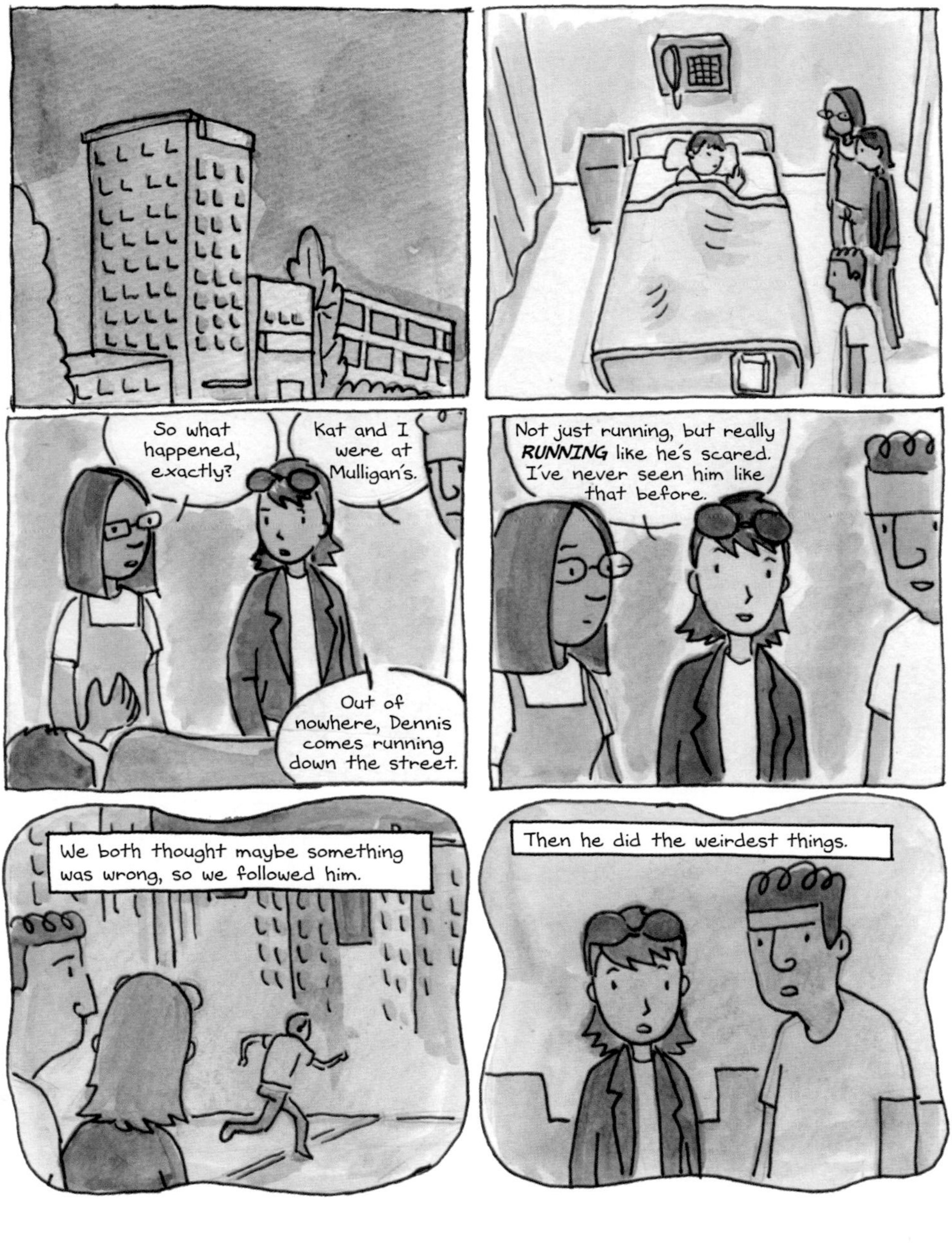

So what happened, exactly?
Kat and I were at Mulligan's.
Out of nowhere, Dennis comes running down the street.
Not just running, but really RUNNING like he's scared. I've never seen him like that before.
We both thought maybe something was wrong, so we followed him.
Then he did the weirdest things.

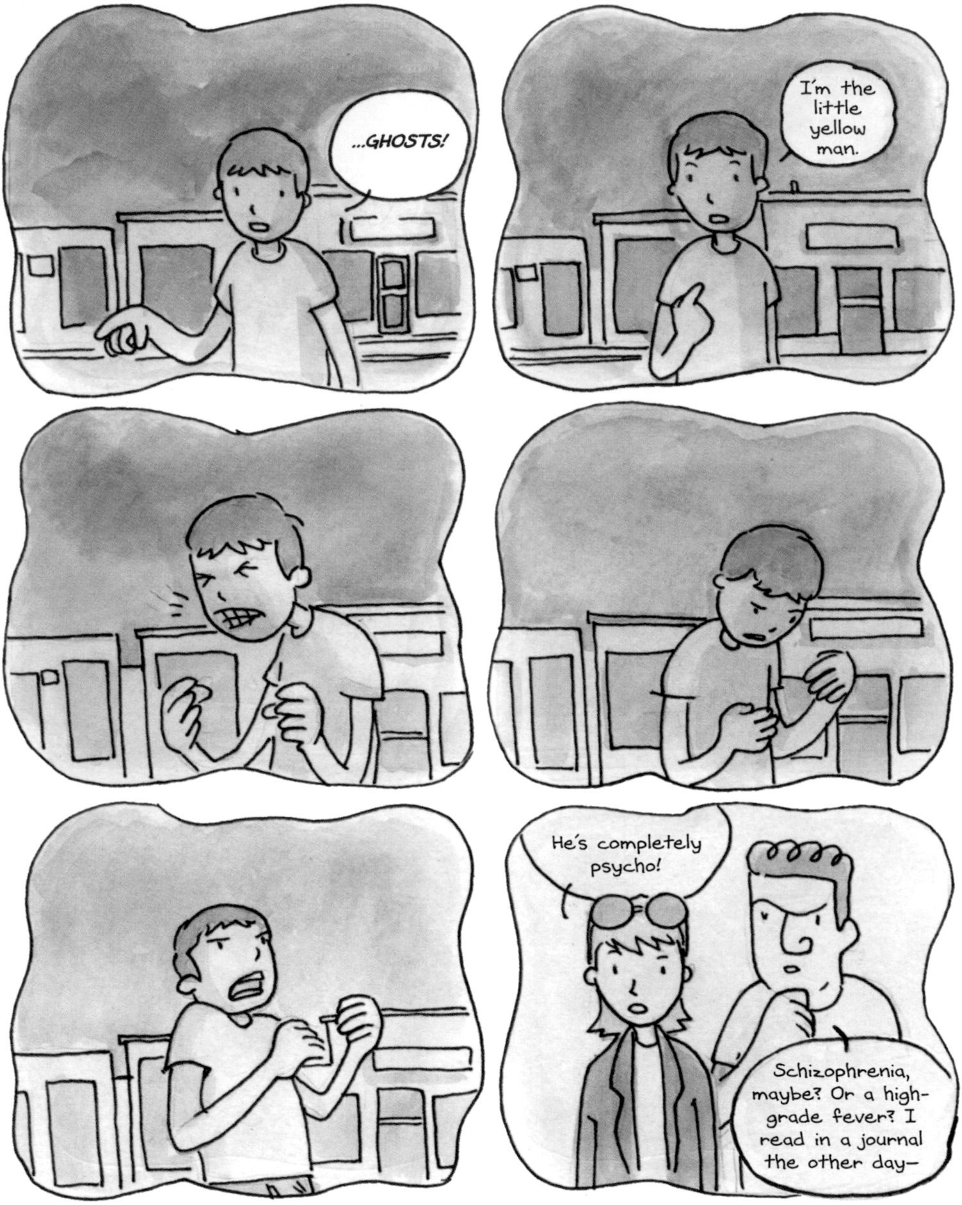
...GHOSTS!
I'm the little yellow man.
He's completely psycho!
Schizophrenia, maybe? Or a high-grade fever? I read in a journal the other day—

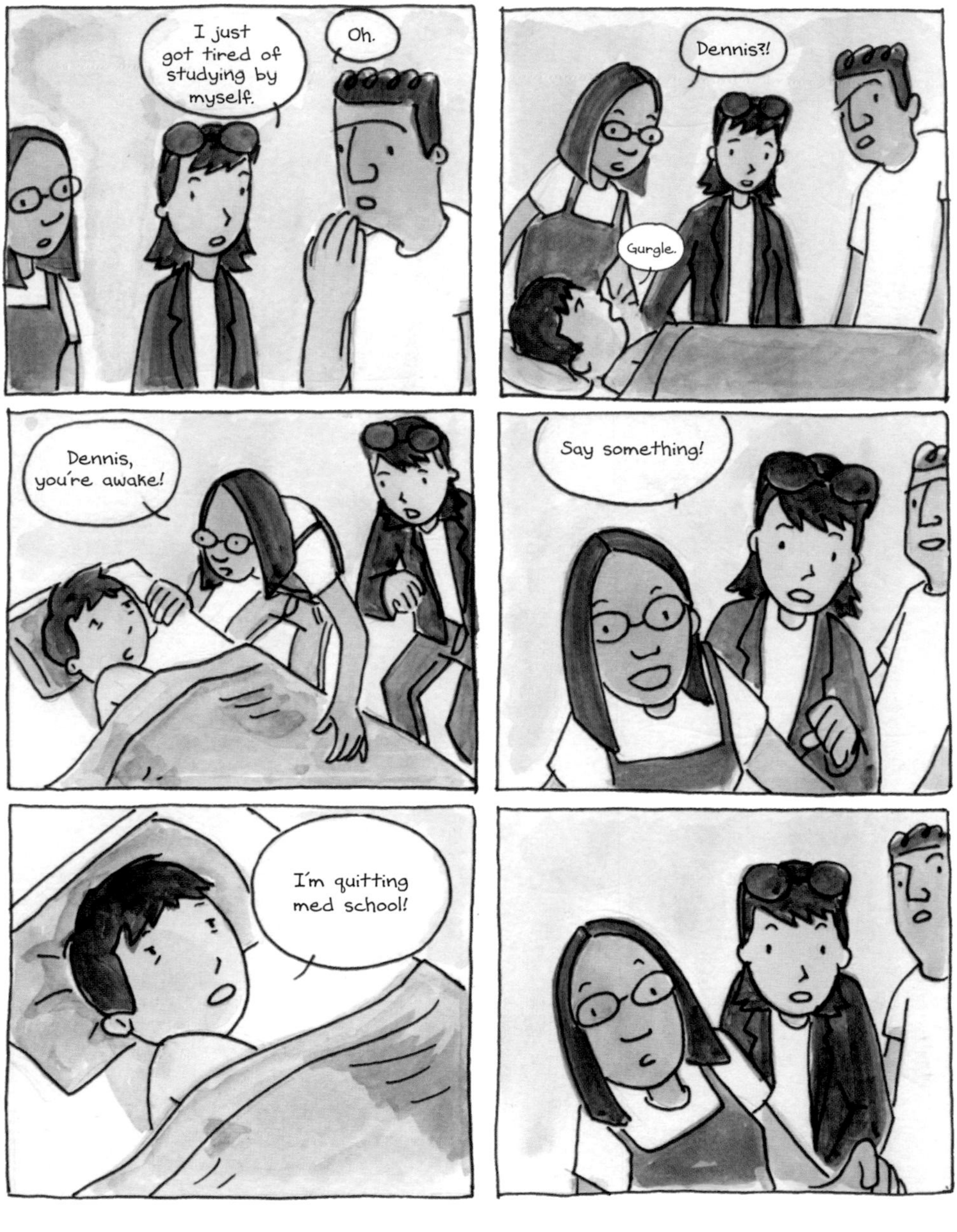
I just got tired of studying by myself.
Oh.
Dennis?!
Gurgle.
Dennis, you're awake!
Say something!
I'm quitting med school!

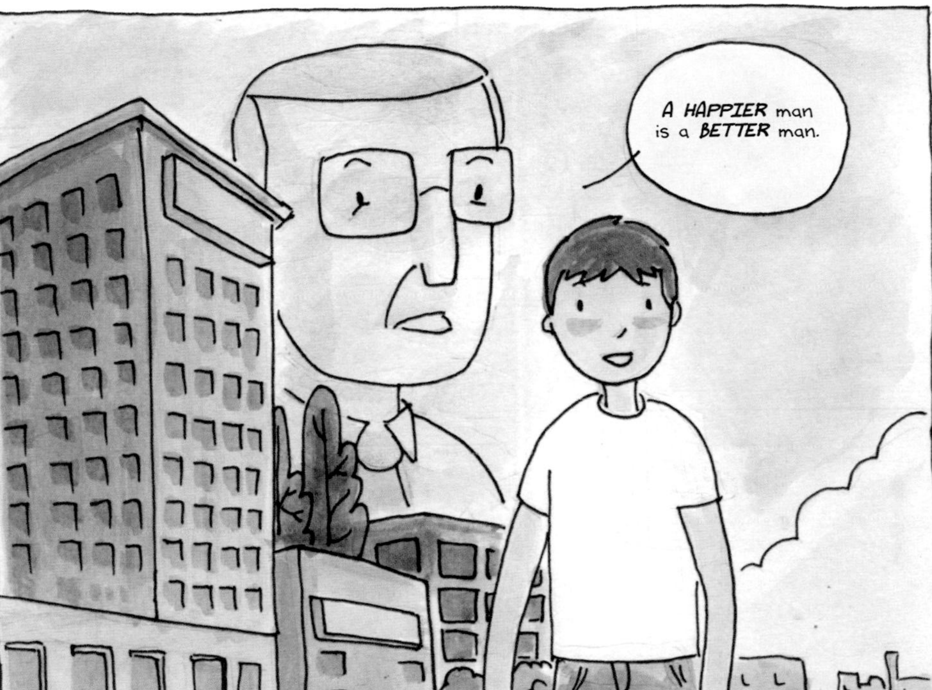
A HAPPIER man is a BETTER man.
The next morning I walked out of med school—

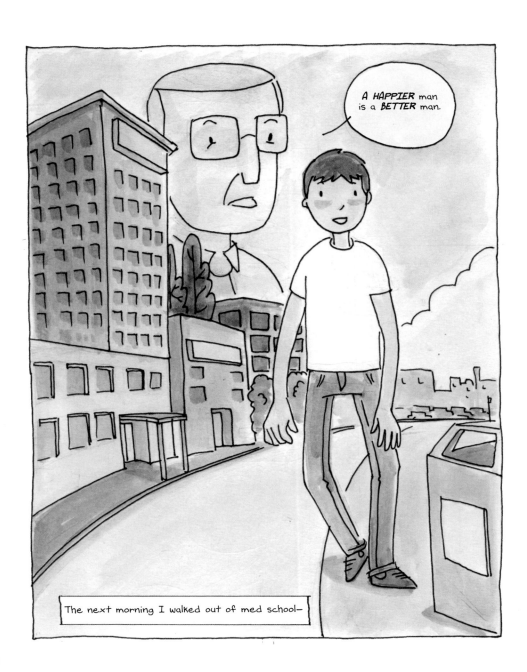

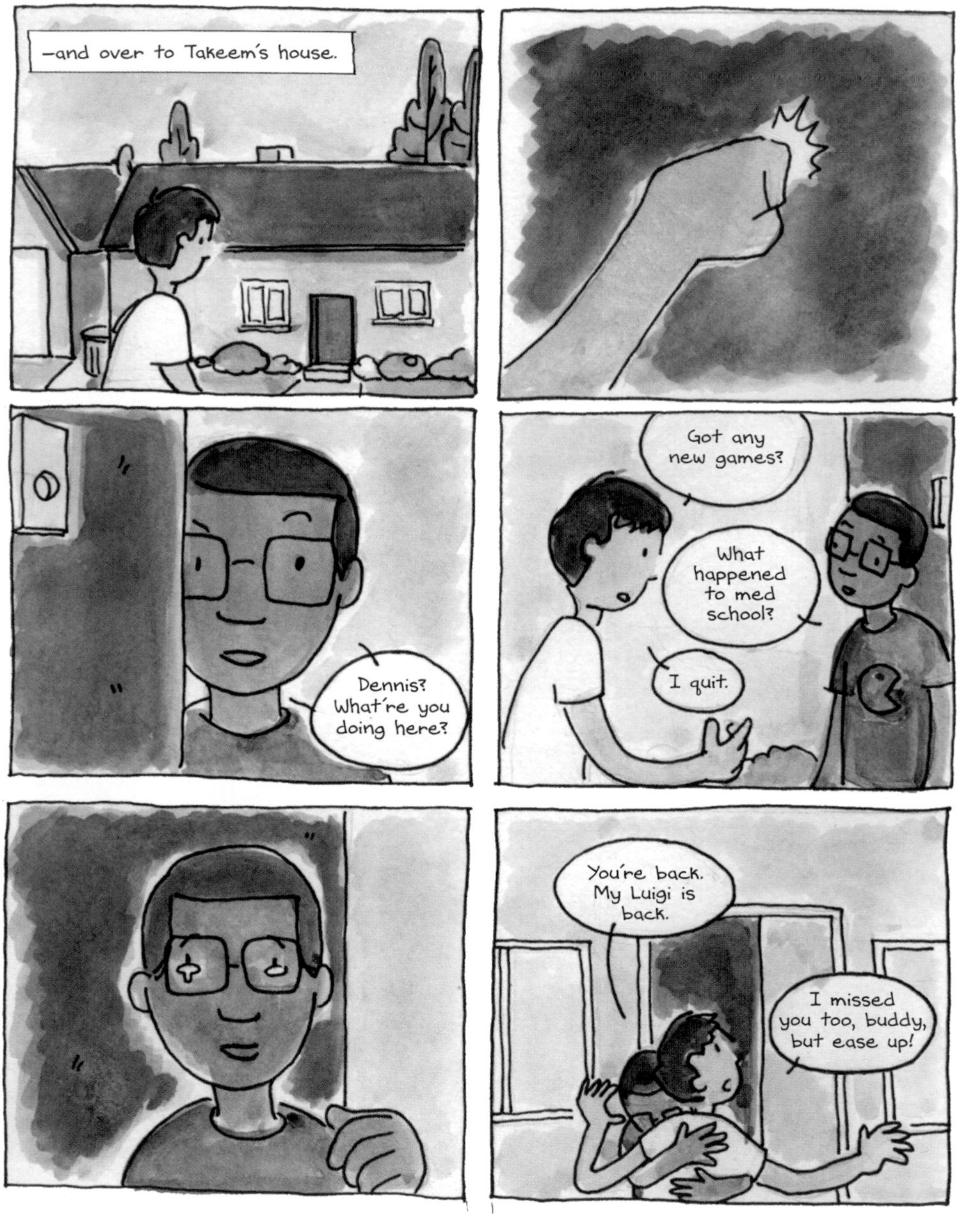
–and over to Takeem's house.
Dennis? What're you doing here?
Got any new games?
What happened to med school?
I quit.
You're back. My Luigi is back.
I missed you too, buddy, but ease up!

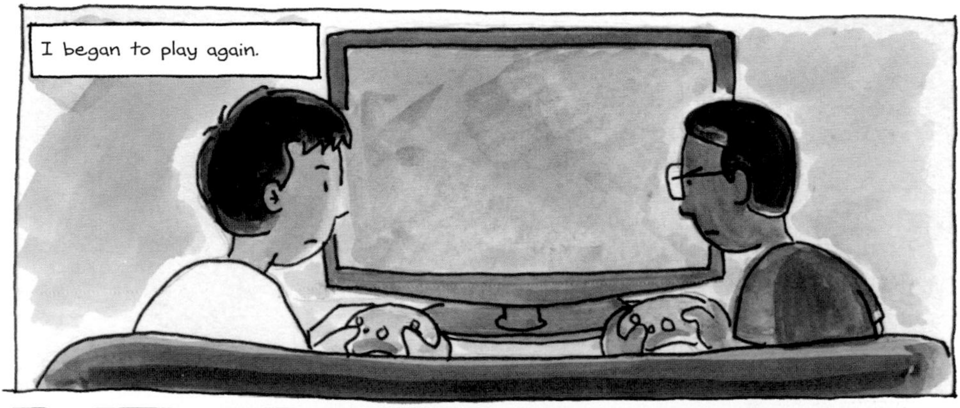
I began to play again.

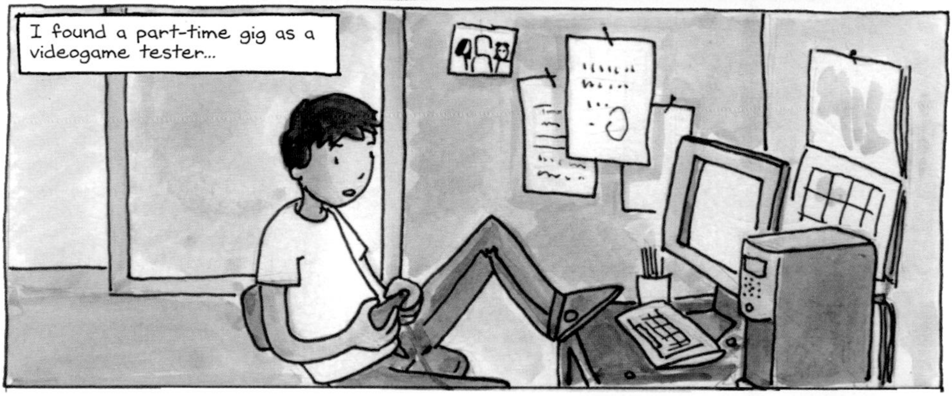
I found a part-time gig as a videogame tester...

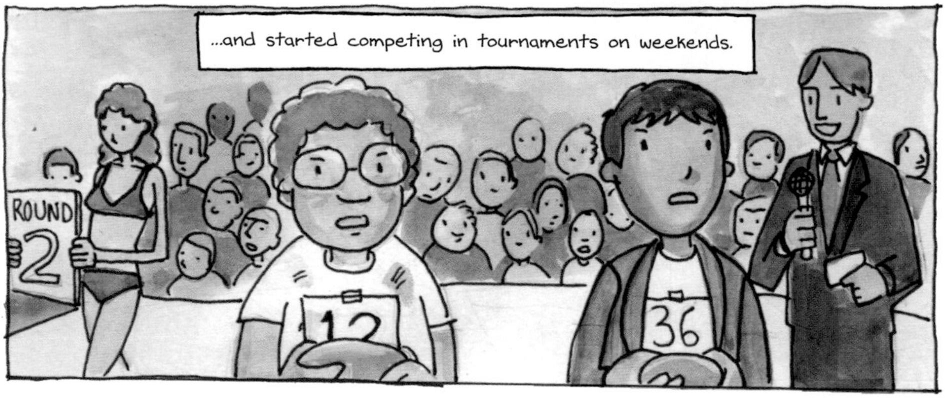
...and started competing in tournaments on weekends.
ROUND 2
12
36

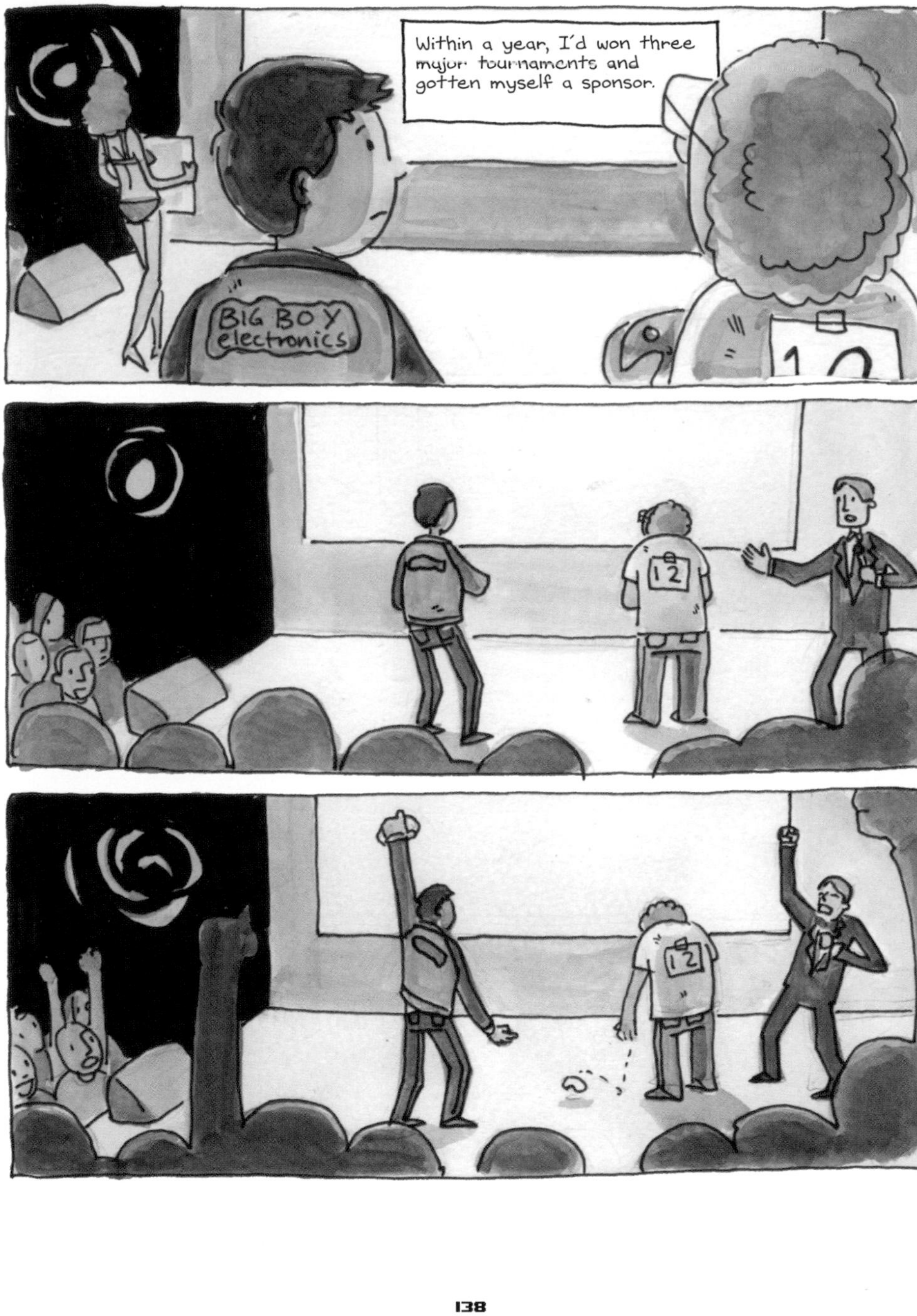
Within a year, I'd won three major tournaments and gotten myself a sponsor.
BIG BOY electronics
12
12

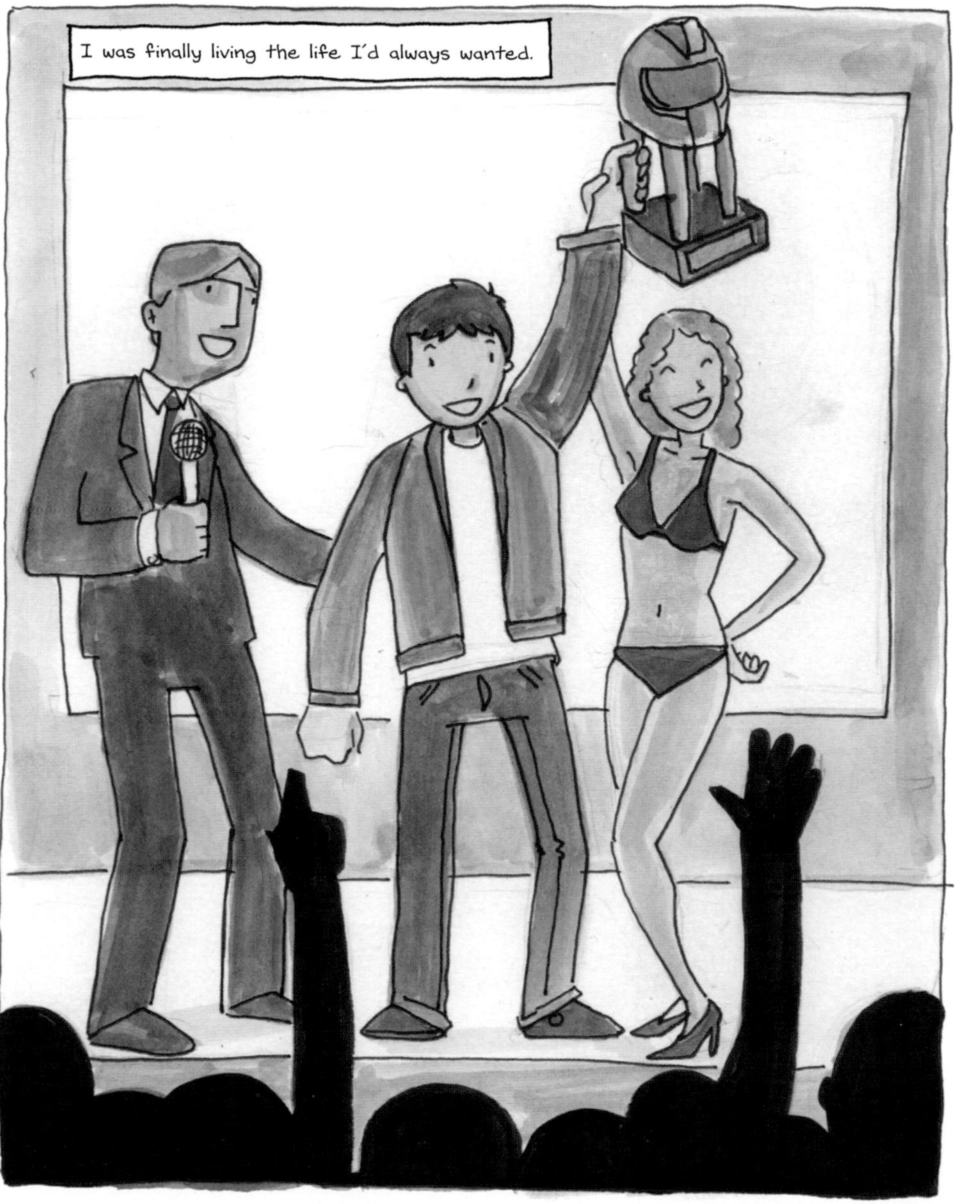
I was finally living the life I'd always wanted.

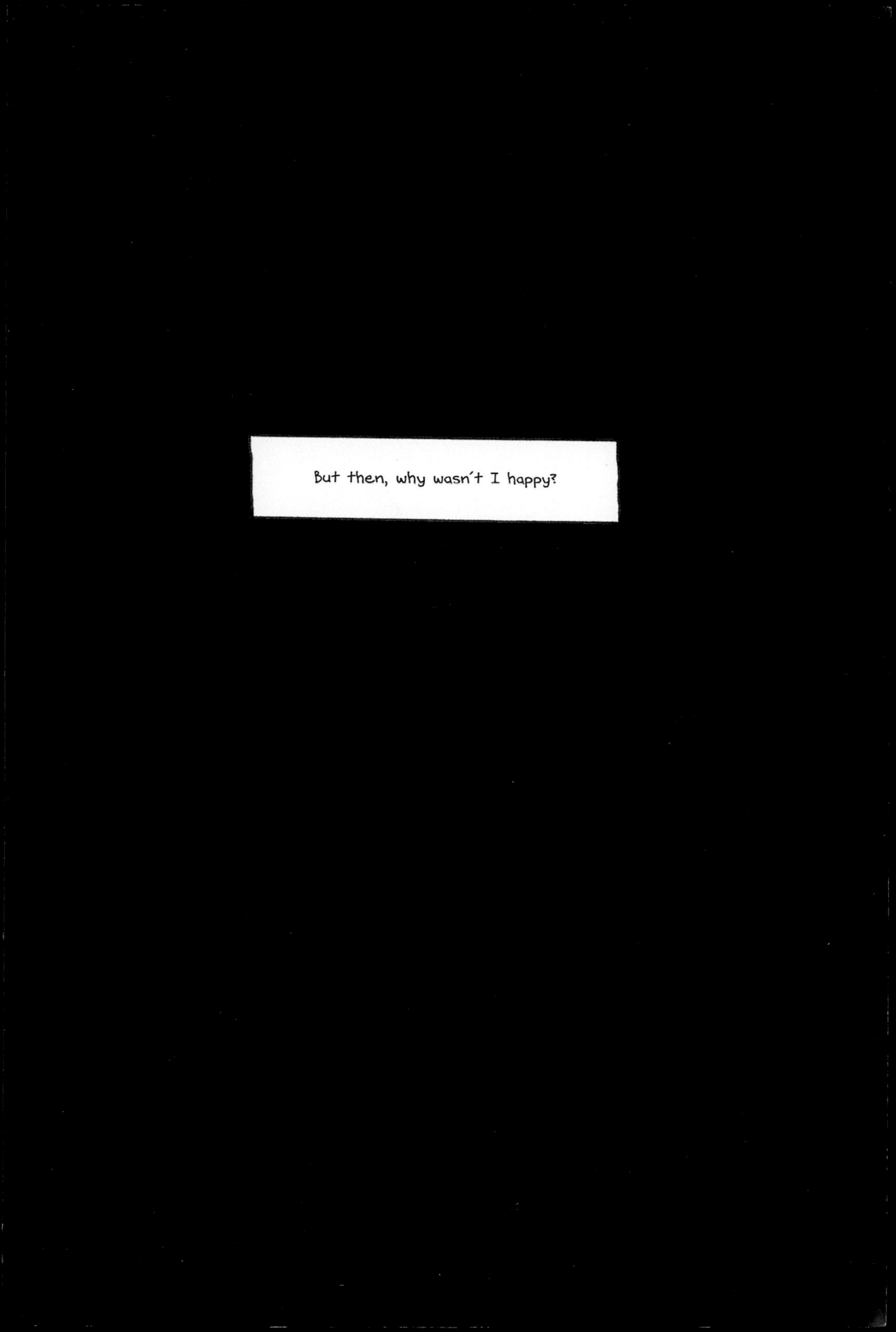
But then, why wasn´t I happy?

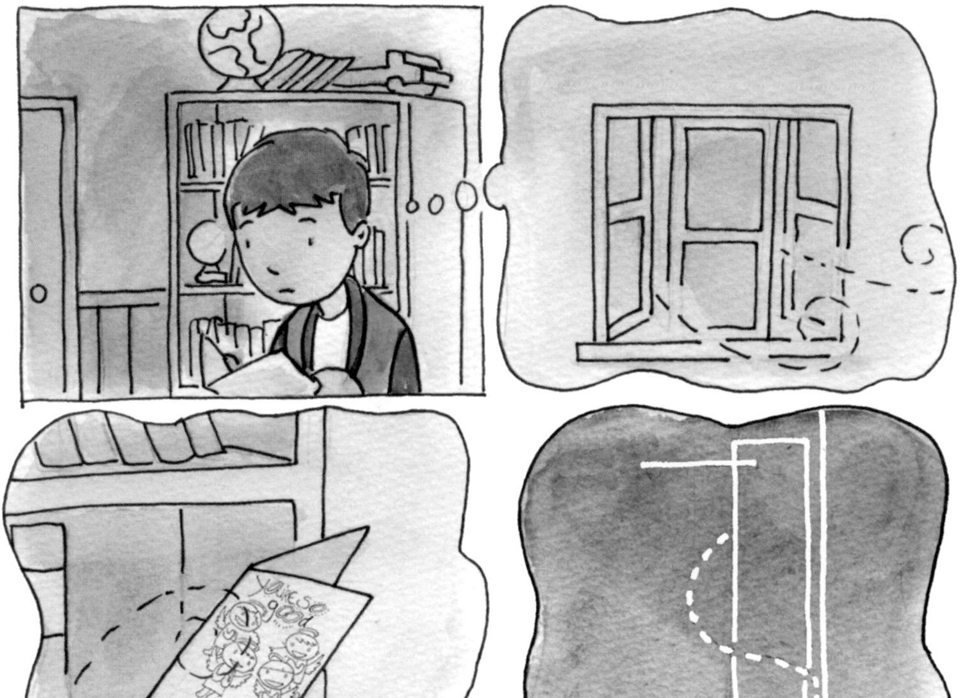
YOU'RE SO
good

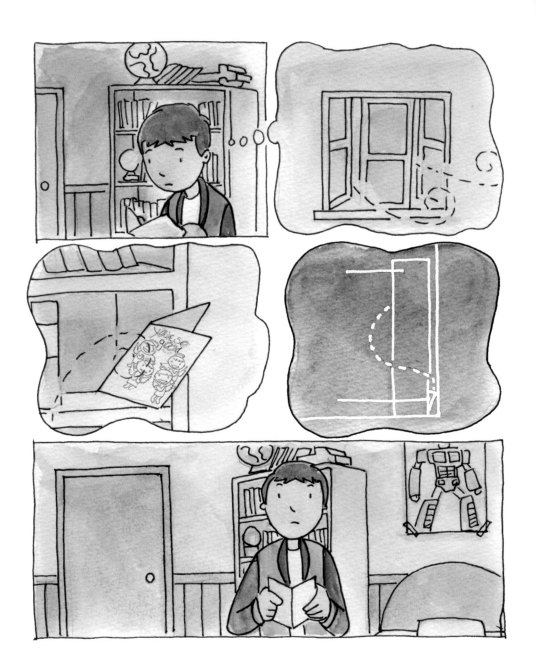

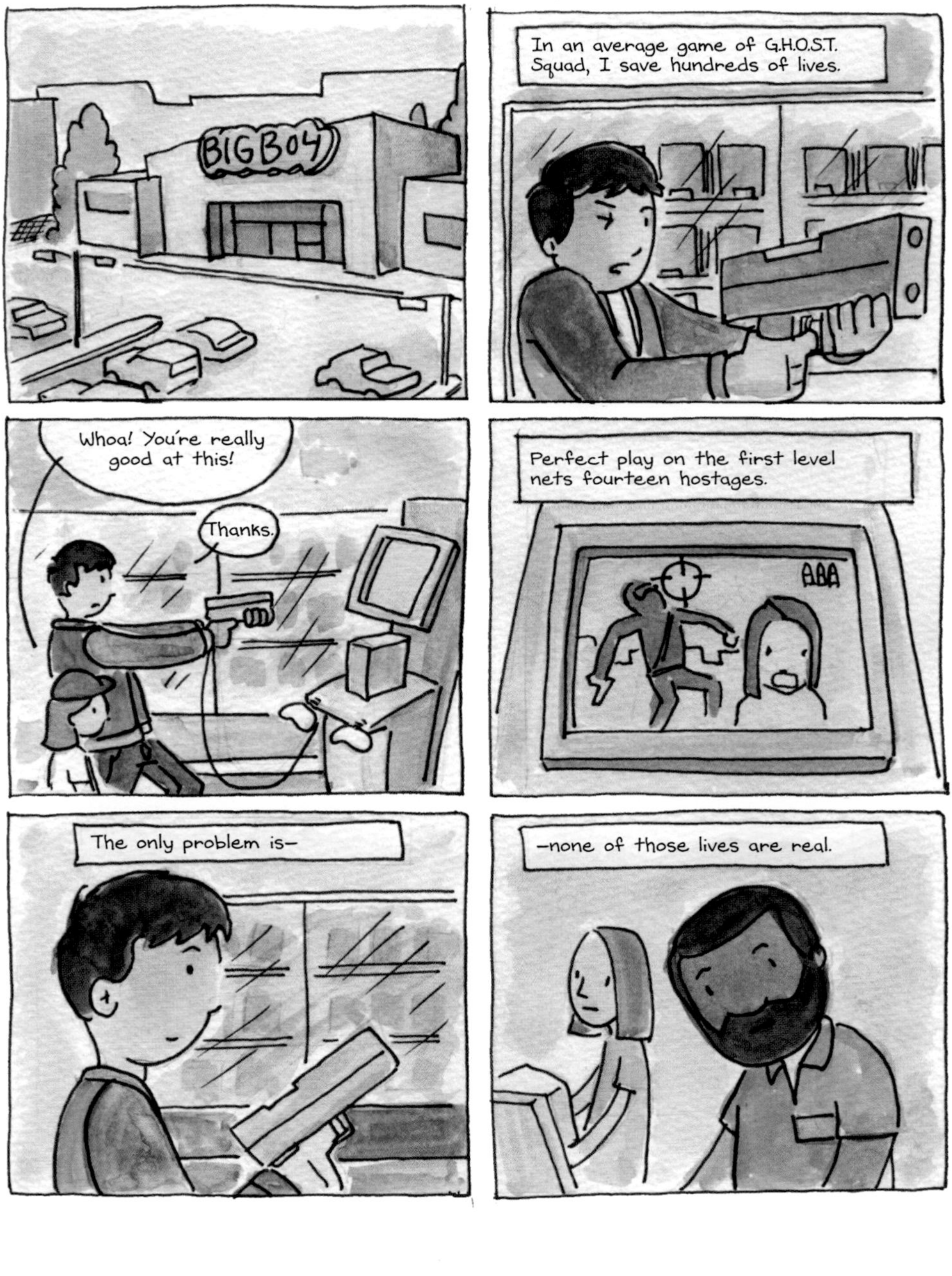
BIG BOY
In an average game of G.H.O.S.T. Squad, I save hundreds of lives.
Whoa! You're really good at this!
Thanks.
Perfect play on the first level nets fourteen hostages.
The only problem is—
—none of those lives are real.

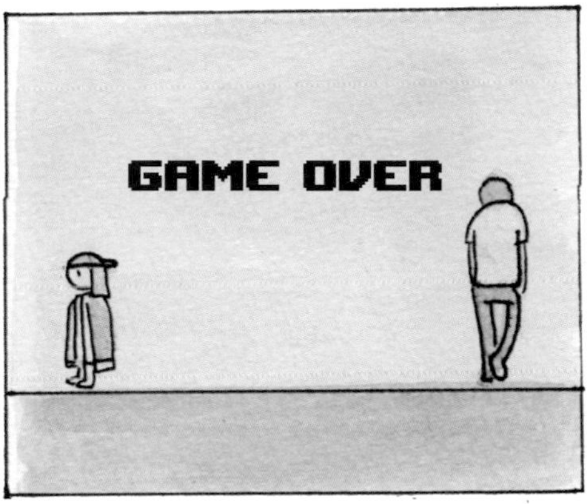
GAME OVER

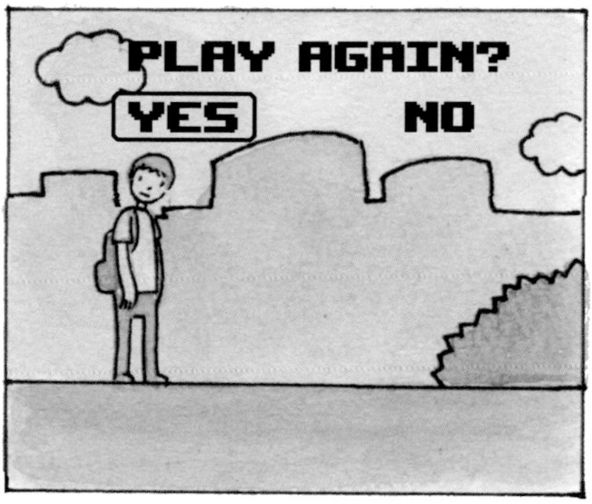
PLAY AGAIN?
YES
NO

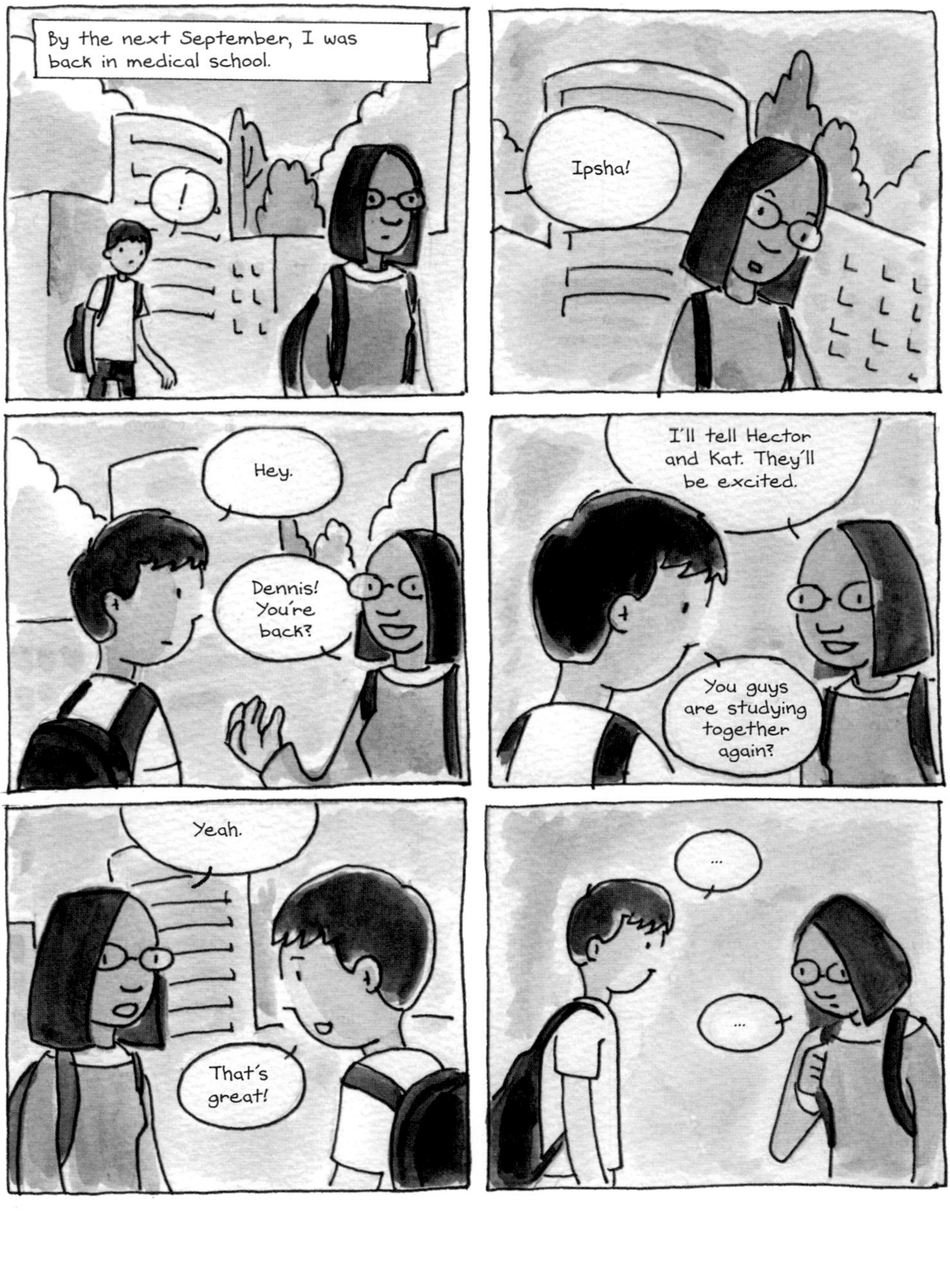
By the next September, I was back in medical school.
!
Ipsha!
Hey.
Dennis! You're back?
I'll tell Hector and Kat. They'll be excited.
You guys are studying together again?
Yeah.
That's great!
...
...

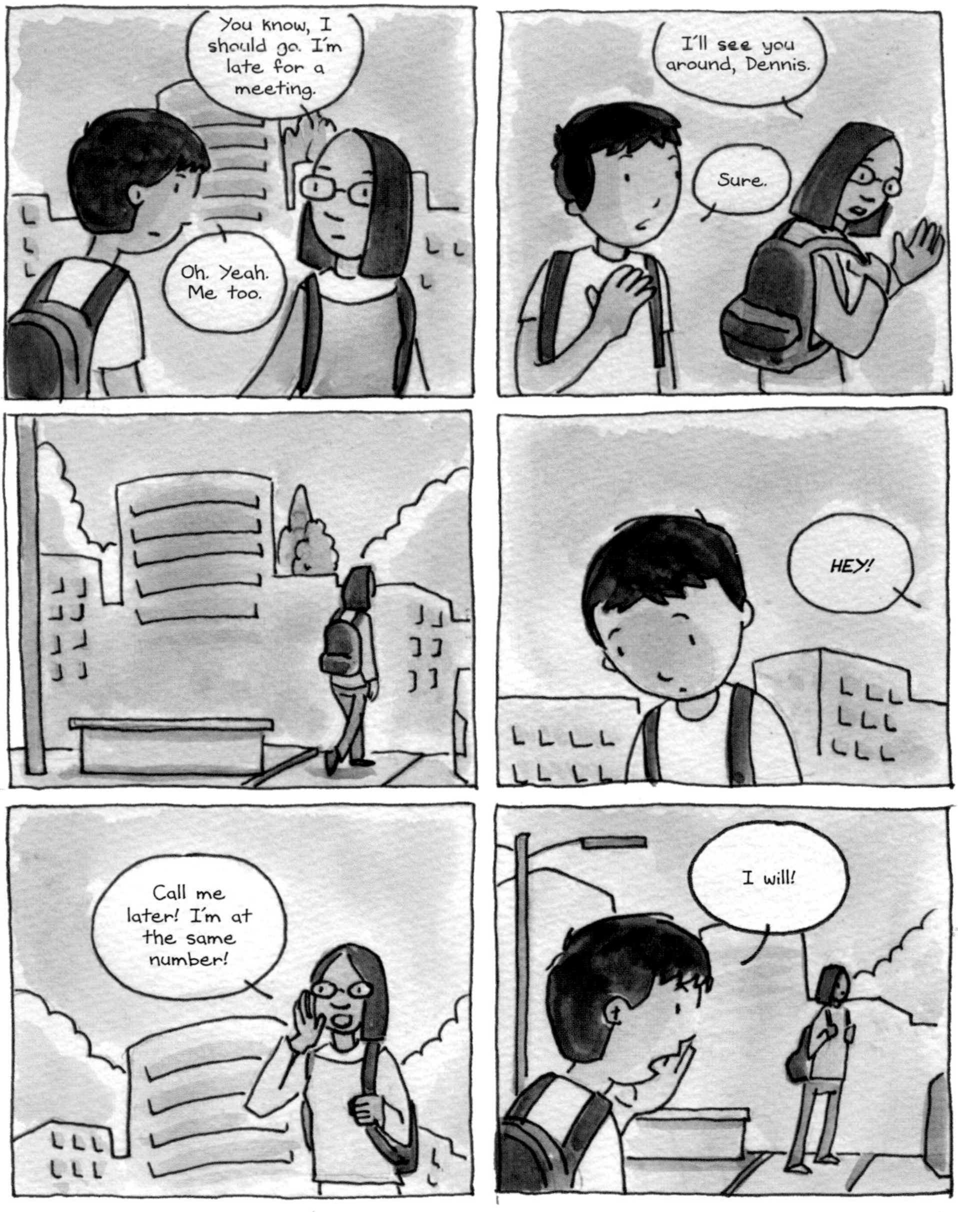
You know, I should go. I'm late for a meeting.
Oh. Yeah. Me too.
I'll see you around, Dennis.
Sure.
HEY!
Call me later! I'm at the same number!
I will!

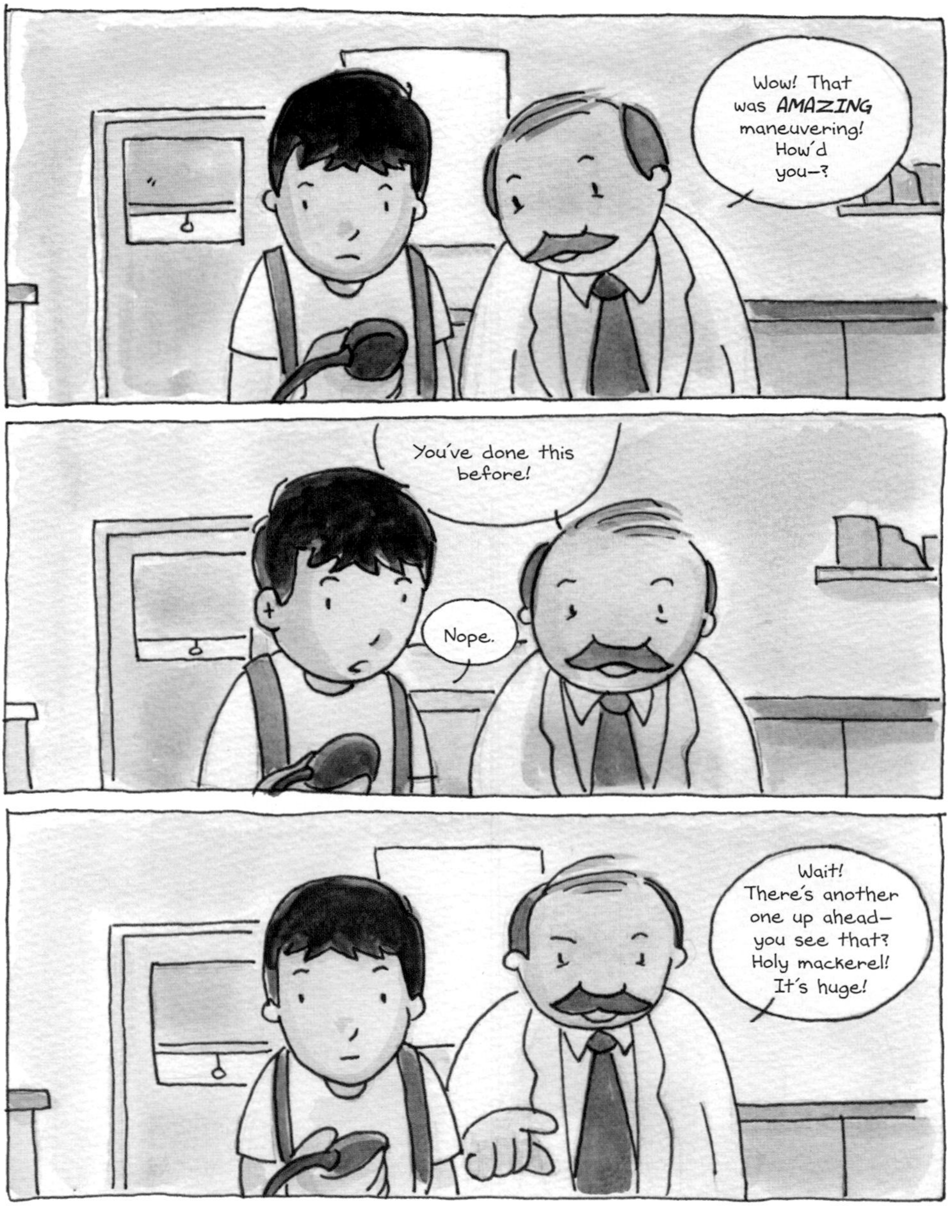
Wow! That was AMAZING maneuvering! How'd you–?
You've done this before!
Nope.
Wait! There's another one up ahead– you see that? Holy mackerel! It's huge!

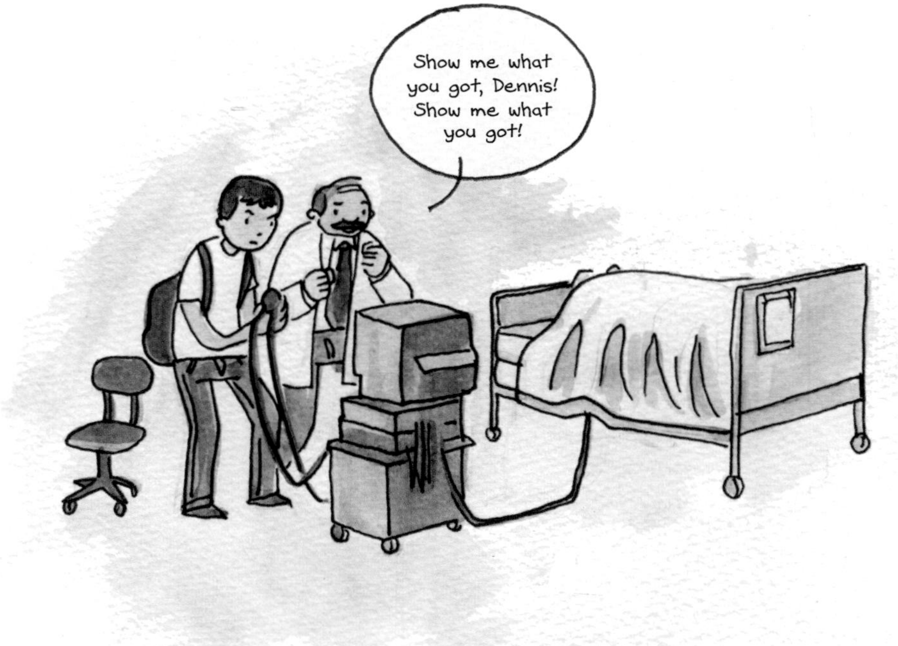
Show me what you got, Dennis! Show me what you got!